ARMAGEDDON

AND THE 4TH TIMELINE

ARMAGEDDON

AND THE 4TH TIMELINE

DON MARDAK

GCP

GRAND CIRCLE PUBLICATIONS LLC
NEW BERLIN, WISCONSIN

Armageddon and the 4th Timeline
Copyright © 2011 by Donald F. Mardak

This book is a work of fiction. Names, characters, places, and incidents are the product of the author's imagination, or are used fictitiously. Any resemblance to actual events, locales, or persons, living or dead, is coincidental.

ISBN: 978-0-9644228-1-0
Library of Congress Catalog Card Number: 2011928514

Also Available as a Kindle e-book, ISBN 978-0-9644228-2-7

For information, contact
Grand Circle Publications LLC
P. O. Box 511307, New Berlin, WI 53151-1307

Cover design and other artwork: Sylvia Maria Edstrom
Layout and design: The Publishing Institute

Printed in the United States of America.

DEDICATION

This book is dedicated to all seekers of Truth—to those people who have been searching for answers to their most basic questions about life and the nature of ultimate reality.

I hope you find a stimulating, thought-provoking blend of entertainment and enlightenment within these pages.

ACKNOWLEDGEMENTS

I wish to thank the following people who have contributed to this work. Kira Henschel, for her wonderful editing, typesetting and design, and for encouraging me to dig deeper within my consciousness to create a more interesting and colorful narrative; Sylvia Maria Edstrom for her creative artwork and graphics; Carol Klose for her insightful and thoughtful early suggestions; and my wife Judy, who has critically reviewed every word but, more importantly, has been my life's inspiration and has kept me on the "path" in my continuing quest for spiritual wisdom.

Without all of your help, this story could not have been told.

AUTHOR'S NOTE

This is a story of the two worlds in which mankind appears to be living: the invisible world of spiritual reality—described by Christ Jesus as *My Kingdom*—and the visible world of material sense, which he characterized as *this world*. In the narrative that follows, you will enter this arena of conflicting forces and see the remarkable contrasts between a life governed by the pairs of opposites—always seeking "an eye for an eye, and a tooth for a tooth"—compared to the joy and harmony that can be achieved through a life lived under Divine Grace.

Because this book is a mystical fantasy based upon the author's imagination, some military and intelligence procedures, along with certain historical figures and events, have been fictionalized. But it also is a stirring reminder of what could happen to our world if the nations and religious followers living on Planet Earth do not reconcile their differences and long-standing hatreds of each other.

With the current level of nuclear proliferation, along with the potential spread of other weapons of mass destruction, people must look beyond their limited concepts of life and deep-seated disagreements about religion and the nature of existence. If we do not soon find a way to cooperate in peaceful pursuits, some of the cataclysmic events portrayed in this book may come to pass in our lifetimes . . . We will be witnesses to *Armageddon*.

However, there still is time for mankind to change course!

Today, there are millions of enlightened beings living among us who have achieved a higher, transcendental level of spiritual awareness. If these illumined souls begin working together with a unity of purpose, they have the capacity to uplift the collective consciousness of all mankind. In this new paradigm, many will be able to ascend into that sublime reality where the great challenges facing our world can be nullified and dissolved in a satisfactory and peaceful manner.

For certain readers, the spiritual principles presented in this book will not ring true. And because this new mysticism may seem quite radical, and contrary to most orthodox religious teachings, some supporters of those teachings may take offense at this message. If that is your reaction, please accept the author's apology. There is no intention here to disparage any religion or to evangelize or proselytize anyone to accept or follow these mystical principles.

At the same time, however, other receptive individuals may find some spiritual insights in these writings that can lead them to their own personal revelation of Divine Truth. If you have that experience, I can promise you a wonderful and exciting journey into a whole new dimension of life—a joyous adventure in living.

Even though this story has been written primarily for the purpose of entertainment, it also is a textbook on how to rise above the conflicting dualisms of this world and achieve the transcendental consciousness that, when embraced and followed, will go before you to *"make your crooked places straight."* And once you have risen into this higher level of awareness, it will forever unfold for you as an uplifting, life-enhancing experience.

I hope you enjoy the trip!

—Don Mardak

INTRODUCTION

When Albert Einstein proposed his special theory of relativity, he provided encouragement and hope that time travel was possible, if not probable. Yet today, many in the scientific community still believe that time travel is highly unlikely—especially traveling backward in time. And since there currently is no single theory combining relativity and quantum mechanics, it is impossible to determine whether this speculation has any basis in fact.

For those who still dream the dream of time travel, some of the most commonly conceived vehicles and methods are: a ship that could travel faster than the speed of light; the ability to find and pass through traversable worm holes; the creation of dense rotating cylinders or cosmic streams; the use of closed time-like curves which would allow transmission through curvature in space-time, plus a few other theoretical possibilities.

But any method of time travel also produces the potential for creating paradoxes. What if you could go back in time and, as a result, caused the death of one of your grandparents before the birth of either your mother or father? If that happened, you could never be born.

A similar theory suggests that if a person were to travel to the past, he could affect some events which might alter the present. In that case, he would have created different outcomes, or possibly even an alternate reality from the one he had left behind.

But all of those speculations are based upon the belief that matter and the four-dimensional universe of space-time constitute the sum and substance of all existence. Mystical Truth, however, has revealed that there is a higher plane of consciousness to which we have access. This transcendental, five-dimensional place—often described as *My Kingdom or the Kingdom of God*—actually is an eternal, spiritual unfoldment of the infinite God-consciousness revealing and manifesting Itself as the substance and reality of all that is.

Consequently, as we begin to abide in this higher state of awareness, we will break the shackles of living solely in this four-dimensional life-experience in space-time. Then, once we attain that elevated degree of illumination, we will gain the capacity to transcend our present parenthesis in eternity, and that will allow us to live in, and traverse through, the *Grand Circle of Eternity.*

This is the story of a world gone mad. But it also is a story of hope and adventure, as one enlightened man achieves that mystical consciousness and, ultimately, learns the secret of transcending time and space.

PROLOGUE

These are the generations of mankind: the progeny of Adam and Eve. The *"man of earth"* lives in an imaginary world of dualistic distortions. This world of material sense is the arena where the pairs of opposites are operating, a battleground for the hypothetical powers of good and evil. The following timeline outlines some of the historical circumstances that have led us to our present, tenuous state of armed strife and danger.

The land east of the Garden of Eden, sometime between 10,000 and 15,000 BCE: After a disagreement while working in the field, Cain, the son of Adam and Eve, murders his brother Abel.

Mt. Horeb in the Sinai Peninsula, 1342 BCE: Moses ascends the holy mountain and meets God face to face. The patriarch is given the sacred name, *"I AM,"* and is told to return to Egypt to free the Hebrew nation from slavery. He travels back to Egypt, but does not share the hallowed name with mankind.

Jerusalem, Judaea, 32 CE: Jesus of Nazareth, also known as Jesus the Christ, or Christ Jesus, is crucified at a place called Golgotha on a charge of sedition against Imperial Rome.

Rome, Italy, 64 CE, during the reign of the Emperor Nero: The Apostle Peter, a disciple of Jesus of Nazareth, is executed for treason and teaching of a false god. By his own request, he is crucified upside down, with his head toward the ground.

Rome, 66 CE, during the reign of the Emperor Nero: The Apostle Paul, formerly Saul of Tarsus and a late follower of Jesus of Nazareth, is executed by beheading.

The Arabian city of Mecca, August 20, 570 CE: Muhammad ibn 'Abdullah, later known as Mohammed, is born.

Mecca, Saudi Arabia, 610 CE in the month of Ramadan: Muhammad receives his first revelation from God.

Syria and Palestine, 634 CE, two years after the death of Muhammad: Khalid ibn al-Walid, a companion of the Islamic prophet, leads the Rashidun Caliphate forces in their conquest of Syria and Palestine.

The Middle East, 1096 to 1270 CE: In 1076, after the Muslim forces have captured Jerusalem, Pope Urban II calls for a war against Islam so Jerusalem can be regained for the Christian faith. That action leads to the first of eight Crusades that, beginning in 1096, are undertaken over the next 175 years.

Ajaccio, Corsica, August 15, 1769: Letizia Bonaparte, wife of Carlo Bonaparte, gives birth to a son, Napoleon.

Paris, France, 1799: Napoleon Bonaparte stages a coup d'état and installs himself as First Consul. Five years later, the French Senate proclaims him Emperor. In the first decade of the nineteenth century, the Napoleonic Wars eventually involve every major European power.

Trier, Prussia, Germany, May 5, 1818: Karl Heinrich Marx is born to middle-class parents. He comes from a long line of rabbis on both sides of his family.

Brussels, Belgium, February 21, 1848: Karl Marx publishes the Communist Manifesto: *Das Kapital*.

Gori, Georgia, December 21, 1878: Joseph Stalin is born to peasant parents.

Branau, Austria, April 20, 1889: Klara Hitler, wife of Alois Hitler, gives birth to a son, Adolf.

] x [

Moscow, Russia, 1922: Joseph Stalin becomes General Secretary of the Communist Party of the Soviet Union's Central Committee. After the death of Vladimir Ilyich Lenin in 1924, Stalin consolidates his power and rises to become leader of the Soviet Union.

Berlin, Germany, January 30, 1933: Adolf Hitler is sworn in as Chancellor of Germany. He soon transforms the Weimar Republic into the Third Reich and eventually tries to establish a New Order of absolute Nazi German hegemony in Europe. Hitler also rearms Germany, giving it the capacity to launch World War II in Europe.

Warsaw, Poland, September 1, 1939: Adolf Hitler, Fuehrer of Germany and founder of the Third Reich, leads his army in an unprovoked invasion of western Poland.

Pearl Harbor, Hawaii Territory, United States, December 7, 1941: The naval fleet of the Empire of Japan attacks the United States naval base at Pearl Harbor, Hawaii. More than 2,400 personnel are killed and 1,282 are wounded. This aggressive act results in the United States' entry into World War II.

Berlin, Germany, February 22, 1942: Adolf Hitler announces his plan of racial hygiene. It involves the elimination of all Jews in what is referred to as "The Final Solution of the Jewish Question in Europe."

Auschwitz, Poland, January 27, 1945: The Nazi concentration camp at Auschwitz, Poland, is liberated by Soviet troops. The camp is one of the largest in Adolf Hitler's quest to exterminate the Jews. It is believed that up to 1.1 million people died there.

Hiroshima, Japan, August 6, 1945: After an ultimatum of the Potsdam Declaration was ignored by the Hirohito regime, President Harry S. Truman gives an executive order for the United States to drop an atomic bomb on the city of Hiroshima, Japan. The weapon, named "Little Boy," kills between 90,000 and 150,000 people, with approximately half the deaths occurring on the first day.

Nagasaki, Japan, August 9, 1945: Because the government of Japan does not respond to the bombing of Hiroshima, President Truman gives an order to detonate another nuclear bomb, this time over the city of Nagasaki, Japan. That weapon, named "Fat Man," kills between 60,000 and 80,000 people. On August 15th, six days after the detonation over Nagasaki, Japan announces its unconditional surrender to the Allied Powers.

Moscow, USSR, August, 1949: The Union of Soviet Socialist Republics (USSR) announces that it has successfully tested its first nuclear weapon.

Moscow, USSR, April, 1955: The Soviet Union begins the process of nuclear proliferation by transferring a sample atomic bomb and some of its nuclear technology to the People's Republic of China.

Riyadh, Saudi Arabia, March 10, 1957: Osama bin Laden is born as the son of Mohammed bin Laden.

The United Nations / New York, NY, July 1, 1968: By this date, five nations have acquired nuclear weapons. They are the United States, Russia, the United Kingdom, France, and China. These also are the five permanent members of the UN Security Council and signatories to the Nuclear Non-Proliferation Treaty (NPT) on March 5, 1970.

Afghanistan, 1989: Osama bin Laden establishes an international terrorist group known as al-Qaeda.

New York, NY and Arlington, VA, September 11, 2001: The Twin Towers of the World Trade Center in lower Manhattan are reduced to rubble after two hijacked commercial airliners crash into the buildings. A third hijacked commercial airliner flies into the Pentagon in Arlington, VA, and a fourth plane goes down near Shanksville in rural Pennsylvania. It is the most devastating terrorist attack on the American homeland in history. 2,973 victims, along with the 19 hijackers, die as a result of these actions, and more than 6,000 people are injured. The terrorist group al-Qaeda claims responsibility for the attacks.

Danger Across the World: During the 1990s and early years of the 21st century, India, Pakistan, Israel, and North Korea acquire nuclear weapons. None of them signs the Nuclear Non-Proliferation Treaty.

Abbottabad, Pakistan, May 1, 2011: Osama bin Laden is killed by U.S. Navy SEALs and C.I.A. operatives.

Tehran, Iran, sometime in 2012: The Islamic Republic of Iran tests its first nuclear weapon and becomes the world's tenth nuclear power.

Central Intelligence Agency, Langley, VA, the Present: Terrorist chatter reaches an all-time high. The intelligence community receives threats of potential nuclear and biological weapons attacks throughout the world. Most western governments are on high alert—

CHAPTER 1

TERRORISM,
CONFUSION,
AND HOPE

THE PRESENT, THURSDAY, AUGUST 13TH
CENTRAL INTELLIGENCE AGENCY HEADQUARTERS - LANGLEY, VA

It had been four months since the last al-Qaeda attack: a dirty bomb detonated near the center of Hamburg, Germany. More than 24,000 innocent people were killed, and nearly 56,000 were injured, many critically. The death toll continues to mount.

On that gloomy Thursday in Langley, an unincorporated community located along the Potomac River a few miles west of Washington, D.C., CIA director Scott Cunningham was addressing his Counterintelligence Center Analysis Group, the Director of National Intelligence (DNI), and a few other members of his agency.

Standing five feet, eleven inches tall, Cunningham had a trim and fit physique to go along with his brown, wavy hair and handsome, movie star looks. The former Navy SEAL, at

48, had also spent twelve years in the field in covert operations, and was considered by colleagues to be a true American hero.

The director opened the meeting by saying, "As all of you know, since the attack in Hamburg, the terrorist chatter has been at a fever pitch. We have intercepted threats against at least a half dozen major western capitals. It appears that something huge is imminent. You are also aware of the three al-Qaeda cells that recently were disrupted in the planning stages: one in Yonkers, New York, one in North Chicago, and one in Ventura, California. Yet the threatening communications continue, and are getting stronger every minute. And even though we don't have any specific information, I intend to inform the President and the Joint Chiefs of Staff about the severity of the situation. Unless any of you disagree, I will suggest that the Secretary of Homeland Security raise the National Terrorism Advisory System's threat level from its present status of '*Elevated*,' to '*Imminent*,' our most critical condition indicating a strong threat of an attack."

Assistant CIA director Lori Colbert then spoke up. "Do we really want to go there, Scott? I know the chatter has been high, but we've seen that many times before . . . and in this case, we don't have any specific dates, times, or places. In the past, these noisy periods turned out to be nothing more than idle chitchat. There hasn't been a major hit on America since 9/11/2001. If we raise the threat level to *Imminent*, we could cause panic in the streets, not to mention wreaking havoc on our air traffic system. The airport delays and missed connections could be staggering. And what would

Wall Street's response be tomorrow morning? Do the nine people in this room have the right to negatively impact hundreds of billions, if not trillions, of dollars of the nation's wealth? Our economy is just getting back to normal since the Bush-Obama recession. Only recently has the dollar stabilized against the other major currencies. So why would we want to take such risky action?"

A no-nonsense, divorced mother of two college-age sons, Lori was totally committed and devoted to her job as the CIA's second-in-command. In fact, some agency employees believed she was the power behind the scenes of the organization, often implementing the minute details of each mission, while Scott Cunningham was the high profile, public face of the agency. The five-foot, seven-inch, slightly overweight assistant director took a deep breath, tugged at her rumpled navy blue blazer for emphasis, and concluded. "Anyway, those are my opinions. I think we should wait for more concrete information."

"Thank you, Lori," Cunningham replied. "Does anyone else have some thoughts?"

Retired General Sean Larkin, Director of National Intelligence, commented, "I appreciate your concerns, Lori. But from all that I've seen, I believe this is the most menacing threat we have yet encountered. These jihadists are serious; they really want to bring America down. Wouldn't it be worse to not give our countrymen some warning? And even more important, what if going to our highest threat level actually helps us prevent an attack, or mitigate the damage if there is one? I believe we have to do it."

Cunningham surveyed the eight, all of them earnest and focused, then asked, "Any other comments?"

Dennis Jacoby, the five-foot, six-inch, intellectual and bookish director of the National Clandestine Service (NCS), responded, "I agree with Scott and Sean. We can't just sit on this news; it's much too volatile. We have a responsibility to the American people and to the rest of the world to help them take every precaution. I think you should request the action, Scott."

Lori Colbert raised her left hand as she slowly looked around the table. Speaking up again, she said somewhat apologetically, "Sorry, guys, I get a little emotional some-times. Maybe the other considerations are more important than mine. As compilers of intelligence, it is not our job to make the decisions; we just need to share our information with those who actually have the power and the duty to do that—and who may even have to walk the plank if they are wrong. Feel free to do what you have to do, Scott. I withdraw my objection."

"All right, then it's settled," Cunningham replied resolutely. "I will be meeting with the President and VP, the Joint Chiefs, the Director of Homeland Security, and the other important players tomorrow morning. I'll let you know how they react to the news."

After those comments, the group adjourned for the day, with each of them returning to his or her regular duties.

THURSDAY, AUGUST 13TH
LHASA, CAPITAL OF THE TIBET AUTONOMOUS REGION IN THE PEOPLE'S REPUBLIC OF CHINA

Kathy and I arrived in Lhasa Tuesday afternoon on a direct flight from Beijing. Since our ride to Shimahn's residence would not be available until Friday, we spent much of Wednesday and Thursday sightseeing around the ancient capital city. A good part of our first afternoon was devoted to studying the heritage and history of the Jokhang Temple, one of the city's most famous landmarks. The temple, which was built early in the seventh century CE during the reign of King Songsten Gampo, is regarded by many Tibetan Buddhists as the most sacred shrine in the country.

Jokhang Temple is situated on Barkhor Square in the old section of Lhasa, with the entire four-story complex covering approximately 25,000 square meters. Having roofs covered with gilded bronze tiles, the temple was originally constructed to house a revered image of Siddhartha Gautama the Buddha. That statue is still enshrined in the temple today and is considered to be the most hallowed object in all of Tibet. The interior of Jokhang Temple is quite dark, but is illuminated by a number of votive candles, and there also is a constant, fragrant aroma of burning incense.

On Thursday, we spent some time touring the majestic Potala Palace, the former residence of the Dalai Lama. Resting atop Marpo Ri—the Red Hill—the structure rises more than 300 meters above the valley floor making it the highest palace in the world. It consists of thirteen stories of buildings containing over 1,000 rooms, 10,000 shrines and about 200,000 statues. This majestic Tibetan landmark is composed of two parts, which are referred to as the Red Palace—located in the center of the complex and devoted exclusively to religious study and Buddhist prayer—and the White Palace, consisting of two wings, which formerly made up the living quarters of the Dalai Lama. Today, the palace is a museum housing a remarkable collection of classic art. Some of the scriptures and paintings date back more than several thousand years.

Kathy, my wife of seven years, loves history and could spend hours delving into ancient documents, monuments and structures. I, on the other hand, am more intrigued by pondering abstract metaphysical principles and practicing other consciousness-expanding exercises.

Though following my beautiful blond wife around is usually a pleasure, palace gazing, temple watching and general sightseeing were not our real purpose in coming to Tibet. Since the takeover of the country by the People's Republic of China, the ancient city, along with the rest of the nation, had lost much of its luster as a center of enlightenment. The Dalai Lama was living in exile in Dharamsala, India, in the foothills of the Himalayas. Numerous Tibetan monasteries and ashrams had been forced to shut down, and the citizens now walked the streets with one eye constantly over their shoulders. While they no longer were being outwardly persecuted for their religious practices, memories of the past still haunted the older residents, as they often reacted in fear whenever they were in the presence of their hostile, pagan occupiers.

When I first received the unexpected, urgent request from Shimahn, I thought I was dreaming. I hadn't seen nor heard from him since my parents and I had traveled to the Holy Land when I was just twelve years old. At that time, I experienced a profound spiritual initiation in the presence of this illumined Himalayan mystic. I had become separated from my parents during a tour of the Old City section of Jerusalem. After visiting the Church of the Holy Sepulchre on Golgotha, our family was walking down the Via Dolorosa with a large group of other tourists. As we were strolling down the crowded street, I became distracted when I saw a very old man sitting silently in meditation a short distance off the main road.

The sight of the man was so intriguing that I slowly approached him and started a conversation. With his long white beard and drab, ethnic clothing—specifically the long gray robe and worn-out sandals he was wearing—he looked much like the historical patriarchs often portrayed in biblical movies. A bit surprised by my intrusion into his inner peace, the old man gently opened his eyes and greeted me with a warm, endearing smile. He said his name was Nehemiah. He also told me that he was there assisting a man named Shimahn, whom he described as an enlightened Himalayan Master. And that intrigued me even more and set my youthful, inquisitive mind into overdrive. After a few moments of additional small talk and pleasantries, Nehemiah bid me goodbye, as he claimed he had to meet someone. By that time, I was so captivated and inspired by what I was hearing that I secretly followed him to the building where Shimahn was residing. I then had an opportunity to spend several hours with the two men, discussing spiritual truths and learning mystical principles I had never heard before. Among other things, I learned about what they described as "the nature of ultimate reality," and I was introduced to a very special book of ancient wisdoms they possessed. But most importantly, they taught me how to meditate and gave me some unique spiritual insights on the true meaning of existence.

That entire episode was an overwhelming spiritual awakening for me. By the time the three of us had finished our animated conversation, my head was spinning. I wondered how I would remember all the profound truths I had heard that afternoon. But Nehemiah told me not to be concerned, as he confidently assured me that I would recall most of the principles. I still remember his final words to me. He said, "Your real teacher is within you and will always be available to instruct you."

As a result of that incident in Old Jerusalem, my life has since become a series of adventures in mysticism, and I have witnessed many unexplainable miracles in my daily experience.

Kathy and I first met as young teenagers during one of my family's trips to St. Louis, Missouri. After that first meeting, we lost contact with each other for more than six years, but were fortuitously reunited as undergraduate students at Purdue University in West Lafayette, Indiana. In my collegiate studies, I majored in business administration and marketing, subjects that I never had an opportunity to utilize in my future life's work.

Because of that unexpected encounter with Shimahn and Nehemiah in the Holy Land, and as a further consequence of my later reunion with Kathy, I was ultimately led to my true spiritual destiny. I have become a practitioner of spiritual healing and have spent several years sharing and teaching the mystical message that has continued to unfold in my consciousness.

Our reunion at college was quite remarkable, as I learned that Kathy, too, was an exceptionally receptive soul and had also had several unique mystical experiences of her own. We were married just six months after Kathy's graduation from Purdue.

Shimahn's letter asking us to come to Tibet was rather short, but projected a very mysterious, and ominous tone. Hand-written on an old, wrinkled piece of yellowed paper, the document was quite disconcerting. Because I had not had any contact with this enlightened mystic since the day he and Nehemiah left me in Old Jerusalem, I wondered how he possibly could have known where to find me . . . yet somehow he did.

The first words of the letter were: "*Eric, it is important that I meet with you. Please try to come to Tibet as soon as possible. You may also bring your wife along to share in the important decision I will be asking you to make. This is of great significance; the future of mankind could be at stake.*" And then he closed with directions on when and where to meet him.

I wondered how he knew that I was married. Kathy also was quite perplexed by the letter and its inexplicable content. She realized how much I had longed to see Shimahn again; for many years, I spoke of nothing else. But since I had left this Himalayan Master in Old Jerusalem all those years ago, I never knew where to find him—until today. So now that we had a location and directions, she readily agreed that we should make the trip.

On Friday, August 14th, Kathy and I were to take the train ride on the Qingzang railway to Nakchu, a fairly large city in northern Tibet located about 100 kilometers from Lhasa. Shimahn told us that two of his students would meet us at the railway station in Nakchu and would drive us to the ashram where he was living. We later learned that it is one of the few ashrams still remaining in Tibet but, because it is so small and far out of the way, the country's Chinese rulers were allowing it to continue operating.

THURSDAY, AUGUST 13TH
THE FATA REGION OF THE ISLAMIC REPUBLIC OF PAKISTAN

After Indonesia, the Islamic Republic of Pakistan has the second largest Muslim population in the world. The northern and western highlands of Pakistan contain the towering Karakoram and Pamir mountain ranges, which incorporate some of the world's highest peaks. In 2001, after the September 11th attacks on the World Trade Center and the Pentagon, the Taliban and al-Qaeda began leaving their sanctuaries in Afghanistan and entering into the nearby FATA region, the Federally Administered Tribal Areas.

As they gradually infiltrated the region, these two violent terrorist groups virtually achieved the same level of organization and sophistication they had before 9/11. And it was here that the newest plot against the civilized world was being hatched. On that foreboding Thursday in August, the small, ragged band of mujahedin was gathering in the cave for the third time that week. Their patience was wearing thin. Ever since the capture and killing of Osama bin Laden, they had become galvanized and totally committed to this undertaking. But now, they were primed and ready to give the signal to implement "Project World Capitals." Their guerrilla insurgents were in place in the various locations, prepared to begin the attacks. It was amazing that all of this could have been accomplished without detection. So why was their revered leader holding them back? Most of their lives had been lived primarily for this day and this project. Soon they would bring the *Great Satan* to its knees.

Their cause is just. *Allahu akbar!* (God is great!)

Shortly after noon on that hot, dry day in the lower mountain range, Hasan Mohammed Farouk, the second highest-ranking figure in the al-Qaeda network, entered the cave. The somber, heavily bearded terrorist leader was wearing a soiled turban, a lightly woven, dark brown field jacket and loose-fitting khaki fatigues.

Looking around at his group of zealous freedom fighters he said, "The hour is almost at hand. We want to have the most damaging impact possible, so the attacks will begin in

Europe on a busy morning next week. Then, while the Americans are still reeling from the bad news of London and Paris, the first blows will be struck in their precious home-land. Before they can react, the horror will be upon them, as their vile pagan monuments come tumbling down."

Unconsciously tugging on his graying beard, he then said, "The rest of the week should create a great deal of confusion and indecisiveness, and will completely destabilize the world's financial markets. We believe several western economies will collapse under the weight of this burden. I know that all of you have been waiting a long time for this moment. But soon your waiting will be over. Our glorious leader, along with all the other devoted servants of Islam thank you for your commitment to this very worthy and just cause. We will prevail."

Then the sinister-looking jihadist bent over to grab his rifle, held it high in the air, and shouted, "*Allahu akbar! Death to the infidels!*"

The little band of devotees couldn't hold back its enthusiasm as a great roar went up in the cave, and the dusky sandstone walls of the arid cavern echoed with the cries of twenty-three rabid warriors. Finally, the time had come. Just five or six more days to wait.

CHAPTER 2

INNER PEACE
IN A WORLD
OF VIOLENCE

After getting his morning briefing from CIA Director Scott Cunningham, President Darwin Thompson was addressing a group of the most powerful people in the United States government. In addition to Cunningham, they included Vice President Jason Tucker, Attorney General Harvey Klemmer, DNI Director Sean Larkin, White House Chief of Staff Donald Bergstrom, the Director of Homeland Security Domenic Fiorenza, the Secretaries of State and Defense, along with the six members of the Joint Chiefs of Staff.

The President began by having Director Cunningham present his portentous report. He then asked for comments and questions from the group. Vice President Tucker was the first to respond. "I believe we must take these threats and this information very seriously. These people have only one agenda, and that is to inflict as much damage on the United States as they can."

General Anthony Fabretti, Commandant of the Marine Corps, replied, "I say screw the bastards!"

Fabretti was short and squat, with a body of steel. After many years of daily workouts in the gym, he was as muscular as any bodybuilding enthusiast. His hair was worn in a short crew cut, shaved almost to baldness over his ears, and still was mostly solid black, despite his 56 years of age. General Fabretti was also known as the only officer in the last few decades whose mouth was as foul as General Patton's.

"If they hit just one of our cities," he shouted—"and I don't care if it's someplace as irrelevant as Sheboygan, Wisconsin or Waterloo, Iowa—we should come back at them and take out Tehran, Damascus, Riyadh, and the Gaza fuckin' Strip—and do it all in the same day. Next, we wait a few months for the air to clear, and then we start bringin' in boatloads of asphalt, so we can have the places turned into parking lots by Christmas."

General Mary Jane Wichman, Chief of Staff of the U.S. Air Force, spoke up next. "Thanks for the nice, thoughtful comments, Tony. Now why don't you tell us how you really feel?"

At a slender five feet, eleven inches tall and wearing high heels, the auburn-haired Air Force Chief of Staff towered over the Marine Commandant, who then said, "Sorry if I offended you, Mary Jane, but I think we have to get rid of these heathens once and for all. Then if they still have the guts to hit a second city, we need to show them how much we mean business by taking Mecca and Medina off the face of the earth. That way, the next time they get on their goddamned knees to face the East, there won't be anything there for them to pray to."

At that point, General of the Army John Cabot Daniels, Chairman of the Joint Chiefs of Staff, stepped in. "Okay, boys and girls, let's keep it civil. This really is a very serious matter."

Chairman Daniels was the most popular military commander in America since generals MacArthur and Eisenhower in World War II. He was affectionately called "Old Whiskey" by the men he had commanded in Afghanistan, in honor of his nickname, Jack Daniels. At 61 years old, General Daniels was another remarkable physical specimen. His blond crew cut still covered most of his scalp and had just a few traces of gray. Standing six feet, two inches tall, with broad shoulders and a rugged jaw line, Daniels seemed born to play the role he now was fulfilling as leader of military operations for what is ostensibly called the world's only Superpower.

The Chairman then said, "This is a very difficult situation, Tony. If we do get hit, I will understand your anger and desire for revenge. But as a military man, I also appreciate the need for a reasoned reaction. I am not suggesting that we try to negotiate with these people, because they are radical, jihadist lunatics who won't accept any compromise except the annihilation of America, Israel, and most of the civilized western world. Yet we have to look at all options.

"What you are proposing, General, is for us to nuke the capitals of several Islamic countries. And while those governments may not like us very much, they will not be the ones perpetrating the attacks—if attacks do come. Rather, it will be independent terrorist cells that are loosely bound under the al-Qaeda banner, or under some other lesser-known groups. In order to prevent those attacks from happening, we need to uncover their lairs here in the States and offshore, just as we did in Yonkers, North Chicago, and Ventura. And aside from that, I don't think President Thompson wants to be remembered as the Commander-in-Chief who started World War III—if there still would be anyone here to remember him after such an event."

Attorney General Klemmer then replied, "That's the problem, my friends. Under United States laws, and under the rules of the Geneva Convention, there is only so much we can do from a pre-emptive standpoint."

Fabretti again interrupted. "I'm not talking about pre-empting anything. I'm talking about kickin' the shit out of them if they do hit us first."

President Thompson then took control of the dialogue. In line with his lofty office, the President, as usual, was the tallest person in the room. His six-foot-seven-inch frame had served him well when he was an all-American power forward at Georgetown University, and still commanded respect and gawking eyes wherever he appeared. As an economics major, both his intellectual capacity and his knowledge of the financial markets were unchallenged. After two-and-a-half years in office, his approval rating was still above 60 percent and his thinning silver hair was just the crowning touch needed to complete the package.

In his resonant, deep voice, the President said, "Based upon the intelligence reports, we all recognize the severity of the problem. So the question is: What do we do about the NTAS threat level? I tend to agree with Scott that we should raise it to *Imminent*. I fully understand the ramifications of going there, since it has never been done before. But this threat is very real. So aside from those complications that we all are aware of, do you really feel we can do anything other than taking this radical step?"

The Attorney General, a balding, extremely overweight, former trial lawyer, commented, "I agree that as painful as it might be, we have to do it . . . What are your thoughts, Domenic?"

Fiorenza, the dark-haired and dark-eyed Director of Homeland Security, replied, "As difficult as it has been for me to come to this conclusion, I see no other choice. I'll give the order, unless someone can show me a real reason not to."

After a brief silence, all those in attendance nodded their heads, along with a few murmurs of verbal assent.

Joint Chiefs Chairman Daniels then said, "I believe we should also raise the defense readiness condition to DEFCON 2, just as John F. Kennedy did during the Cuban missile crisis."

President Thompson replied, "I concur with your assessment, Jack. Do any of you have a problem with that?"

When no one responded, the President stated affirmatively, "Okay, let's go to DEFCON 2 . . . but try not to be too public about it." Turning to the CIA Director, he said, "Now, as to any disruptive or preventive activity, Scott, please do everything you can on intelligence with every resource at your disposal. If we do get any specific information as to time or place, we will certainly want you people back here ASAP."

Glancing then at his Director of Homeland Security, Thompson commented, "And by the way, Domenic, why don't you wait until Sunday afternoon before raising the threat levels. Then Monday morning we can see how the markets react. If there is panic selling, we can have SEC Chairman Bronstein shut them down for a few days.

"So with that," the President rose, spreading his arms in an embracing gesture, "I once again thank all of you for your dedicated service to America, and even more especially in these very trying times." Then with his eyes uncharacteristically welling up with tears, and his voice choking with emotion, he passively said, "And may God be with us."

FRIDAY, AUGUST 14TH
THE RAILWAY STATION - NAKCHU, NORTHERN TIBET AUTONOMOUS REGION

Kathy and I boarded our antiquated, steam-engine train right on time Friday morning. The ride from the captive nation's capital was quite scenic, but also a bit tiring—mostly because of the uncomfortable wooden benches. Along the way on our journey, we saw numerous wild yaks and Tibetan antelope roaming the countryside, all oblivious to the glorious Himalayan backdrop. But at least we were dressed for the occasion.

We had also been able to do some shopping while we were in Lhasa, and that gave us an opportunity to purchase clothing more appropriate for the trip. Nakchu is situated in the vast land of the northern Tibet Autonomous Region. The area is guarded by the snow-capped Dargo Mountain in the west and Burgyi Mountain in the east. The region's extreme altitude—more than 4,500 meters (14,760 feet)—means that winters can be severely cold, as much as 25 degrees Fahrenheit below zero. Fortunately, we were there in August, and temperatures were in the balmy 70s.

As we arrived at the Nakchu railroad station, Kathy and I shouldered our backpacks, tossed our duffle bags, and stepped off the train. Though I had expected the station to be quaint and rustic, it, instead, was a small, fairly modern facility with very little charm. The day was bright and unseasonably warm, as we waited about twenty minutes without anyone approaching us. After the train had pulled away and most of the travelers had left the station, the two of us felt eerily isolated and alone until two dark-skinned young men suddenly appeared, seemingly out of nowhere. Both of them had wide smiles on their faces and began bowing to us. Their names were Tenzing and Mingma. They told us Shimahn's ashram was about 125 kilometers northwest of the city, but because of the difficult terrain, the trip could take as long as three hours.

The two young Tibetans then carried our bags as they led us out of the train station to a very old, rusty vehicle that seemed to be half car and half truck. It reminded me some-what of the dusty old tour buses my parents and I rode in on our trip to the Old City of Jerusalem when I was twelve years old.

Much of the area around Nakchu is surrounded by the rather barren Changtang Prairie. As we drove north and west from the city, however, the terrain became quite rocky and considerably more scenic. I felt the drive was a bit boring but, as I glanced across the back seat at Kathy, I still mar-veled at her remarkable natural beauty. I once again recalled the first time we had met at Purdue University when she was hosting a tape-recorded lecture on what she referred to as *Primitive Christian Mysticism*. At that time, I could not have conceived of just how much she would eventually come to mean to me. The mysterious spiritual backgrounds we shared, along with the deep love we soon would feel for each other, proved that she truly was my pre-destined soul mate.

Nevertheless, in spite of the slow, tedious drive on those bumpy, winding roads from Nakchu, this car-truck, or whatever it was, did its job, and exactly three hours after leaving the train station, we arrived at Shimahn's ashram.

After we entered the charming nineteenth-century facility, Tenzing, whose English was far better than Mingma's, led us to our room and promised that Shimahn would join us in about an hour. So after unpacking our bags and refreshing ourselves with some savory green tea and delicious fresh fruit, Kathy and I took a short stroll around the lush ashram grounds. The serene beauty of the premises was almost overwhelming. There were exotic flowers and plants climbing small rock walls that surrounded clear, placid ponds filled with several varieties of tropical fish. Two mini-waterfalls created a steady flow of fresh water through gentle streams that fed the ponds. And even though the area immediately outside the grounds was a bit barren, the perpetually snow-capped mountain peaks in the distance were quite majestic, providing a sensation of impregnability and protection to the surroundings.

For a moment, I wondered if this magical place was our own personal Shangri-la, where all this natural beauty and these precious living things could survive the bitter winters. But most impressive was the atmosphere of peace and harmony seeming to be ever present in and around the ashram. Indeed, the feeling was so intense that this dwelling felt like home to Kathy and me—a place in which we belonged and had always lived.

When we finished our tour of the ashram grounds, Tenzing escorted us down a long hallway lined with slender wooden doors to a sparsely furnished room at the east end of the building. As we entered the room, we found Shimahn sitting quietly in a soft, high-backed chair. The emotions I felt at that moment were virtually indescribable—as was the appearance of my long-lost Himalayan Master. At first glance, Shimahn's entire being seemed to be clothed in an aura of illumination and peace. As we approached him, his olive-colored skin appeared to be almost translucent, though his eyes still were dark and probing. He looked so fragile sitting there I was somewhat reluctant to touch him. Yet he had an enchanting beatific smile on his face while extending his hands to us. For an instant, my eyes met Kathy's, as we simultaneously sensed we were standing on *"holy ground"*— that we were in the presence of a truly enlightened being.

After we had retired to our room that evening, Kathy told me she now understood my enduring desire to see Shimahn once more.

Yet, just as my mind had done when I first met him all those years ago, it started to wander and, being there now in his commanding presence, I again tried to determine just how old this man was. Based upon what Nehemiah had told me back then, Shimahn must now be over 100, and possibly even as much as 105 or 110 years old. But before I could dwell too deeply on such an irrelevant thought, our Tibetan Master brought my mind back to the present by inviting us to sit in two thinly padded wooden chairs stationed about five feet across from him. Because some of the blinds were drawn, the room was a bit dark for that time of day, and was filled with a pleasant bouquet of burning incense.

Knowing that we must have been puzzled by his urgent summons, he gave us a partial explanation that evening. But those preliminary words were only a small foretaste of what he really had in mind and would share with us in the days to come.

Shimahn began his comments much as he had his class work in Old Jerusalem. He once again stressed the all-inclusive nature of God. He said, "God is infinite, which means that God is all that exists—the only Life, Substance and Intelligence, the one infinite Consciousness. I am certain both of you have heard those words before, but now you must take them within your souls and make them *'bone of your bones and flesh of your flesh.'* If you accept the all-ness of God, you will then realize that there can be only goodness and perfection in God's true creation. Therefore, any appearances of evil must be illusions, or errors in belief."

He paused briefly, and then said, "This universe of space-time that we seem to be living in is a false concept of the divine reality. Yet we still must be concerned about the growing turmoil and violence that is evident all around us. Without some intervention in the very near future, I believe we could witness another holocaust, but this time, on a much grander scale. This world, as we perceive it today, is on an irrational path to oblivion, and its only hope for survival may depend upon the three of us."

Seeing the puzzled expressions on our faces, Shimahn seemed to be waiting for a response. When we didn't reply, he continued. "Eric and Kathy, out of all the enlightened souls on this plane of consciousness, I have chosen you to help me in an endeavor that has never before been attempted, and certainly has never been achieved. But I believe that, together, we can prevail."

Our spiritual teacher studied the two of us for a moment and, before we could respond with any questions, raised his left hand slightly and said, "I assume both of you must be quite exhausted from your long journey. So why don't you have a nice warm dinner that Mingma will prepare for you, and then retire early tonight. We will have ample time tomorrow to discuss the situation."

And with that, he closed his eyes. Obediently following his instructions, Kathy and I rose from our chairs and quietly left the room, as Tenzing was attentively waiting in the long hallway outside Shimahn's door.

CHAPTER 3

A RAY OF LIGHT
IN A DARK SKY

Even though it was Saturday and the traditional Jewish day of rest, or Shabbat, Mossad Director Amram Yehuda called the meeting on very short notice. His Institute for Intelligence and Special Operations was responsible for Israel's intelligence collection, covert operations, and counter-terrorism duties, including paramilitary activities. The Mossad has a total of eight departments and a staff of about 1,200 personnel. The highly secretive organization functions much like America's CIA, focusing on external high-threat activities. The Mossad is complemented by Shin Bet, or Shabak, the Israeli counterintelligence and internal security service, along with Aman, the country's military intelligence unit.

On that fateful morning, Yehuda was addressing the leaders of all Israeli intelligence agencies. His first words were: "Are you absolutely certain of this information, Yitzhak? Are they really that close to full assembly? We just don't want to be wrong on this one."

Major General Yitzhak Feldman, chief of Intelligence for Aman, replied, "No question about it, sir. This is real. Our mole was on the premises in Gaza City late last night. He told us the device is only hours away from being ready for detonation. We must take it out tonight by hitting them sometime after dark."

Aaron Leibowitz, Director of Shabak, then commented, "Remember, we don't have many feet on the ground in the Gaza Strip, thanks to that foolish 1993 Oslo agreement. So this operation will be more difficult than going after something in Tel Aviv, or even in the West Bank. Nonetheless, we've been planning for days and have about a dozen members of the Sayeret Tzanhanim unit ready to move. We just needed to learn the specific location."

Sayeret Tzanhanim is an Israeli commando force trained in the use of many weapons. The group functions much like the United States Army's Rangers. All recruits to this service are put through a rigorous three-day-long training and testing period known as the Gibush. Out of hundreds of candidates who enter the program, only a few survive this difficult exercise.

Liebowitz continued, "For the moment, these elite special-forces people are situated in safe houses in Gaza City and Dayr al Balah. They should require only a few hours notice before hitting the target."

"All right, Aaron, you take the lead," said Mossad Director Yehuda, "but please feel free to use any of our other resources for support. We'll be right behind you. We cannot accept failure in this mission."

So without any further discussion, all parties present agreed to take this dangerous, but necessary, action. After all, the very survival of Israel was at stake.

It was just two days earlier that Israeli intelligence had learned of the plot and its unimaginable level of progress. The device was not just a so-called dirty bomb, but a full-scale nuclear weapon, with enough fissionable materials to do a horrific amount of damage. And though no one understood how those materials could have been brought into Gaza City without detection, somehow they were there.

As soon as the decision was made, the elite forces in the field were given their orders. It was precisely at 11:45 that evening when the Sayeret commandos descended on the facility. Their superb training served them well, as they came in like a bolt of lightning. Wearing night-vision goggles and carrying riflescopes, monoculars and other night-vision accessories, they had the advantage of complete surprise, as they simultaneously burst through every door and window. Consequently, the groggy, and in some cases still-sleeping jihadists, didn't have a chance. Because of the attackers' swiftness and efficiency, every enemy combatant in the building was terminated, without a single Israeli casualty. Then with astounding precision, the nuclear device was quickly secured, disarmed, and loaded on the waiting truck.

Mission accomplished!

By the time word of the operation reached President Thompson and the CIA, it had long been successfully concluded. This secretive undertaking was carried out by the same organization that had participated in the July 1967 raid on the Entebbe airport in Uganda. In that earlier operation, the other participants had been Sayeret Matkal and Sayeret Golani.

While the seriousness of the new attempted attack on Israel couldn't be discounted, the fact that the strike was thwarted gave some comfort to other governments around the world. *Was this the anticipated "big one" they all had been waiting for? Could they now let their guard down a bit?* But the two big unanswered questions still were: How many nukes or dirty bombs could these jihadists produce? And did they have the resources to launch a similar attack anywhere else?

Thank God for the amazing proficiency of the Israeli intelligence and security systems.

On Saturday morning, Mingma prepared a wonderful early breakfast of foods that I cannot even describe; but I know there were at least three eggs and some exotic fruit juices in the mix. Then about 8:30 a.m., Tenzing escorted us back to Shimahn's living quarters where, because of the partially open windows, the room was illuminated much more than it had been the previous day. I was surprised to see our Tibetan Master appear so alert and fresh that early in the morning. Once again, he was seated in his soft, high-backed chair and, as he had the previous evening, invited us to sit in the two chairs located across from him. We were separated from our teacher by a low, hand-carved round table made of highly polished teakwood. A little book and a few loose papers with some scrawled notes were lying on the table. The book looked very much like my treasured *The Gospel According to I AM*.

To be certain we would understand everything he was about to propose, Shimahn tested us on our current knowledge of mystical Truth, and then gave us additional instructions and insights. His initial question was, "Have the two of you been spending a sufficient amount of time in meditation and prayer?"

Both of us nodded our heads in the affirmative. Kathy and I always set aside some time each day for that very purpose. We realize how helpful it is to start every day grounded in Truth, to be assured that we have established contact with our Source.

"That is extremely important," Shimahn continued. "Because living in this illusory, four-dimensional world of space-time, it is very easy to get caught up in the problems and temptations we see all around us; yet we must find a way to rise above them.

"Spiritual reality exists in a different dimension of life, at a higher, transcendental level of consciousness. So you must always keep our most basic premise at the forefront of your thought process. Because God is infinite, God fills all space and is the sum and substance of all existence. Most people find that fact quite difficult to accept, primarily because they have been living with, and accepting, a false concept of God. They perceive their Deity as a physical entity, as some type of superhuman, man-like being—maybe even an old man sitting up on a cloud somewhere.

"But the one true God is an incorporeal infinite Consciousness, the only Substance and Intelligence. This God is also Life Itself—the one universal Life, the Life of all being.

"So our only task on the mystical path is to accept these facts and then take them within our souls, making them an integral part of our conscious awareness. Every moment we spend in that transcendental reality lessens our dependence on the illusory world of cause and effect, of action and reaction."

Seeing that Kathy and I were in agreement with everything he was saying, Shimahn continued. "While we try to devote much of our time to dwelling in the five-dimensional consciousness of *My Kingdom*, we still are being presented with problems in the outer world of sense perceptions. But all of those circumstances can be ameliorated by an enlightened soul who understands and realizes his or her Oneness with God. And that is how spiritual healings are brought about. A consciousness imbued with Truth becomes a healing agency.

"In every case, the restoration to health occurs, not because we are doing something to the specific condition but, rather, because we see it for what it is: an illusion. And then, if we reach a high enough level of receptivity to the inflow of the Spirit, the so-called disease will dissolve into its native state of nothingness."

Shimahn paused here, waiting for our affirmative nods, which we gave. The morning sunlight streaming in through the tall windows lit the air behind him, as he went on.

"To an outside observer, this appears as a healing; but to the illumined consciousness, it is a revealing of that which already is. Knowing these facts, we should never have to deal with a problem at the level of the problem. But because the circumstances facing the world today are so perilous, I feel we must address them from a different perspective.

"And even though the three of us can most likely lift ourselves above the conflict to a place in consciousness where we will not be affected by what is happening around us, there are many others who cannot do that. Yet some of these people have been awakened from the dream of material sense and have already achieved a measure of enlightenment. For the first time in the history of mankind, there are millions of receptive souls living on this planet.

"These are the people I want to help. They have acquired a level of awareness and understanding high enough to survive the holocaust that is coming, and then to assist us in uplifting the collective consciousness of mankind"

Pausing once more and taking a deep breath, the Master concluded this discourse. "So for those reasons, I believe that, together, you and I can alter some events that would affect the future and help this world avoid the imminent calamity that may soon be upon us."

Shimahn then asked if we had any questions. Neither of us responded, because we were totally in awe of his presentation. Both of us understood the words; we had heard those many times in the past. But they were spoken with such conviction that we knew he was not just a learned intellectual speaking. The infinite God-consciousness was speaking through this being who at that time was so much more than just a mortal man.

Though both Kathy and I understood much of what our Master was saying, neither of us knew exactly where he was leading us. He still hadn't revealed his grand plan. But so well did my wife and I understand each other that no words were necessary. With only a brief glance between us, we decided to just let him explain it in his own way and at his own chosen time.

Shimahn then invited us to meditate with him. We all closed our eyes and sat quietly for more than an hour. It was one of the most profound and enlightening meditations I have ever experienced. I truly felt the presence of God with us, and I reached that place in consciousness where there is a supernal feeling of only peace, joy and harmony.

After the meditation, Shimahn suggested that Kathy and I spend some time enjoying the beautiful and serene atmosphere of the ashram grounds. He said Mingma would be preparing a nutritious lunch for us in the dining room. With a gentle gesture of his elegant hands, he asked us to come back to his quarters at 2:30 that afternoon.

Our spiritual teacher further piqued our curiosity as he told us in closing that he would then outline his plan on how the three of us could change the course of human history.

CHAPTER 4

A CHANCE ENCOUNTER, AND THE PLAN IS REVEALED

SATURDAY AFTERNOON AND EVENING, AUGUST 15TH
THE ATLANTIC OCEAN - 152 NAUTICAL MILES
NORTHEAST OF VIRGINIA BEACH, VA

After four days of partying in Bermuda, followed by another raucous bash Friday night on the ship, the scantily clad revelers on the sleek, 185-foot luxury yacht were just getting ready to start up again. Christened *Midnight Lace*, the opulent craft was a floating display of overindulgent extravagance. But on that fortuitous Saturday evening, there was an unexpected moment of tension, as a foreboding pall suddenly hovered over the travelers.

Shortly before dusk, Captain Richard Bauer summoned the vessel's owner—dot-com billionaire Larry Archibald—to the bridge deck. Handing his binoculars to Archibald, Bauer asked him to look over the portside railing to the southwest.

The captain then began describing what he believed they were seeing.

The fifty-something seasoned sailor said in a gruff voice, "No question about it, Larry, that looks just like a Somali pirate ship. I can't imagine what the heck they are doing way out here so far from Africa, but you may remember that I had a horrific run-in with one of those before I came to work for you."

Seeing the potential adversary with his own eyes, Archibald asked, "What makes you think it's a pirate ship? Maybe it's just a fishing boat."

"I have a sixth sense about the way it looks and is moving. It appears to be a pirate mother ship. Notice all the rust, and the lack of any identification. Since my run-in, I know one when I see it."

"So what do you suggest we do, Rich?"

The captain answered, "Well, we are not heavily armed and couldn't put up much of a fight if they do decide to come after us. I suggest we act as though we haven't seen them, and start sailing due north. With our horsepower, maybe we can outrun them."

"Okay, you're the captain, Rich . . . Uh, do you think we should notify the Coast Guard?"

"Yes, I'll do it right away. Sorry to put a damper on your passengers' evening, but they should be made aware of the threat."

Archibald rejoined his guests to share the bad news, and Captain Bauer made his report to the Coast Guard. He received a puzzled response from the maritime branch's radio operator.

"How and why would a group of Somali pirates even think of coming near our coastal waters? That sounds awfully suspicious. Are you sure you're not mistaken?"

"Nope," Bauer replied. "I've been in a dogfight with those guys before. But it's strange that they haven't made any move toward us, because we certainly are one of the best targets they could find. They're not moving, but just sitting there dead in the water."

After giving a description of the vessel, along with its coordinates, Captain Bauer signed off and began heading north. As he did so, there was no movement in his direction by the other craft. A short while later, as the *Midnight Lace* sailed on, the pirate ship disappeared into the distant receding horizon.

When the maritime base's radio operator relayed the message to his superiors, it was greeted with alarm, so it took only a few minutes for it to travel all the way up the line to the Coast Guard Commandant, Admiral Arthur Kelbe.

The Commandant is not a participant on the Joint Chiefs of Staff but, rather, answers to the Department of Homeland Security. In wartime, however, the Coast Guard may operate under the Department of the Navy. And since this present environment was approaching a wartime level of tension, the message from the *Midnight Lace* was also passed all the way up that chain of command to Admiral Casey McGraw, Chief of U.S. Naval Operations, and a member of the Joint Chiefs.

Admiral McGraw had been present at the Friday morning meeting at the White House, so he knew that any out-of-the-ordinary events had to be taken seriously and had to be checked out. But dusk had already settled on the nation's Capital, and it was even darker out there over the Atlantic Ocean. The 58-year-old admiral, who was the smallest member of the Joint Chiefs, standing five-feet, five-inches in height, wasn't certain of just how much searching they could, or should, do in the dark, especially if this were just a wild goose chase. So he decided to have the process ready to go first thing Sunday morning by utilizing some of the assets of the Coast Guard's interception and interdiction operation in the drug war. But first they had to determine just what hardware would be available to cover the wide search area. And that would be the responsibility of people lower in the chain of command.

SATURDAY AFTERNOON, AUGUST 15TH
SHIMAHN'S ASHRAM - NAKCHU PREFECTURE -
NORTHERN TIBET AUTONOMOUS REGION

After a lunch consisting of a plate of food that looked and tasted a little like seaweed—we were afraid to ask what it was—Kathy and I returned to Shimahn's quarters right at 2:30 that afternoon. When we arrived, our Himalayan Master was sitting in his chair with his eyes closed. But as we entered the room, he gently looked up and greeted us with a warm smile, as we took our customary seats in the two chairs across from him.

In that session, Shimahn didn't waste any time getting to the substance of his plan. He said, "As I mentioned this morning, this world is blindly and mindlessly headed on a path toward oblivion. And amazingly, it has all transpired very quickly. Even during the darkest days of the Cold War, with the world's Superpowers pointing their nuclear weapons at each other, circumstances were not as catastrophic or explosive as they are today. During those years, we had nations dealing with other nations. And even though they had disagreements, they also were all very concerned about their own survival. But today, because the radical elements have perverted a great religion, they are actually willing to sacrifice their own lives in suicidal fashion, by dying for their misguided, jihadist cause."

Shimahn took a deep breath, and then continued. "Eric, I believe that you can be an instrument for change—that you can affect the outcome of this present dilemma."

"And how could I do that, sir?"

"I would like you to go back in time and change certain events in the past that could then alter future circumstances, especially some of the perilous conditions we are facing today."

Both Kathy and I gasped at that statement. Was this spiritually inspired man losing it in his old age? My wife was the first to speak up. "Surely, you're not talking about time travel, are you?"

"Yes," he replied simply, a barely concealed smile on his face.

Puzzled by his last comments, I then said, "Shimahn, what makes you think time travel is possible? Many of the world's most renowned scientists don't believe that it is."

"Because I have already done it," he stated firmly.

With her eyes as wide as saucers, Kathy asked, "Do you have a time machine? Have you invented one?"

He chuckled for a moment and said, "No, Kathy, you don't need a machine to travel through time. Time travel is an activity in consciousness."

"How would that work?" was my next question.

"It begins by understanding the true nature of eternal life. Eternal Life can be compared to an infinite Circle that has no beginning or ending. In our real life-experience, each of us lives forever in that Grand Circle. We are spiritual beings who were never born and will never die. The Life of God—the Life that is God—is flowing *in* and *through* each of us forever . . . or as the Bible states: *'from everlasting to everlasting.'* "

"I understand that," I interjected, "but how does that make time travel possible?"

Shimahn replied, "Because you must also realize that this present life-unfoldment in which you are living today is a very small, almost infinitesimal part of the eternal Circle. Actually it is just a parenthesis superimposed on that Circle. But it is only one of many such parentheses."

The Master paused for a moment to let us digest that statement, then said, "Let us close our eyes now and try to conceptualize this picture. We will proceed very slowly.

"First of all, visualize an enormous, never-ending, infinite Circle which represents eternal Life . . . Then imagine a set of parentheses placed upon a small part of that Circle . . . The left bracket of the parenthesis represents your birth into this life, and the right bracket represents your death, or transition out of this life.

"Now take some time to establish that picture in your mind's eye."

Shimahn paused once again to give us enough time to do that.

After a few minutes, he continued. "Now envision a whole series of those parentheses placed at various intervals around the Circle—

"Those additional sets of parentheses represent other lives you have lived in the past, or will live in the future.

"Once you realize that you have lived before in numerous lifetimes—all of which have occurred at some interval in the Grand Circle of Eternity—you will be able to step in and out of those other lives with some frequency, and almost at will."

The enlightened mystic then asked if we had any questions.

I commented, "So if I understand this correctly, you are saying that somehow we have the ability to rise out of our present lifetime—a parenthesis as you called it—and enter the Grand Circle?"

"Yes," he answered authoritatively. "And while that may seem to be an imposing challenge, you already have done it many times. Whenever you make a transition out of a given

lifetime—that process which the world perceives as death—
you reenter the Grand Circle of Eternity."

Kathy then asked, "Shimahn, if after a death experience
we are living once more in the infinite Circle, why would we
come back and live again in another earthly lifetime?"

"We don't always have a choice," he replied gently.
"Usually, it is because we have not risen to a high enough
level of awareness in the previous lifetime to avoid the need
for another reincarnation.

"That is our purpose in every new life-journey. We are
here to function as instruments through which the God-Life
is lived in perfection and harmony. When we achieve a
perpetual or permanent realization of that perfection by living
in constant Oneness with our Source, we will break the cycle
of endless reincarnations and ultimately achieve conscious
union with God."

The Master shifted slightly in his chair, crossed his legs,
and then said, "The Buddhists and Hindus refer to this as
nirvana, a blissful state of enlightenment in which we rise
above all physicality. In that illumined environment, we
recognize our true identity as an immaculate, perfect spiritual
being—a being that has been created in the image and
likeness of God. That is our divine birthright and our spiritual
destiny."

As the light in the room was beginning to darken with
the approaching dusk, Shimahn suggested we stop our
instructions for the day. He told us to have a nice dinner and
then spend some time pondering these latest revelations
before going to sleep. He recommended that we continue

visualizing our life as being lived in the Grand Circle of Eternity, and to know that we have the ability to re-enter and exit any one of the parentheses appearing in that circle. In other words to revisit our past lives—

Wow, what a mind-boggling concept!

CHAPTER 5

POLITICAL CONFUSION VERSUS SPIRITUAL CLARITY

EARLY SUNDAY MORNING, AUGUST 16TH
CENTRAL INTELLIGENCE AGENCY HEADQUARTERS - LANGLEY, VA

For the second time in three days, CIA Director Scott Cunningham called an emergency meeting of his inner circle of intelligence specialists. After sharing the information about the aborted Israeli attack, he stressed the seriousness of that situation and updated the group on the ever-increasing, incendiary chatter being picked up by agents across the globe. The Mossad had learned from an Israeli mole that the Gaza terrorist group had been trained by Hamas and was based in Yemen. Most of the bomb-making materials had been supplied by the Iranians.

Ever since they attained the highest level of uranium enrichment, the Ayatollahs and their lunatic president were wreaking havoc all over the world. It was always assumed that once Iran had the bomb, they would try to annihilate

Israel. But because of President Thompson's stern warning that "any strike against Israel would be responded to as a strike on America," the mullahs knew we would take their country off the face of the earth if they openly fired the missile. And so up until now, the dreaded, potential nuclear event in the Middle East had never occurred. It appeared that rather than hitting Israel with one of their own missiles—which could be traced back to them—the mad men in Tehran chose just to disseminate weapons and other materials to surrogates, who would do all the dirty work while appearing to be nothing more than isolated terrorists. That was why the previous night's Sayeret mission had been so important.

Opening the meeting, Cunningham said, "The key questions at the moment are: Is this the end of it, or only the beginning? Is this what all the chatter was about, or are more attacks being planned?"

Lori Colbert commented, "It's too bad the Israelis are so darned efficient. They took everybody out at the site, and now there are no subjects available for interrogation. Some of those people might have known something about what is going on."

"I agree with you, Lori," the CIA Director acknowledged. "It would have been nice to have gotten more information. But sometimes I wish we could be as secretive and adept as the Mossad. They really know how to execute a mission."

Cunningham surveyed his intelligence community people seated at the table and asked, "Do we have any updates since yesterday?"

DNI Director Sean Larkin replied, "We do, and we don't, Scott."

"What's that supposed to mean, Sean?" asked Jacoby of NCS.

As the president's principal advisor on intelligence matters, Larkin was a retired three-star army general, with many honors for his service in the first Gulf War, Iraq, and Afghanistan. At sixty years old and a stocky five feet, nine inches tall, he had his head shaved bald, sported lots of gray stubble on his pockmarked, ruddy face, and looked "tough as nails."

Replying to Jacoby, General Larkin said, "We're hoping this attempt in Israel is the one that was causing all the noise in the intelligence-gathering fraternity. If the bad guys have another attack planned, we aren't aware of it—at least not with any degree of certainty. However, there is something else—

"Last night, a luxury yacht was sailing back from Bermuda to Newport, Rhode Island, when the captain thought he saw a Somali pirate ship sitting about 150 nautical miles off the coast of Southern Virginia."

"That's crazy!" Cunningham interrupted. "Why would some pirates from Somalia take a chance like that? By coming so close to America, they'd be sitting ducks out there . . . They'd have no place to hide."

"I thought so, too, Scott. And so did Admiral Kelbe of the Coast Guard . . . That is, until he learned that the yacht's captain is Richard Bauer.

"He's the guy who was commanding a different ship a few years ago that really was attacked by pirates off the east coast of Africa. Unknown to the attackers, Bauer had a shitload of weapons on board, so he suckered the buccaneers by passively letting them board his boat. Then, seemingly out of nowhere, his hidden crew jumped the bastards and cut their balls off. Bauer also had enough firepower on board to sink the friggin' privateer. And you know the best part? He threw the dead pirates overboard—and didn't pick up any of the survivors still in the water.

"Now that's my kind of guy!"

General Larkin concluded his discourse by saying, "Admiral McGraw of Naval Operations told us that because Richard Bauer has dealt with pirates before, his sighting carries some credibility. And since it seems odd for any Somali pirates to be this close to our shores, the boat might be a fake, a cover for a more deadly cargo. Anyway, to be sure that nothing bad slips through our defenses, the Admiral said the Navy is joining forces with the Coast Guard to go out and search for that little bucket this morning. We'll let you know if they find it, and if it turns out to have any significance."

Director Cunningham thanked Larkin for the update and then asked if there were any additional comments. Hearing none, he said, "For your information, General Larkin and I will be going to the White House for another briefing in a little while. President Thompson has been in constant communication with the Israeli, British, French, Russian and Chinese heads of state. Most people in intelligence don't believe this is the end of the aggressive acts, because this was a Hamas-trained group based in Yemen, and the bulk of their activities are carried out in the Middle East. On the contrary, the three aborted attacks here—in New York, Illinois and California—were al-Qaeda inspired. And that group is much more aggressive in far-away places around the world. So we have to believe there still is something in the works; we just don't know when or where."

Cunningham stood, then said, "Well that should be all for now. I'd like to suggest that any of you who are church-going people to please consider attending your respective services today to say a special prayer at this time. Either way, keep your cell phones and beepers turned on in case we need you back here real fast . . . Hopefully, we won't!"

LATER SUNDAY MORNING - AUGUST 16TH
THE CABINET ROOM, WEST WING OF THE WHITE HOUSE
WASHINGTON, D.C.

In addition to the people who had attended the White House meeting on Friday, Sunday's group included SEC Chairman Sheldon Bronstein and several more cabinet members. Among them were the secretaries of Treasury, Transportation, and Health and Human Services. Also present were the President pro tempore of the Senate and the Speaker of the House of Representatives.

With a serious frown on his face, CIA Director Cunningham gave a synopsis of the events in Israel on Saturday night and an update on any other information now available.

"Unfortunately, we don't know very much," he told them. He also mentioned the possible pirate ship sighting, but said he had very little information about it. He looked at Admiral McGraw for help, but the diminutive Chief of Naval Operations could only say that his people, along with the Coast Guard, were investigating it.

President Thompson then reviewed whatever news he could share from his discussions with the other worldwide heads of state. Though some of them were cautiously optimistic and happy about the Israeli action, most were still unsure of what steps to take next.

After a brief period of introspective silence, General Daniels said, "Mr. President, I expect to give the order to go to DEFCON 2 later today at about 1830 hours. He then looked at the Director of Homeland Security and asked, "When are you raising the airport security levels, Domenic?"

"I plan on doing that after 5:00 p.m. Eastern Time tonight."

Vice-President Tucker spoke next. "What about Wall Street, Sheldon? Are you gonna let the markets open Monday morning?"

Bronstein, a frizzy-haired, six-footer whose trademark was the colorful bow ties that he wore, responded, "My first inclination is to let them open and see how it goes. Since the Israelis were successful in aborting the attempt there, the news isn't all that bad. So if the Dow does drop 500 or 600 points in the morning, I believe we can weather that, and probably even see it come back a bit with a nice bounce in the afternoon. However, if it looks like all the downtick safeguards are being triggered, we will close early.

"Does anyone here disagree with that strategy?" he asked.

"Sounds right to me," the President replied. "But there is another serious matter we must discuss.

"In the event there is a hit somewhere else, and especially if it appears that anything is aimed at Washington, D.C., we need to immediately implement our contingency evacuation plans for the government." Looking directly at Vice President Tucker, Thompson said, "Jason, what would you think about taking your family on a quick, unexpected and unannounced fishing vacation to your cabin in Northern Minnesota?"

Tucker looked a bit puzzled, but then asked, "Uh, when would you want me to do that, sir?"

"How about sometime in the next three or four hours?" the President answered. "Air Force Two is ready to go, if you can be."

The vice president, a slight man who reminded some people of Mr. Rogers, the old children's-television-show host, shrugged his shoulders, and with an obedient smile on his face also nodded his head while at the same time saying, "Uh-huh."

"We must take all precautions for the continuity of our government," the President stated with strong conviction in his voice. "I believe that you and I should not be in the same place again until this thing blows over."

Then addressing the two leaders of Congress, he said, "If things get hairy by tomorrow or Tuesday, I'd like the two of you to call for a Congressional recess. To avoid too much panic, let's not make it an official adjournment, but just a temporary recess. Since we currently don't have much legislation on the front burner, that shouldn't cause any real problems. Then I want all members of Congress to head back to their home districts ASAP. Those who are close enough could maybe just drive home, even if they have to rent cars. But those who live farther away will need to fly. And since the air traffic system may be extremely frantic, or possibly even shut down by that time, we will try to make as much military transport available as possible.

"Can you work that out, Mary Jane?"

The Air Force Chief of Staff replied, "I'll get on it immediately, Mr. President."

Thompson then addressed Congressman Robert Berkley of Texas, the Speaker of the House of Representatives. "Bob, since you are second in line to the presidency should something happen to me, I suggest you also head home to your ranch as soon as possible. If you can't get away later tonight, then do it first thing in the morning."

His eyes surveying the table, the President asked, "Are there any other questions or comments at this time?"

Getting no response, he closed the meeting by addressing Admiral McGraw. "Casey, please let us know what you learn about that so-called pirate ship. Hopefully it's nothing more than an over-active imagination by that yacht captain.

"All right, that should be all for now. But everyone please stay alert and ready in case we need you back here anytime soon."

On Sunday morning, Kathy and I had an earlier-than-usual breakfast and then joined Shimahn at 8:00 a.m. He started that session by asking if we had any questions about what he had been telling us thus far.

Kathy spoke up first. "Uh, Shimahn, when you originally suggested the idea of time travel, you also mentioned that you had already done it."

"Yes, I have."

"Then why do you need Eric or me to help you? Can't you just go back and do whatever needs to be done by yourself?"

"Good question, Kathy, but it's not that simple—

"You see, this is not like climbing inside a Jules Verne or H. G. Wells time machine, where you can set a random date on the monitor and then just get out at any point in history.

"No such machine has ever been invented. And even if one had been, the eminent scientist Stephen Hawking has suggested that time travel might be possible only in a region of space-time that is warped in the right way. Hawking also claims that if we cannot create such a region until the future, then time travelers would not be able to travel back to a time prior to that date.

"Notwithstanding all those other considerations, our mystical method of time travel involves returning only to one of your own previous lives. In other words, you cannot go back in time and suddenly become Julius Caesar, Napoleon or George Washington, if you were not one of those people in your past lifetime. You can only be yourself . . . This immortal soul that you are can only enter one of your previous parentheses and, then, it can fuse with, and take over, the body you were using in that parenthesis."

Shimahn paused for a moment so we could digest and comprehend his astonishing theories. He then said, "When you do enter one of those previous bodies, it would be at the same age you were when you left here . . . the age you are today in this present reality. Your soul or consciousness does not fuse with that other body as a six-year-old child, as an adolescent, or as a seventy-year-old man or woman.

"It is the present *you* that is appearing as, and temporarily replacing, the old *you*."

"That's incredible!" was all that Kathy could say at that time.

The Master spoke again. "As a further illustration, let us use the example of a hypnotist taking a person through a series of past-life regressions. In that process, the subject may be able to see events from those previous incarnations and might become an observer. He may even have some memories of that time period, but he will seldom actually enter those bodies and relive those lives.

"And that is what makes our approach so different. We can return to a previous parenthesis and take control of the host body."

I then asked, "Shimahn, when did you go back in time? What age were you?"

"I didn't discover the secret of mystical time travel until I was already 88 years old in this lifetime. As a result, I was able to find only one other incarnation in which I had lived to such a ripe old age."

"And when, or where was that?" I pressed him again.

"The trip took place about 18 years ago," he replied. "In that particular past, I was living in a Carmelite Priory in Paris in the seventeenth century CE . . . I believe the year was around 1687."

"What was life like at that time? Were you anyone famous?"

"Sorry to disappoint you, Eric, but I was merely a simple monk doing menial chores in the monastery. However, I did work alongside a very spiritually enlightened man. He was Brother Lawrence, the Carmelite monk whose *Conversations and Letters* became the foundation for the book: *The Practice of the Presence of God*."

Kathy asked enthusiastically, "Did you help Brother Lawrence write his book?"

"No, Kathy, I had no role in the authorship. I was just another humble servant of God who had the privilege of living in that wonderful spiritual environment. But I did make one important contribution: I was the one who sug-gested the title for the manuscript. And it was another coworker of ours, Father Joseph de Beaufort, who saw to it that Brother Lawrence's famous book was published. Father de Beaufort later became vicar general to the Archbishop of Paris."

So even if Shimahn hadn't done anything of major significance in his journey back in time, this story gave me a better indication of his current age. He would have to be 106 years old today.

After hearing this most fascinating narrative, both Kathy and I were sitting dumbfounded at the edges of our chairs with our mouths open.

Shimahn looked at us and smiled demurely as he said, "Now that the two of you have heard my account, maybe you will understand why I have asked for your help. Eric, you are at the ideal age to make the journey through time. You will have many parentheses—many past lifetimes—that you can visit."

I then asked, "But what makes you believe that either Kathy or I would be able to rise into the Grand Circle of Eternity as easily as you did? You are a truly enlightened Tibetan mystic. We are just two kids from Chicago."

"That is not true, Eric . . . You, too, are a very illumined soul. I know you were told long ago that not only have you had numerous lifetimes of mystical training, but also that you were my spiritual teacher in a previous incarnation. And even now in America, you are doing healing work and conducting classes in spiritual living. Furthermore, you must know that in an earlier lifetime, you were the author of *The Gospel According to I AM*."

We should have been totally shocked by Shimahn's last statement but, when he said it, I realized this was the second time someone had told us that I was the writer of the ancient mystical Gospel. When Kathy and I had first met as young teenagers in St. Louis, Missouri, we had an encounter with a very fascinating enlightened man named Jeremy Hunt, who evidently was endowed with remarkable extra-sensory abilities. In an astounding revelation at that time, Mr. Hunt declared that I had authored the profound esoteric book of spiritual wisdom. So to hear Shimahn repeat that suggestion in our conversation in Tibet was a bit unsettling for both of us.

Nonetheless, when the Master saw that I was quietly agreeing with everything he was telling us, he authoritatively concluded this discussion by saying, "Eric, you have the capacity within you to very quickly practice and master this special art of time travel. And you not only *can* do it, but you *must* do it.

"The future of mankind hangs in the balance!"

CHAPTER 6

THE OUTER SEARCH
AND
THE INNER MISSION

I t is virtually impossible for United States counter-terror organizations to keep track of all the ships and aircraft that could possibly pose a threat to the homeland. At sea, there are more than 30,000 ocean-going ships, along with thousands of smaller craft cruising nearer to the nation's coastlines. In addition, there are 300,000 non-military aircraft flying worldwide that operate from more than 40,000 airfields.

As a result, threats that terrorists pose to America's ports, waterways and airways remain persistent and grave. In response to these threats, the Office of the Director of National Intelligence, or ODNI, was established in 2005. This is the agency now headed by retired General Sean

Larkin. Nevertheless, the challenges in monitoring all of this traffic remain formidable, so to find a rather small boat that had been described by a yacht captain as a pirate ship would also be nearly impossible. Yet because of the many rumors and potential threats reverberating through the intelligence community on that Sunday morning, an attempt had to be made.

After receiving the coordinates and a description of the suspicious boat on Saturday evening, the Coast Guard responded quickly. By mid-morning Sunday the maritime service dispatched three "Sentinel Class" fast-response cutters, three Island Class patrol boats, two of the new HH-65 multi-mission cutter helicopters, and two H-65 Dolphin helicopters to handle the search. These are some of the most sophisticated and commonly used vessels for this type of operation.

Though the coverage area was wide, the choppers were able to traverse a large expanse in a reasonably short time. Jokingly naming the target *The Jolly Roger*, the helicopter pilots were actually enjoying themselves, as they still were able to find some levity in the midst of a potentially grave situation.

It was at 1318 hours that the initial contact was made. The boat in question—a rusty 78-foot vessel—was sighted by one of the choppers about 135 nautical miles off the southern coast of Maryland. Moving slowly, the craft was meandering somewhat, without any objective and with no apparent targeted destination.

So as not to alarm the ship's crew, the helicopter moved away, but kept watch from a safe distance. After contacting their home base, the airborne team learned that one of the Sentinel Class cutters was within forty-five minutes from the site of interception, and one of the patrol boats was a little more than an hour away.

The Sentinel-Design cutter is 154 feet long and is armed with a remote-control 25mm Bushmaster autocannon and four M2HB.50 caliber machine guns. These ships also have bow thrusters, which aid in maneuvering in crowded areas, along with underwater fins, which help fight against the rolling and pitching that can be caused by large waves. While the cutters are true "fighting ships," the older Island-class 110-foot patrol boats usually perform surveillance, law enforcement, and drug interdiction operations in addition to their search and rescue work.

If this really was a pirate ship, the people at Mission Control assumed those two Coast Guard vessels should have had enough manpower and firepower to handle the situation. Yet, if the craft was carrying any weapons of mass destruction, it may not have mattered how many warships came to the scene.

Before the Coast Guard vessels had arrived at the point of contact, it was learned that the Navy also had one of its Arleigh Burke class guided-missile destroyers in the vicinity. When that fact became known, the planners decided to have the closest ships wait until all three could converge on the target simultaneously. Then as a backup, the choppers would enter the air space to provide any additional coverage and support needed.

The all-steel, fire-resistant Arleigh Burke destroyers carry a Collective Protection System, which makes them more responsive to nuclear, biological and chemical attacks. The destroyers are powerfully armed, with weapons and systems ranging from BGM 109 Tomahawk missiles, to SM-e Standard Ballistic defense missiles, to several varieties of lightweight guns and MK-50 torpedoes.

And while all of that armor might have seemed like overkill for this present operation, the proximity of the ship to the suspect vessel was too good an opportunity to pass up. It also was a very symbolic way of scaring the heck out of any small group of pirates, or other people with bad intentions.

The perfect moment for interception occurred at 1525 hours that afternoon. Coast Guard Commander Stanley Pakulski was in charge of the cutter, which had positioned itself approximately sixty yards from the potential adversary, and the customary signals for boarding were given by the boarding officer.

At that time, the United States' maritime crews still didn't know if this really was a pirate ship, a group of people out for a leisurely cruise, or something more dangerous. While the day was bright and sunny over the Atlantic Ocean, the water in the interdiction area was quite choppy, giving the heavily armed American ships an even greater advantage.

As the three military vessels moved closer, the Navy destroyer and the cutter had their snipers poised and ready in case of any hostile action. But the shooters had been fore-warned not to kill all combatants, if that's what they turned out to be. A few shots in the legs would be enough to maim some of the crewmen and take them out of commission, while still leaving them available for interrogation.

The Navy's Arleigh Burke destroyer was commanded by Captain Kevin O'Connell, a veteran of twenty-three years of maritime service to his country. As the ranking officer in this operation, Captain O'Connell would have ultimate responsibility for determining the response level in case of hostile activity.

Then suddenly and without any warning, AKM assault-rifle shots were fired from the so-called "pirate ship," aimed mainly at the Coast Guard cutter. The Russian-built semi- and fully automatic weapons are readily available to terrorist groups and other soldiers of fortune around the world. However, since no United States' crewmen were hit by the randomly fired shots, it was obvious that the foreign sailors were not trained militants. But at least the American seamen now knew this wasn't just a pleasure cruise.

Within seconds, several rounds came flying back in response, as two of the foreign shooters' heads were blown off. Once the aggressive action began, eight Navy SEALs entered the water behind the destroyer. As the Coast Guard and Navy ships moved closer, it appeared there were about ten or eleven crewmembers on the enemy boat, including the two who had just been taken out.

"Lay down your weapons," the voice from the bullhorn said. "You are completely surrounded and cannot get away."

More shots were fired at the cutter, and then, almost instantaneously, another enemy shooter was eliminated. Pirates usually don't fight this hard when it is obvious they are outnumbered and outmanned. The American seamen wondered why these guys were being so combative? Once the U.S. ships were that close, it became apparent that all the crewmembers on the "pirate ship" were of Middle East extraction, which meant there now was one consolation for the current survivors: their three late friends have just been sent off to meet their awaiting virgins.

While the cutter was creating a huge distraction along the portside of the smaller boat, the Navy SEALs had reached the base of the rusty, barnacle-covered hull at the starboard side.

Captain O'Connell told the cutter's boarding officer to give one final warning. When that was responded to by another volley of shooting, O'Connell gave his snipers the order to take out three more of the enemy combatants: "anybody with a weapon in his hands," he said. "Then let's draw all of their attention to the cutter and have the SEALs quickly board the ship. They should be able to handle what's left of that crew. But be sure they keep three or four of them alive for interrogation."

As expected, the remaining adversaries were fully absorbed in the portside action, so the SEALs effortlessly blindsided them from behind. In spite of being so over-whelmingly outnumbered, the militants continued to battle fiercely and seemed willing to fight to the death. Two more of the insurgents were killed in hand-to-hand combat with the

SEALs, and it took all their skills for the amphibian strike force to capture any of the combatants alive. Fortunately, three of them were subdued and taken prisoner, and there were no American casualties. All of the scruffy, apprehended Middle-Eastern crewmen were heavily bearded and continued to struggle, even while their hands were tightly tied behind their backs.

Once the intruding vessel's combat zone was secured, the boarding crew from the cutter joined the SEALs on the deck. And it was only a few minutes later that they found the reason for all of the aggressive action.

In the cabin below, a partially armed tactical nuclear bomb was resting securely in a custom-built compartment of the ship. As the Navy specialists disarmed the device, the prisoners were transferred to the destroyer. Captain O'Connell immediately relayed a brief report of the mission to Naval Operations. When he described the discovery of a nuclear weapon on board, he was instructed to give *The Jolly Roger* a full military escort to the U.S. Naval Station in Norfolk, Virginia . . . and to do it very gently.

SUNDAY AFTERNOON, AUGUST 16TH
SHIMAHN'S ASHRAM - NAKCHU PREFECTURE -
NORTHERN TIBET AUTONOMOUS REGION

As had been our practice for the past two days, Kathy and I had another "nutritious lunch"—as Shimahn usually referred to them—with ingredients direct from the ashram's organic garden. After heartily satisfying our palates, we then returned to his room at 2:00 p.m.

Once we were back in our respective chairs, the enlightened Master revisited the subject of time travel.

"How do you feel about my proposal, Eric?" he inquired.

"A little strange, and a little concerned," I responded cautiously. "I don't know what to expect or whether I will be able to pull it off. So why don't you tell us more about the process and how the experience actually feels. For example, how long can a person be gone . . . and does time pass here just as quickly as it does for the traveler? If I were gone for twelve years, would Kathy age right along with me? When I get there, will I remember where I came from? And most important, how do I get back here?"

"Good questions, Eric," he said. "Let us take them one at a time.

"First of all, you can be gone as long as needed to complete your mission. And in my experience, I learned there is a strange phenomenon to all of this . . . No matter how long you may be away, no time will have elapsed in the present. You will come back to the exact same moment in which you left here."

"How can that be?" Kathy asked.

"I believe it happens because *you*—your true identity or soul—cannot be in two places at the same time," he replied.

"You may recall how in some time-travel movies or books, the character goes back in time and sees an older version of himself when he arrives there. In those fictional scripts, the character is often warned not to interact with his other self, because that may cause a paradox of some sort.

"In our mystical time-travel model, however, you don't just *see* your old self . . . you actually *become* that. And when the *you* of today fuses with, and controls, that body of the past, the older *you* enters a state of dormancy until the present *you* exits the body.

"Does that sound logical?" he asked thoughtfully.

"Not really," I mumbled. "Frankly, none of this sounds logical."

Shimahn chuckled, and then said, "All right, Eric, let us try to answer your other questions.

"No time will pass in the present—at least not for you— because you wouldn't be there to experience that passage of time. Remember, you will be returning to the exact moment in this life as it was when you originally left.

"And as for memories," he said, "it all depends on how strong your attraction will be to the life to which you are going. If you are entering a parenthesis in which you are merely a temporary visitor and have no commitments or soul mates waiting for you, you will have greater memories of this life that you just left behind. However, if you become immersed in that previous lifetime and have other strong ties to that environment, it will seem more real for you, and there will be less remembrance of this present parenthesis.

"Yet even under those circumstances, you still will be subjected to occasional memory lapses where you will feel out of place there and may experience an affinity or attraction to another time or place.

"But because *you*, Eric, are a highly illumined soul, you will always know at the core of your being where you really belong. And that will give you the ability to return to the present. Even in the previous lifetime, you will discover or be reintroduced to the secret of mystical time travel; you will find your way back to the Grand Circle of Eternity."

He then said, "One final point about memory: When you return here, you will remember most of the events you experienced in your sojourn into that previous lifetime."

With a worried frown on her face Kathy then asked, "Shimahn, what if something bad were to happen to Eric? What if he were arrested and put in prison, or worse yet, what if he found himself in a very dangerous place and was killed? I couldn't bear that."

Sensing Kathy's deep apprehension about the potential danger of this undertaking, the Master answered compassionately. "Do not be concerned, Kathy, because even in those extreme circumstances, Eric would find his way back to us.

"Let us take a moment to analyze the possibilities you just described.

"If for some reason Eric ended up in prison, his highly developed consciousness could lift him right out of that situation by making a transition out of that entire parenthesis. Remember, the Apostle Paul had a similar experience when he and Silas were arrested and incarcerated in Phillippi. After being placed in shackles, Paul's revelation of Truth was so strong that an earthquake occurred, reducing the entire facility to rubble and breaking the chains on Paul, Silas and all the other prisoners. And though, outwardly, the saving event in Paul's case appeared to be an earthquake, in reality it was an inner activity of his enlightened consciousness that effectuated the miracle.

"So even if some unforeseen circumstance led to Eric being arrested and imprisoned, the presence of God active in his consciousness could release him, not from just the prison, but from that entire parenthesis."

I glanced at the side window and noticed that the sun was setting, creating a gorgeous array of colors across the clouds resting so peacefully above the mountains. While I was relishing the beauty outside, my enchantment with nature was quickly dissolved by the alarm in my wife's voice.

"But what if he were killed?" she asked gravely.

Shimahn tried to console her. "Even death would not be a problem, Kathy, because he has already died in that lifetime. So with this second transition, Eric would merely be lifted back into the Grand Circle of Eternity and, from there, would have a clearer path back to this present time.

"Furthermore, you and I will be here doing spiritual work for him, seeking to realize the perfection of his being as God-consciousness individually expressed. Hence, wherever he may be at that time, and in whatever situation he may find himself, he will feel that 'pull' and will be led back here to us.

"Because of all these factors, Kathy, I have no fear for Eric. He will be doing God's work and cannot be harmed by any illusory temporal powers."

After another twenty minutes of that type of give and take, Shimahn said, "Having covered all of these principles, my good friends, I now would like to offer you an exercise that you can use to help lift yourselves out of your physical bodies and into pure consciousness. Would you like to try it?"

"Yes," we replied simultaneously. My dear wife and I briefly held hands, and the warm feeling of her delicate fingers gave the assurance and courage to move forward.

"All right," he said. "Make yourselves comfortable in your chairs and close your eyes . . . This is one of the most powerful mystical practices that I have learned; it is a procedure I have been using for the past sixty years.

"Now I am going to lead you through a series of steps which will enable you to actually discern your true identity and rise above your physical sense of body.

"First of all, look down at your feet . . . or with your eyes closed, visualize your feet . . . take them into your mind—

"Are those feet you, or are they yours?"

"They are mine," we both responded audibly.

"Good," he said. "Now lift your thought up to your legs... Once again, ask yourself the question, are those legs me, or are they mine? You may just contemplate the answer, you do not have to speak it aloud."

As with my feet, I realized that my legs also are not me, but are mine . . . I use the feet and legs for my own purposes. They enable me to walk, run and jump. I use them to move around. Therefore, *I* must be separate from those appendages. If they were to be amputated from my body, I would have less mobility, but I would still be *I*, my selfsame immortal soul, the divine identity that *I* am.

Shimahn then continued. "Now consider your hands and arms. Are those limbs you, or are they yours?"

Within me, I could only give the inevitable answer. They are mine. Of themselves, my hands and arms are inanimate objects; they can only be used if I move them. He then had us begin contemplating all the organs of our bodies: the stomach, intestines, liver, kidneys, lungs, the heart, and even our organs of reproduction and elimination.

The same question elicited the identical reply. I am not those organs, but they are mine.

In a flash, I also realized that medical science has evolved to a level where most of those internal organs can be transplanted from one person to another. And when that surgery is completed, the recipient awakens from the operation with his unaltered identity and soul—the same essence as before—even though he no longer has his original heart, lung or liver. So therefore, none of those organs can be *me* but, rather, all of them are *mine*.

The good Master then had us lift our thought process up to our heads. He asked if we considered our brain to be us— the essence of what we are. In other words, am I the brain, or do *I* have a brain?

Once again, that question brought forth the same answer. The human brain is much like the memory bank of a computer. I can program it, and I can use it for many other purposes. I think with it, I calculate and reason through it.

And since I am the user of the brain, I must be separate from it. Therefore, *I* cannot be it.

But then came the final and most thought-provoking question of all. Shimahn asked, "What about your mind? Are you the mind, or is the mind yours?"

In response, I could only conclude: I am neither my mind, nor am I in my mind . . . instead, *I* use my mind.

That then begs the questions: If I cannot be found anywhere in my body . . . If I am not my mind, and if I am not in my mind, then where am I? What am I? Who am I?

This answer then came to me: *I* am consciousness . . . a spiritual, omniscient consciousness that is living as the individualized expression of the one infinite Consciousness.

In other words, I am not a material organism living in a physical body. Instead, I am one with the eternal Godhead. I and my Father are One.

But this line of thinking led to an amazing occurrence. As I came to the full realization that I do not reside anywhere in my physical body, I now beheld myself living above and beyond the body as pure consciousness . . . and then it happened—

I had my first out-of-body experience!

With my eyes still closed, I found myself floating high above my body, and I was looking down at it sitting there in the chair. From that elevated vantage point, I achieved a much grander view of the Universe. I perceived the infinite nature of creation, not as just a physical structure but, rather, as an incorporeal, spiritual unfoldment of the one universal God-consciousness.

Initially, I saw bright lights all around me and, far beyond that, a seemingly illimitable darkness. Shortly thereafter, I acquired a fleeting glimpse of the Grand Circle of Eternity. I now more fully understood the real meaning of infinity. The boundless and timeless nature of ultimate reality was coming more vividly into view.

I then was overcome by a tremendous desire to soar deeper into this fathomless openness of endless space. I yearned to just let go of any attraction to my physical body and my present life-stream. But before I could relish and truly experience that risky undertaking, I heard Shimahn's voice calling me back.

"Eric," he said emphatically, "I believe you have experienced enough for now."

At first, I didn't want to relinquish the expansive joy and freedom I was feeling. I wanted to stay at that elevated level of consciousness, so I clung to the rapture of the moment.

But my teacher spoke again, this time in an even louder voice. *"Eric, it is time to come back!"*

And then, as if a hypnotic spell had been broken, I opened my eyes to find myself sitting in my chair next to Kathy. As our eyes met, I realized that she also was extremely moved by this exercise, although she told me later that evening that she did not share in my deep mystical experience.

Once I had an opportunity to settle in and comprehend what had just happened, Shimahn said, "Eric, you now must realize that you are capable of rising into the Grand Circle of

Eternity—of making your all-important journey back in time."

I silently nodded my head in agreement. He then told me to spend time that evening trying to recreate that out-of-body experience and to envision the infinite Circle. But he also cautioned me not to attempt entering any parenthesis I might observe there. He said we would discuss how to take that higher step the next morning, after we all had had a good night's rest.

CHAPTER 7

THE LATEST REPORT AND A TIME OF DECISION

MONDAY MORNING, AUGUST 17TH
THE CABINET ROOM, WEST WING OF THE WHITE HOUSE,
WASHINGTON, D.C.

Even though the morning sky over the nation's capital was bright and sunny, the atmosphere in the White House Cabinet Room was gray and filled with gloom. President Thompson had just called another emergency meeting of his war council.

Admiral McGraw, Chief of Naval Operations, opened the meeting by reviewing the Sunday afternoon incident in the Atlantic Ocean with the nuclear-armed terrorist ship.

"After dissecting the weapon," he said somberly, "we have determined that the device was a full-scale nuclear bomb that could have produced a 10- to 15-kiloton blast. Though that is small compared with most Cold War-era warheads, it is considerably more powerful and lethal than a dirty bomb. And while our interrogators haven't gotten much information yet from the three prisoners, we did learn from one of them that the target was New York City, and more specifically, Lower Manhattan. As the subject described it, the plan was to *'completely disrupt and destroy the infidels' financial system.'*

"They had intended to bring the boat through the Verrazano Narrows into New York Harbor on Wednesday morning, and get as close as they could to Lower Manhattan. Then, they were going to detonate the weapon right after the stock markets opened. Other than that, we haven't been able to get much information out of them."

Marine Commandant Fabretti spoke up. "How are we interrogating them? Are we just playing by the rules that the previous spineless president gave us, or are we actually trying to learn something? Have they been water-boarded yet?"

Attorney General Klemmer answered sternly. "You know we don't do that anymore, General . . . we are more civilized now and are restricted by today's guidelines."

"Are you shittin' me?" Fabretti yelled. "They were gonna nuke New York! Do you call that being civil? This is war, dammit!

"Just let me in the room with those terrorist bastards for about twenty minutes, and I'll have 'em squealin' like pigs!"

General Larkin agreed. "I'm with you, Tony . . . This is no time to be playing footsie. We need to know what else is planned, and we need to know it now!"

He chuckled, and then said, "Maybe I should join General Fabretti in those interrogation rooms."

The attorney general defended his previous statement. "Look, guys, I'm not saying that I like the new rules, but they are the current law of the land. Still, because of the seriousness of this situation, I'll certainly consider looking the other way, no matter what action you take . . . Just don't tell me about it."

Joint Chiefs Chairman Daniels then said, "Mr. President, if you are in agreement, we will handle the interrogation however we have to, and we will get some answers. It appears that the world is going mad, and there is no time for civility."

"All right, General, do what you must do," Thompson answered pensively. "The security, and possibly even the very existence of America are at stake.

"Now on another subject, how are we doing in getting Congress shut down?"

Senator Brett (B.B.) Barrett of Georgia, the President pro tempore of the Senate, replied, "We can be finished with our work by Tuesday afternoon, sir. All the committee chairmen are prepared to recess for a week or two, and Speaker Berkley also has everything ready to go in the House."

"Great, Brett. Thank you for such quick action."

The President then said, "I cannot stress enough the severity of the current situation, or how fortunate we have been up to now. Both the Israeli covert operations and our maritime forces have intercepted and disrupted potential nuclear attacks . . . and these weren't just dirty bombs. Those loony Iranians have really gone over the edge with their proliferation. Their fingerprints are all over those weapons, but we just can't prove it at this time."

General Fabretti spoke up again. "So if the Ayatollahs have made all of this possible, why don't we warn them that if anything goes off here, we're takin' out Tehran?"

"Nothing is off the table, Tony," the President replied. "That is part of the conversations I have been having with the other heads of state. We are trying to get a consensus on a proper response if there are any attacks. The problem, as usual, is in getting the Russians and Chinese to go along, or at least not to throw up any roadblocks. We should have some answers in the next day or two, and I will keep you all posted."

He paused for a moment, and then gave his final thoughts. "Okay, that's about it for now. Uh, Scott, is there anything new from the intelligence community?"

"Nothing, sir, except that it's getting even noisier. We seem to be in a race against time, yet we have nothing more concrete to report."

The Commander in Chief then said, "At any rate, I want to thank you and every one of your people for a job well done; the intelligence work has been superb."

"Don't thank me, Mr. President. We had very little to do with the bomb interception. That was just a stroke of luck. We were fortunate the rich guy's yacht was in those waters at the same time the terrorists were in the area. And we also were blessed that the ship's captain had such alert eyes. Maybe there really is some divine intervention in all of this.

"But the key questions now are: Do they have even more in their arsenal, along with delivery capability? And where are their next targets? Unfortunately, since we haven't been able to get any specific information, I can't give you the answers, folks."

"Well, just stay with it, Scott. You can only do your best."

And with those comments, the President concluded the meeting.

MONDAY MORNING, AUGUST 17TH
SHIMAHN'S ASHRAM - NAKCHU PREFECTURE -
NORTHERN TIBET AUTONOMOUS REGION

Following Shimahn's suggestions of Sunday afternoon, I spent most of that evening practicing the exercise he had given us. Each time, as I worked my thought process up and through my physical body, I achieved the realization that my true identity is spiritual consciousness. And in my second attempt that evening, I had another out-of-body experience. This time, I achieved an even higher level of receptivity and attained a temporary immersion into the Grand Circle of Eternity. I was no longer just an outside observer, but I virtually became a part of the infinite flow of Life.

As I relaxed and rested in that transcendental conscious-ness, I was able to faintly identify several of my own parentheses off in the distance. But I also followed Shi-mahn's instructions and did not attempt to enter any of them. Then, after reposing in that state of serenity and tranquility for a while, I allowed myself to return once again to this four-dimensional sense of awareness.

At 8:00 on Monday morning, the three of us were ready to resume our metaphysical work. Shimahn asked if we had any questions on the principles and ideas he had presented during the previous two days.

Kathy spoke up first. "I am still a little confused about the passage, or non-passage, of time while someone has gone back to a previous lifetime. For example, if Eric went back, and you and I stayed here, why wouldn't the two of us live on and continue to experience the passage of time for as long as he is gone?"

"Oh, we will," he replied knowingly.

"But you told us yesterday that he would return to the same moment in which he left."

"That is also true, Kathy."

"How can that be?" I asked.

"Please remember, my young friends, that time, as described by Albert Einstein, is relative. It exists only in this four-dimensional universe of space-time. When we transcend this illusory sense of existence and rise into the fifth dimension of *My Kingdom*, there is no onward movement of time for us. There is only the *Eternal Now*.

"In embarking on his historic journey, Eric will be entering the infinite Grand Circle of Eternity. In that state, he will not be affected by the passage of time, because time does not exist in eternity. Then, when he enters a previous parenthesis—even if he stays there for twenty years—it will be the host body of that lifetime that will age. His immortal soul will not age with it, any more than our souls are aging in this present lifetime. Only your physical sense of body goes through the aging process. Your soul exists forever in the fifth dimension of Eternal Life.

"That is why we continuously practice the presence of God. We strive to lift ourselves out of these temporal bodies and to spend more time in the divine reality of *My Kingdom*."

"Okay," Kathy stated, "let's concede that you are right about time and eternity. But if Eric is gone for twenty years and he doesn't age, why wouldn't I be twenty years older than he is when he comes back? I would have lived through that passage of time."

"Yes, you would have, Kathy, but only in an extension or continuation of this present timeline. If Eric returns on the day he left, you and I will also still be there in the then-present age we were at that moment, without having yet experienced the progression of time you just described.

"In other words, from that point forward, there will be an alternate reality—the one with Eric in it, as opposed to the other in which he was not present. So anything that might have happened in that previous reality will not affect the new future.

"As a result, the life-stream of the new reality will continue to flow, and all three of us will share it together. And that is why it doesn't matter how long Eric may be gone, or what might, or might not, happen to him while he is away. His soul lives endlessly in the infinite Circle of Eternity, and time measurements are just temporal markings that we humans erroneously impose in each parenthesis."

When we finished that eye-opening discussion, both Kathy and I were speechless, as our beloved Master had taken us on this newest mind-bending excursion into the uncharted abstract.

He then asked, "Do either of you have any more questions?"

Visibly showing her deep apprehension about all of this, Kathy pleaded once more, "Are you absolutely certain that Eric will be protected in this undertaking, Shimahn? I still am very concerned about his safety."

He responded empathetically, "I would not be asking your husband to embark on a risky, perilous journey, Kathy. And since I have already made a trip back in time, I can assure you that it is safe, and is a profoundly exhilarating and exciting experience."

After that exchange, I spoke up. "Well, if I do agree to try this experiment, when would you suggest we begin?"

"Because of the seriousness of the circumstances facing the world today, I would like you to make your initial journey in time this afternoon."

My God, this man was persistent.

He then said, "Why don't the two of you have a relaxing lunch, and then come back at 1:30 to give me your decision."

A relaxing lunch . . . ? I felt like I was being offered my last meal before the executioner comes into the room.

CHAPTER 8

THE HISTORIC
JOURNEY
BEGINS

MONDAY AFTERNOON, AUGUST 17TH - 1:30 P.M.
SHIMAHN'S ASHRAM - NAKCHU PREFECTURE -
NORTHERN TIBET AUTONOMOUS REGION

ollowing a period of much soul-searching over lunch, Kathy and I returned to Shimahn's quarters and informed him that I would be willing to participate in his highly improbable undertaking.

Considering everything I had learned since my first encounter with this mystical being, and after having had numerous other spiritual adventures, I truly believed that he would not be sending me on a frivolous or dangerous journey. Furthermore, since God is my life, that life can never be lost. But even more important, Life is not confined to any specific physical body.

Life, Soul and Consciousness are synonymous. I am Life, I am Soul, I am Consciousness, and I cannot be separated from what I am.

But before I began the process that would take me on this remarkable adventure, Shimahn had a few additional comments.

"Eric, neither you nor I know exactly when you lived before, or where those lives took place. So when you merge into the Circle of Eternity, you will have to select a specific parenthesis to enter. You might feel a strong attraction to a certain life-stream. That may be the one with which you should coalesce. Remember, I had only one choice in my experiment in time travel, but you will have many. Ideally, I would like you to enter a lifetime where something you do there could have a significant impact on the future—specifically on today's present. Yet, I have no idea when or where those opportunities will lie. We will need to trust your instincts. Hopefully, if a lifetime has no significance, you will quickly realize that and will return here sooner rather than later."

Shimahn then asked if I had any other questions. I said, "Do I need to take anything with me? Does it matter how I am dressed?"

He responded, "Did you take anything in your sojourns out of your body yesterday? Were you concerned about the clothes you were wearing?"

"No, I just ascended into the fifth dimension."

"Well, that is how it will be on this journey. It is your soul—the *I* of you—that is making the trip; it does not need any possessions. When you arrive in that other place and time, you will inhabit the body you were using during that specific life-experience."

I looked at Kathy one last time seeking visible assurance, as we reached our hands out to each other. With a hesitant smile on her face, her soft fingers delicately squeezed my palms, and she gently nodded her head, giving me a final gesture of tentative approval of the plan.

The Master then suggested that I should be alone when I attempt to become the world's second time traveler. He had a cozy library-study in his living quarters just off to the right of the main room where we had been meeting. So after saying my emotional good-byes to both Shimahn and my devoted and understanding wife, I slowly entered the other room, shut the door, and made myself comfortable in a firmly cushioned chair.

I closed my eyes in meditation and again performed that special, deductive exercise our teacher had given us. I mentally worked my way through the limbs, organs, muscles and tissues of my physical body. Within minutes I achieved a transcendental level of awareness and quickly found myself outside of that body, floating above the earth and rising deeper into the heart of the Universe. Everything had a cosmic, out-of-this-world sensation to it.

For a moment, I gained a brief glimpse of the Grand Circle of Eternity, but then without any warning, I actually became a part of it. As I entered the great Circle, I realized it was three-dimensional, but so vast that I could look in all directions and see what appeared to be an endless number of stars and planets. It was as though I were soaring at the center of the Milky Way or some other galaxy. I quickly gained a clearer conception of the meaning and drift of the Universe.

Shortly thereafter, there was a sensory change. While I still experienced my identity and remembered my past, the degree of body I was carrying became far more ethereal, almost a kind of energy or vibration. Then suddenly, I was rising even higher into this vast unknown.

The next sensation was of an enormous spiritual spectrum of bright lights that were far in the distance, but soon were all around me. I was floating in an infinite ocean of life; it was eternal Life, the Life we refer to as God. But I also realized I was at one with that Life. It is the very essence and substance of what I am.

Gradually, the various parentheses in the Circle came more sharply into focus. While hovering above them I counted at least thirty sets of brackets. Did they represent thirty previous lifetimes for this soul that I am?

I also noticed a unique phenomenon regarding the different parentheses. Some were brilliantly illuminated, glistening with lights, while others were rather dark and shadowy. Another group fell somewhere in between those polar opposites. Did those levels of light describe happy and successful lives, versus others that were sad and unsuccessful?

And then, just as quickly as it all began, the movement and activity quieted down, as I started to gently linger over the inviting parentheses. Because I was an integral part of this endless Circle, I could not distinguish which lifetimes occurred far in the past, or more recently. So I just continued to hover until I felt a strong attraction to a certain parenthesis that was moderately bright. I drifted down to that area and then felt a powerful magnetic pull urging me to enter. As I moved closer to that particular life-stream, memories of my recent past began to fade, and my mind became an empty, but receptive vacuum. Gradually all the lights dimmed, and I drifted down into a black fathomless void—

At first it seemed as though this soul—named Eric in his last life—had fallen asleep and was dreaming. But then, he was gently awakened by the sound of sheep bleating all around him, and he was slightly blinded by the early after-noon's bright sunlight.

CHAPTER 9

THE WILDERNESS OF SINAI, 1346 BCE

On that summer day long ago in the Sinai Peninsula, the desert air was hot and dry, and the midday sun baked down with a ferocious intensity. For most of the shepherds and nomadic people living in the area, it was a day much like any other. Their ancestors had walked up and down this barren, mostly uninhabited region ever since their heralded father—the revered Patriarch Abraham—had settled in the land of Canaan. But during the time of Joseph, when the seven years of famine consumed the land, many of their kinsmen from the north had migrated to Egypt. Yet this little band of Midianites, situated in this arid wasteland near the foot of the fabled Mount Horeb, persisted in their struggle for survival.

Yaacov, son of Boaz, was surveying the familiar countryside as he tended his large flock of sheep. Walking near his tribe's life-sustaining oasis, he entered the lush patch of green and approached the ancient well located in the middle of the grove. The handsome young shepherd's curly dark-brown hair reached to a level just below the shoulders of his burgundy robe. Yet unlike so many of his kinsmen, Yaacov was unable to grow the dense, heavy beard that most of them sported. As a result, he looked even younger than his actual age.

Seeking to cool himself on that scorching afternoon, Yaacov splashed a handful of water on his face. While doing that, his attention was drawn to the small clump of bushes on his left. A sudden rustling sound indicated that something was moving in the brush. Had one of his sheep wandered away from the flock?

Using his shepherd's staff to part the bushes, Yaacov was suddenly startled as a violent-looking hulk of a man, who apparently had been sleeping under the foliage, leaped to his feet and drew back his rod, as if to strike the inquisitive shepherd. The man had a weather-beaten complexion, and his face was covered by a heavy beard that obviously had been growing wildly for several months. Furthermore, the eyes of this strange intruder were very dark, projecting an electrifying intensity that bordered on being a look of madness.

Gazing directly into the demonic eyes of this creature that appeared to be half man and half beast, Yaacov quickly realized he would have a difficult time defending himself if this confrontation degenerated to the level of hand-to-hand combat. In fact, as he stood there before this potential adversary, his mind seemed to go blank. Not only could he not remember if he was capable of holding his own in a fight but, at that very moment, he couldn't remember anything about his personal human history. However, before he could further analyze this apparent mental lapse, the stranger lunged at him in an unprovoked attack. But then, at the very instant the young herdsman expected to feel the crushing blow to his skull, the hairy man's eyes rolled in his head, as he dropped his rod and collapsed to the ground at the shepherd's feet.

At first, Yaacov stepped back to observe the fallen body from a distance. After reassuring himself that his attacker really was unconscious, he moved closer to further scrutinize this intruder. It was only then that the relieved shepherd became aware of the robe the man was wearing. On it was the emblem of the Levite tribe of the Children of Israel.

This was the first time Yaacov had seen a person of that particular tribe in this area. According to legends he had heard, most of the Levites had migrated to Egypt years ago, and now were living in captivity, in forced servitude to Pharaoh. So rather than try to arouse the stranger and possibly face another physical confrontation, the shepherd decided to return to the tents of his people to seek some help.

As he hurried back to the simple, makeshift village, Yaacov once again realized that he was unable to recall many events of his past. He was familiar with his surroundings and knew he spoke the language of the area. He also remembered that he was working under an oral contract for Jethro, a wealthy merchant-priest who had seven beautiful daughters. For the present, Yaacov was laboring as a shepherd, with the understanding that he would receive the hand of one of

Jethro's lovely daughters when he completed the terms of his contract. The young man also believed that, if he performed the sheepherding assignment competently, he could ultimately rise to a higher level of responsibility, possibly even helping the desert patriarch manage his varied business interests.

But while all of this was clear to Yaacov, for some unexplained reason, he could not recall any other previous events pertaining to himself. He was not aware of having had a childhood, or of having gone through any period of adolescence. It was as though he had just been placed in this environment a few moments ago, without having experienced the processes of birth, education and growth. Yet at the same time, he felt that he must have had some degree of education, because he was hearing puzzling, complex words, thoughts and ideas that he didn't remember hearing before. They seemed to be flowing through his mind from some outside source. But before he could solve his dilemma, Yaacov came upon his peaceful village. There, he quickly sought out four strong young men and convinced them to go back to the oasis with him. He aroused their interest by telling them of his encounter with a hairy manlike beast who had the strength of ten men. For the benefit of the villagers who were listening, the young shepherd added a bit of color to the story by claiming he had single-handedly subdued the creature.

When the little band of Midianites arrived at the oasis, the fallen body of the Levite stranger was still lying on the ground. Not wanting to take any chances, they bound the man's hands and feet with leather straps and laid him in a crude stretcher made of tent cloth and some wooden poles. The four hardy men then followed Yaacov, dragging the heavy stretcher all the way back to the village. By the time the now-weary group of helpers arrived there, most of their tribesmen had gathered together to witness the scene. Yaacov proudly led the other men into the center section of the village where all the events of public interest took place. As he did that, he was rather surprised to see his future father-in-law, Jethro, standing there.

Normally, Jethro didn't have time for such frivolous activities yet, for some unexplained reason, he seemed to be taking an unusual interest in this uninvited stranger. And he wasn't just taking a passive interest. The desert patriarch instructed several of his servants to carry the man to one of his own tents where he would be kept for observation.

As Yaacov glanced around the square, he noticed the rich man's second-youngest daughter, Leah, standing in the midst of the crowd, proudly smiling at him. While Jethro had promised the loyal herdsman that he could choose any of his daughters as a wife when the work contract was completed, Yaacov already knew that Leah was the one for him. They truly shared something special. If only she would wait for him until he had fulfilled the terms of his agreement with her father.

Yaacov then tried walking toward Leah, but he was having trouble making his way through the boisterous crowd, as many of the villagers wanted to congratulate him on his magnificent conquest. While this should have been a very exciting and glorious moment for Yaacov, he suddenly was oblivious to the scene going on around him. Once again, he became rather bewildered because his mind was almost a total blank. He was aware of a strong emotional feeling toward Leah and, based upon the expression on her face, she seemed to be experiencing a reciprocal sentiment toward him. But at that very moment, he could not remember any specific events of their past relationship. *How did they meet? Where did he first see her?*

By the time he reached Leah, she was beaming from ear to ear. She squeezed his hand and pulled him after her as she skipped down a narrow passage between several tents. Very quickly, they were at the edge of the village, near a rocky area where they apparently had often gone to talk. Yaacov then suggested they go back out to the oasis so he could check up on his flock. Walking together on the path to their ever-vital water supply, Leah told him of the immense pride she was feeling. She always suspected that Yaacov had a wonderful future and was destined for greatness, and now, through this heroic conquest, he had taken the first step in that direction by gaining the respect of all their people.

The young herdsman was enraptured with Leah's natural beauty and innocent freshness. Except for Jethro's daughters, most of the women in the village were quite plain, having severely sun-damaged skin, which amplified their overall primitive coarseness. Very few had the delicate femininity of Leah. She had unusually fair skin and the face of an angel, topped off by her long reddish-brown hair. To Yaacov, it seemed as though she had come from somewhere else, and was not really a member of the tribe.

As Leah continued expounding on the day's events, Yaacov's mind contemplated the great irony illustrated by all that had happened in the past few hours. *What a fine line between success and failure,* he thought. *Just tell a little white lie and you win the respect of an entire village. That is how to create a reputation built on sand.* But then he became aware of an even greater enigma: *What a fine line between life and death!*

If the Levite stranger hadn't collapsed during their confrontation, it might have been Yaacov himself who would have been lying in the oasis. Why, at this very moment, he could still be unconscious, or possibly even dead. *Is that all there is to life?* he asked himself. *Is our very being so fragile that it is based on nothing more than the winds of chance? Surely, there must be a higher purpose to the true nature of existence.* But then Yaacov became somewhat perplexed as he wondered where those vexing, thought-provoking questions were coming from. He usually spent his time dwelling on more mundane worldly matters.

Over the next several days, much of the villagers' attention was directed to the tent where the fallen Levite was being nursed back to health. As the days passed, many conflicting stories began circulating among the people.

One version claimed the hairy creature was an advance spy who was checking out the village to see if it was worthy of attack. According to this account, the intruder was not really a Levite, but was merely wearing that robe as a disguise. Supposedly, his people were a group of rebellious and outcast Persians, who themselves survived by plundering small towns in the desert hill country east of Sinai. Another tale portrayed the stranger as a former high priest of Moab who had fallen into disfavor when he began preaching of the One True God. And though this Moabite had been wandering in the desert for more than a year and was so weak that he was near death from starvation, Yahweh, the Lord God of the Hebrew nation, had saved him.

But the story getting the most traction among the villagers told of a legendary Prince of Egypt who, after learning that he was born a Hebrew, murdered one of Pharaoh's overseers. To avoid being captured, this prince, who was the adopted son of Pharaoh's daughter, fled into the desert wilderness with his rod, a Levite robe, and a minimal ration of food and water. Since this event had taken place more than six months ago and he had never been heard from again, Pharaoh and the Egyptian people concluded that the missing prince was dead.

While several other variations of these stories were also being circulated, Yaacov assumed he could learn the truth about the situation from Leah. He was aware of the local gossip, which claimed that she and her six sisters were all spending a good deal of time in the stranger's tent. But the next time they were together, Yaacov didn't need to ask any questions. Leah could speak of nothing else. She animatedly described how her sisters had dismissed the servants and now were personally taking care of the Levite's needs. She also explained that the stranger was not a hairy beast, and most certainly was not violent but, instead, was a very handsome and gentle man. Leah's cheeks flushed as she giggled and told Yaacov how Jethro's daughters had literally been falling all over each other trying to make the man comfortable. They had bathed him, and shaved him, and—

As she rambled on, Yaacov was overcome with jealousy. He thought: *Maybe this isn't the missing Prince of Egypt, but he certainly is being treated like royalty.*

Sensing his jealous reaction, Leah quickly consoled him. "Oh, Yaacov, don't be concerned," she said tenderly. "This event has brought some unexpected excitement into our lives—all of us in the village—and it has been entertaining to watch my sisters vying for the Levite's attention. But you know how I feel about you. I really haven't been very involved in their actions. And neither has my oldest sister Zipporah; she feels the other girls are making fools of themselves. Even though she and I occasionally look in on the visitor, Zipporah does not want to appear as frivolous as the rest of them and spends almost no time in his tent."

The relieved herdsman then asked, "Do you have any idea who the man is? Do you know where he came from?"

"No, I don't, Yaacov, but I do know that my father has spent a good deal of time with him. The two of them seem to have much in common."

The next day, Yaacov received an unexpected surprise, as he was summoned by one of Jethro's servants. The priest wanted the young shepherd to join him at his afternoon meal. Yaacov wondered what could have precipitated that invitation. He had certainly had conversations with Jethro in the past, but he never had been accorded the honor of joining the desert patriarch at his private table.

Upon entering Jethro's dining tent, Yaacov was quickly taken aback, as he immediately was approached by a tall, handsome stranger who extended his hands in a warm greeting. Squeezing the shepherd's shoulders, the man said, "So you are Yaacov, son of Boaz. I want to thank you for saving my life!"

Without replying, Yaacov quizzically stared at the clean-shaven large man. Before he could say anything, Jethro stepped into the tent and interrupted them.

"Oh, Yaacov, welcome! Let me introduce you to my new friend, Moses, the son of Amram and Joshebed of the tribe of Levi."

Yaacov nodded his head as he wondered, *is it possible this obviously well-bred man is that same hairy creature I encountered at the oasis?*

All of his questions were quickly answered, as the loyal shepherd spent the balance of the afternoon in Jethro's tent. There he learned that this man, Moses, was indeed the missing Egyptian prince. Yet, while Moses had lived most of his life in complete luxury, and had even been considered as a potential successor to the throne of Egypt, in truth, he was the humble son of Hebrew slaves.

During Moses' years in the land of the Pharaohs, his ancestry had never been disclosed to him. The facts of his birth were an extremely well-guarded secret, known only to Pharaoh's daughter—whom Moses had always thought of as being his mother—and to a few of her servants. But now that his real identity was known, and he had compounded the problem by committing the heinous crime of murder, he obviously could not return to Egypt.

As their conversation progressed, it became evident to Yaacov that Jethro was extremely impressed with Moses. The wealthy priest had asked the former prince to stay on and work for him, even offering Moses an opportunity to some-day become his business partner. And as an additional incentive, Jethro made several references to his seven beautiful daughters. Maybe one of them could make Moses very happy as his wife and could produce many sons for him.

Apparently, the two men had discussed this subject before, while Moses was still recuperating from his long ordeal in the desert. But it was not until that fateful afternoon in Jethro's tent—fully realizing he did not have many other options—that Moses, the Levite son of Amram and Joshebed, willingly agreed to make his new home here in this barren wasteland resting so quietly in the ever-present shadow of Mount Horeb.

When the three men concluded their conversation, Jethro asked Yaacov to begin spending most of his time with Moses. He wanted the young shepherd to teach the self-exiled prince everything he knew about tending sheep, and about the other aspects of Jethro's enterprises.

While Yaacov was always willing to do whatever he could to help his future father-in-law, as with everything else in his past, he had no recollection of ever trying to teach anything to anyone. Nevertheless, he readily accepted this new challenge and soon began devoting most of his attention to his new acquaintance.

At first, Moses had a difficult time settling in to the solitude of life in this arid, but peaceful wilderness, since he had spent the major portion of his life right at the center of the social, economic and political power structure of one of the greatest nations in the history of mankind. Yet he had been driven out of Egypt for what he felt was an illegitimate reason. So several years would have to pass before the strong desire for vengeance would be eliminated from the soul of this man who might have become Pharaoh.

As the two young men continued to work together, their relationship evolved, first, to a strong bond of friendship and, soon, to a point where they were closer than brothers. Their individual backgrounds and personalities strongly complemented one another.

While Moses was about twelve years older than Yaacov, and obviously more "worldly," the younger shepherd had developed an introspective, contemplative nature that made him quite adept at philosophizing about abstract concepts and ideas. Often when they were out in the fields with Jethro's sheep, the two men sat at the base of the holy mountain and pondered its majesty and power. Occasionally, Yaacov narrated legends, which claimed that the very Presence of God dwelled there.

Yet, in all the time they had spent together, Yaacov never told Moses of his feelings toward Leah. In fact, no one else—not even Jethro—was aware of the relationship between the loyal shepherd and the desert priest's second-youngest daughter. The romantic couple usually rendez-voused in secret, seldom allowing their true emotions to be revealed in public. So Yaacov received quite a shock one evening when, in the middle of their conversation, Moses said, "Well, my good friend, I feel it is time for me to begin giving some real meaning to my life."

The shepherd looked at him inquisitively as he continued. "As you know, Jethro has often suggested that I marry one of his daughters. I sometimes think the old man is becoming a little concerned that none of them has been claimed yet. So I expect that I will be discussing this matter with him soon."

Yaacov then asked. "Have you decided which daughter you would like to marry?"

Moses replied, "Well, they all are very lovely. But ever since you found me lying in your oasis and brought me to the village, five of the girls have been doing everything in their power to get my attention. But the other two—Zipporah and Leah—have been much more aloof. I like that quality of dignity in a woman."

As Moses continued talking, Yaacov began to feel extremely uncomfortable. The former prince then said, "Both of them are so beautiful. Any man would be proud to claim either young lady as his wife. But there is such an innocence and freshness about Leah. Yes . . . I think Leah's the one. I will ask Jethro for her hand."

Yaacov's face became flushed and his entire body began to tremble as he asked, "But have you discussed this with Leah? Has she told you she loves you?"

"Loves me?" Moses answered. "How could she have any feelings for me? She has hardly even spoken to me. But that's not important. She will learn to love me after we are married."

At that point, Yaacov shouted angrily, "What kind of a creature are you? Have the pagan gods of Egypt taken your soul and made you so heartless that you don't even understand the meaning of true love?"

Moses was shocked by this sudden outburst. In the seven months the two men had worked together, they had not had a single disagreement—at least none that he was aware of. *What is wrong here?* he wondered.

"I am sorry if my customs are somewhat different from yours, Yaacov. But in the larger world outside of this valley, many marriages are arranged merely for political or economic considerations. And in most of those situations, the participants have never even met. At least in our case, Leah and I do know each other. And I certainly am attracted to her. You'll see. This kind of marriage can work."

"But you have no right to just walk into our community and disrupt our lives!" the younger man shouted. "Leah doesn't want you. If you try to take her this way, she will come to revile you. Don't you understand? She loves someone else!"

Suddenly, the meaning of this discussion became clear to Moses.

"Oh, Yaacov," he said sympathetically. "I'm sorry! Are you and Leah . . . ?"

"Yes, we're in love!" the shepherd interrupted, with a little more composure in his voice.

"My dear friend," Moses responded, as he placed his large hands on Yaacov's shoulders. "I had no idea . . . Please forget this conversation. Leah is yours. I will ask Jethro for the hand of Zipporah."

Shaking his head in disbelief, Yaacov replied, "Oh, Moses, Leah and I truly thank you. And I apologize for some of the things I might have said to you . . . But please consider Zipporah's feelings now. She may not want to be treated like just a piece of property that can be sold to the highest bidder. Talk to her first, before you discuss this with Jethro. Show her some affection, and I am certain she'll be willing to share her life with you."

The two men continued exchanging their thoughts on this subject until the early hours of the next morning. Moses was extremely impressed by the younger man's readily apparent intuition and wisdom. So, accepting his good friend's advice, Moses devoted much of his free time during the next several weeks to courting Zipporah. He was quite surprised and thrilled by her willing responses to his over-tures. Within three months, the former Prince of Egypt and the eldest daughter of Jethro were married. The wealthy merchant-priest made their ceremony the biggest social event the little desert community had enjoyed in many years.

During the months following the marriage of Moses and Zipporah, Jethro seemed to undergo a change of conscious-ness. He became more introspective and began exhibiting less worldly desires.

In his business endeavors, the Midian priest relinquished some of his responsibilities, allowing both Moses and Yaacov to take more active roles.

And it was during this same period that Yaacov began having moments of utter confusion. There were times when he wondered where the words and phrases he was hearing subconsciously were coming from. At other times, he experienced additional incidents of memory loss, in which he could not remember anything about his past. He felt like a stranger in a strange land. Then again, there still were other times when the young shepherd was subjected to a completely different sensation. He was overcome by an inner attraction to another time and another place. Something inside of him was suggesting that he did not belong here. But in each instance, before Yaacov could get an explanation of what was happening, those feelings would disappear as quickly as they had appeared. And yet, his love for Leah was so real and intense that he knew this was where he belonged.

By the following spring, Jethro had become aware of the young couple's feelings for each other. And since Yaacov had proven his loyalty, he certainly deserved to become a member of the priest's illustrious family. So even before all the terms of his contract had been fulfilled, Yaacov, son of Boaz, was given the hand of his beloved Leah in marriage.

The next few years seemed to pass quickly in the peaceful valley, as Zipporah gave birth to two sons, Gershom and Eliezer. Their grandfather Jethro shamelessly doted on the boys and finally had become very comfortable with the future. *God is good*, he thought, *and all is right with the*

THE WILDERNESS OF SINAI, 1346 BCE

world. Though he had not been blessed with any sons of his own—having seven wonderful, loving daughters—he now knew that his heritage would be carried on through his two beloved grandsons.

Being a very pious man who spent much time in contemplation, Jethro had also developed a unique sixth sense, which allowed him to recognize the true character of other people. Yet even with this remarkable quality of perception, the desert patriarch had never had what could be described as a *mystical experience*; he had never *"seen God face to face."*

But then one evening during the following autumn, he was walking alone in the low ground near the bottom of Mount Horeb. After reaching one of his favorite resting places, the wealthy merchant-priest decided to sit down on a large rock and enjoy the moment. With the warm fall breeze blowing gently in his face, he closed his eyes in quiet contemplation.

As he later reflected back on this episode, Jethro couldn't be certain if he had merely fallen asleep and had a dream, or if his meditation had actually achieved a new, transcendental level of awareness. But whatever specific circumstances brought about his state of receptivity, Jethro experienced a mystical vision in which he learned that he had a son-in-law who was a "very special soul." The patriarch was told that his son-in-law had the capacity to become an "instrument for God," and through the young man's enlightened consciousness, the revelation of the true meaning of existence could be made available to all mankind. Along with this disclosure of absolute Truth would come the power to free an entire nation, and possibly even the whole world, from bondage.

At that moment, Jethro was incapable of thinking any thoughts. He merely sat quietly and allowed this mystical initiation to continue unfolding. He then was advised that the coming years could usher in a new era of spiritual enlightenment for all mankind.

For the first time since the fall of Adam and Eve, man was capable of receiving the Truth that could set him free. By accepting the revelation of his divine birthright, the *"man of earth"* could overcome centuries of self-inflicted pain and suffering. But he must be willing to relinquish all of his false beliefs about life. "Truth will be revealed," the priest was told, "but it must be accepted in consciousness."

And then the Voice stopped speaking. Jethro continued to sit there in silence, trying to absorb the words he had just heard. He didn't return to his home that evening, as he fell asleep on the ground. And though the ground was hard and he had no bed, it was one of the most restful nights of sleep that Jethro had ever enjoyed.

The next morning, the reborn priest of Midian was awakened by the first rays of sunlight that crept over the holy mountain. For Jethro, it was a glorious new day filled with great promise.

CHAPTER 10

THE TENSION MOUNTS

Now that Vice-president Tucker had left Washington, D.C. to hide away in his Minnesota cabin, and the Speaker of the House of Representatives had gone to his ranch in the Texas Panhandle, the two people next in line to the presidency were in safe places. Congress was winding down its work, and most of the 535 members of the two legislative bodies would be leaving the nation's Capital by Tuesday afternoon. Still, the intelligence services had no specific news to report of any imminent attacks.

As a result, President Thompson, the six members of the Joint Chiefs of Staff, and most cabinet members were continuing their duties in their respective offices.

Wall Street opened that morning with a downward jolt, much as SEC Chairman Bronstein expected. The Dow Jones Industrial Average was down 567 points by 11:00 a.m. But then, just as the chairman had predicted it would, the average rebounded somewhat by 1:30 p.m., gaining back about one-third of the morning's losses.

Then, at 3:10 Eastern Time, while the President was meeting in the Oval Office with Chairman Daniels and the secretaries of State, Defense and Treasury, White House Chief of Staff Donald Bergstrom abruptly burst into the room.

"Quick," he shouted, "turn on CNN and Fox News . . . a Singapore Airlines jet just blew up on its approach to LAX."

After the instantaneous reaction in the room, the first TV voice was that of news anchor Jessica Bremer saying, "Fox News has just learned that Singapore Airlines flight number SQ12 from Tokyo to Los Angeles has exploded while making its descent into LAX. The explosion was visible to air traffic controllers at the airport and to others in the terminal. First reports indicate that 226 passengers were on the plane, along with a nine-member crew. At this time the cause of the blast is unknown, but terrorism is suspected."

Switching to CNN, the people in the Oval Office heard the young blond male announcer say, ". . . and in just the 20 minutes since reports of the detonation hit the street, the Dow has plunged 700 more points and is now below 11,000. As a result, SEC Chairman Sheldon Bronstein announced that the markets will close one-half hour early today . . . And now, over to Stephanie Welles, who is on the scene at LAX . . . Stephanie, what can you tell us?"

Back in the White House, Defense Secretary Roger Bledsoe spoke up. "Mr. President, I am so sorry. It feels as though we are just like defenseless clay pigeons, waiting to be hit. What's next?"

"I wish I knew, Roger."

The President then made a quick call to CIA Headquarters. Immediately getting through to Director Cunningham, he asked, "What do we know, Scott? Where did the flight originate?"

"It started in Singapore with a connection in Tokyo, and then," his voice began choking with emotion, "came so close to landing safely in Los Angeles."

Regaining his composure, Cunningham continued. "As you know, Singapore has the world's largest Muslim population, and we have always believed that terrorist acts would eventually come from there. It looks like one finally has—

"Uh, Mr. President, we have had a lot of noise today implying that something serious is being planned for Washington, D.C. We really would like to get you out of the White House, and we don't feel that Camp David is an option. I have been discussing the situation with Director Marcus at the Secret Service. He has made arrangements for you, Mrs. Thompson, and your daughter to board Air Force One as soon as possible. They want to take you to the NORAD command center at Peterson Air Force Base in Colorado."

"Do you honestly think such a radical move is necessary, Scott?"

"Yes, sir, I do. As you know, during recent years NORAD's day-to-day operations have been conducted out of an ordinary building at Peterson. However, because of the seriousness of the current situation, we want to house you in the underground operations center inside Cheyenne Mountain. Even though many of the workers have moved to the other building, the mountain bunker is fully functional and staffed with support personnel. We believe you can run the government from there while benefiting from the elevated level of security the facility provides. And of course, you can bring anyone else along with you."

"Okay, Scott, if you and David Marcus believe it is in the best interest of the country, we can be ready to leave this evening. I'll make a list of who to bring along."

MONDAY AFTERNOON, AUGUST 17TH - 2:45 P.M.
SHIMAHN'S ASHRAM - NAKCHU PREFECTURE -
NORTHERN TIBET AUTONOMOUS REGION

It had been nearly an hour since Eric had gone into the library to attempt his odyssey in time. Not hearing any sounds during that entire period, Shimahn and Kathy finally decided to determine what had happened. They opened the library door and stepped into the room, only to find no one there. All the books and furniture were in place, but Eric was gone.

Kathy asked, "Do you think he actually was able to make it work?"

"It looks that way, Kathy. I assume that, right now, Eric is in another parenthesis somewhere in the past. Just think of how exciting that is!"

"You may think it's exciting," she replied, "but I am really concerned. What if he gets lost out there in some timeless abyss? What if he can't find his way back to us? I already miss him, and he left just a short while ago."

"Of course you miss him, Kathy," Shimahn responded with sincere empathy in his voice. "I understand your concern. But please trust me on this . . . The oneness the two of you share can never be broken or lost. Eric is safe where he is at this very moment, and will be divinely guided on every step of his journey. It is you and I, along with the rest of mankind, who now will be facing imminent danger.

"Your husband must be successful in this momentous adventure in transcending time. If he is not, I believe the world we have always known will soon cease to exist."

CHAPTER 11

THE SACRED NAME
FROM THE
HOLY MOUNTAIN

THE SINAI PENINSULA, 1342 BCE

Believing that he had heard the voice of God in his meditation, Jethro began having long philosophical conversations with Moses. In his eye-opening encounter alongside the holy mountain, the Midianite priest had been told that his son-in-law was a very special soul—that he could become an "instrument for God" and could free the entire world from bondage. And while Jethro was quite enthusiastic during those exchanges, Moses was not very receptive to the ideas being suggested and seemed just to be humoring his father-in-law. Yaacov was also present for the last three of those discussions, and though he didn't participate in much of the dialogue, the young shepherd was silently pondering everything he was hearing.

However, none of that had any impact on their daily routines until one momentous day in the spring of the next year. Late that afternoon, Moses and Yaakov were tending their flocks near the base of Mount Horeb when they heard some foreboding rumblings coming from the higher elevations. The sounds were not those usually associated with a brewing storm, but had a mysterious, otherworldly character.

Their curiosities aroused, the brothers-in-law began ascending the holy mountain. At a plateau about sixty feet up the eastern slope, they stopped to rest. A few minutes later, and without any warning, the wind began swirling around them and the sky became ominously dark, in a way neither of them had ever witnessed.

Seeking shelter, Moses rose to his feet and began walking toward the entrance of a small cave, with Yaakov slightly behind him. As they approached the cave opening, there was a sudden sharp bolt of lightning followed by a loud burst of thunder from directly above the mountain. Before they could move any farther, a bush began burning right in front of them.

The light from the bush was so intense that both men turned away and shielded their eyes with their arms. When they finally were able to look into the bright light, they realized that, even though the bush was burning, it was not being consumed by the flames.

Standing awestruck before the burning bush, the shepherds heard a commanding, majestic Voice begin to speak. It said, "Remove the sandals from your feet, because the place whereon you stand is holy ground."

The two men followed those instructions, and then the Voice resumed. "I am the God of your forefathers, the God of Abraham, Isaac and Jacob."

Moses covered his face again, but Yaacov continued looking into the flames.

The Voice then said, "Moses and Yaacov, look unto Me."

The intensity of the light was so great that Moses could only look into it intermittently, despite the instructions. Meanwhile, Yaacov continued facing the burning bush.

In that defining moment of transcendent illumination, the two men heard an insightful, sacred message, but each of them interpreted it in his own individual way.

To Moses, the Voice said, "I have seen the misery of my people who are slaves in Egypt. I am sending you to Pharaoh and, through you, I will bring my people out of bondage."

Being reluctant to believe what he was hearing, Moses then asked, "Lord, how could I bring our people out of bondage? Who am I that I should go unto Pharaoh? I do not have an army of men. I am slow of speech and will not be able to say the proper words. If I go to the Israelites and tell them the God of their forefathers has sent me to free them, and they ask me His name, what shall I say?"

The Voice replied, "*I AM* that *I AM*. Tell them that *I AM* has sent you to them. I will be with you in this undertaking. I will be your shield and strength."

At the same time, Yaacov heard the Voice say: "I have seen the misery of all My children upon the earth. Because of their superstitious beliefs and their acceptance of two powers, they are living under a false sense of reality that will keep them subject to material sense. You can free them, Yaacov, if you give them My revelation of Spiritual Truth."

Yaacov replied, "Lord, I am just a humble shepherd with limited vocabulary and am not qualified to speak to the world. Who shall I say has sent me? What is Your name? And what is Your message of Truth?"

"Tell them they have been created in My image and likeness," said the Voice. "Tell them that we are One, and they are here for a singular purpose: that is to show forth My glory.

"*I AM* that *I AM*. Explain to them that we share a common identity. They must learn that My name is the same as their name. It is *I* . . . This is the ultimate revelation of Truth. But also tell them that *My Kingdom* is not of their world—the physical-sense-of-existence in which they believe they are living. That is an imaginary world of matter and illusory concepts. In truth, we all exist together in *My Kingdom*. We live in an immaculate, spiritual realm of consciousness above the pairs of opposites. All men and women can be free from their seeming bondage to material sense if they will only accept this wondrous Word of Truth. Yaacov, from this day forward, I will be with you and will speak through you, providing the words that you must share with all mankind."

And then, just as suddenly as it all had begun, the Voice stopped speaking. The flames ceased burning in the bush, and the darkness faded away, revealing a glorious, majestic sunset across the holy mountain.

For the next several minutes, both men were silent and did not even look at each other. After a while, Moses asked Yaacov, "Did you see and hear all of that?"

"Yes, I did."

"Was that really God speaking, Yaacov? Do we need to follow His instructions? Should we go to Egypt?"

"I do believe it was God speaking," the younger man replied. "But why should we go to Egypt?"

"Because God told me to go," Moses answered. "He said that I can free the Hebrew nation from its subjection to Pharaoh."

"That is not what I heard," said Yaacov. "I was instructed to convey the Truth that man is not a mortal, physical creature, but has been created in the image and likeness of God. When you and I stood before the burning bush, we were given the holy name. God and man are One, and our name is *I*. That is the indelible message we must communicate, but we have to share it with all mankind—not with just a few Hebrews living in Egypt.

"Man was born free, and he will be free, if he will just accept his true identity as a spiritual being living in Oneness with God."

The two men lingered on that hallowed ground for several hours, as they quietly discussed what each of them thought he had heard. Moses was convinced he had been told to go back to Egypt to try to reason with Pharaoh—to persuade the ruler of the most powerful nation in the world to *"let the people go."*

Contrarily, Yaacov believed Moses had a flawed interpretation of the sacred message. The now-awakened shepherd had concluded that his own mission was to share his newly discovered Truth with all mankind. But how could he do that, living in this lonely spot in the desert, with no resources of his own? Because of his limited vocabulary and inability to travel, he assumed it would be almost impossible to explain and disseminate the message to anyone else. Yet, the Voice at the burning bush had promised that It would always be with him and would speak through him. So a spark had been ignited within the young man's soul that would prod him to follow the instructions he had received, and this quest would define the balance of that lifetime.

But none of that would be an easy task 1,340 years before the birth of Christ.

As the days passed into weeks, Moses became even more convinced that he had been chosen for a historic assignment: to go back to Egypt and free the Hebrew nation from slavery. As a result, he had many discussions on the subject with Yaacov and Jethro. Neither of them agreed with him, and Zipporah, being loyal to both her husband and her father, was torn between the two conflicting points of view. But within her soul, she knew that, in the end, she would be faithful to Moses and would follow his lead.

Yaacov, on the other hand, believed freedom would come to mankind only through a realization of the Truth he had heard during the miracle of the burning bush.

"God and man are One, and they share the sacred name 'I.' Man is the begotten son of the Father. Living as the

image and likeness of God, man does not have an identity separate and apart from the infinite Consciousness." Yaacov now knew that only through a recognition and acceptance of this profound revelation could mankind find its freedom from the ills of *this world*.

But how could he communicate this message?

The humble shepherd began by trying to convince Moses that he had misunderstood God's Word. Yaacov saw that Moses did not grasp the meaning of the holy name—if he had even heard it spoken. The younger man tried to persuade his brother-in-law that the *Word of God* active in consciousness was more powerful than any physical weapons Moses could muster, and more convincing than any eloquent words the former prince could speak. But it all fell on deaf ears. Moses had too many physical instincts and was too materially minded to accept a purely mystical message of Truth. It would be many years in the future before another enlightened prophet would ask the questions: "*Having eyes, see ye not, and having ears, hear ye not?*"

For Yaacov, the message was absolutely clear. He must find a way to share the truth of Oneness. "*Hear, O, Israel, the Lord our God is One.*"

But he also was having a perplexing problem that carried another unusual dilemma with it. For the past two years, the shepherd was experiencing periods of confusion and memory lapses, as he often was overcome by an attraction and allegiance to another place and another time. Something seemed wrong with his present environment, yet the other was a place and time he could not recall, locate or describe.

During the same period, Moses came to the conclusion that he had to return to Egypt to fulfill his destiny as the deliverer of the Hebrew nation. And no arguments from Yaacov, Jethro, or even Zipporah could dissuade him. So after ninety days of preparation, the former Prince of Egypt and his family embarked on his highly improbable mission to the *"Land of the Pharaohs."*

To provide comfort and protection on the journey for his oldest daughter and two beloved grandsons, Jethro outfitted them with an entourage of servants and several of the strongest warriors from his tribe.

So it was an extremely emotional separation on that warm day in the month of Tishri (September), as Moses and Yaacov bid each other farewell. Both men realized that, most likely, they would never see each other again. And for Jethro and his wife Naomi, it was a heartbreaking experience.

With the leaving of their beloved daughter and their only grandchildren, the couple would never again feel the remarkable joy of living they had shared for most of their adult lives together. From that point forward, something would be missing; there would always be a godforsaken void . . . *And for what reason? Why did Moses do this to them?*

In the months after the departure of Moses and Zipporah, Yaacov became even more introspective. While he loved his life with Leah, he also knew that he, too, was given a very solemn assignment during the episode at the burning bush.

Though he had never admitted it previously, Yaacov now realized that the spiritual message spoken at the site of the bush was not new to him. He had heard all those words before. They already were *"bone of his bones and flesh of his flesh."* But how could that be? Where in the past had he heard those principles?

While the primary source of the message seemed perplexing, the shepherd also knew he would need help in bringing this awesome Truth to others. So initially, he spent a good deal of time discussing the matter with his father-in-law.

The words carried a ring of familiarity for Jethro, just as they had for Yaacov. During his own experience at Mount Horeb, Jethro also received many of those same spiritual principles. As a result, the wise, older man became a reliable sounding board for his gifted and illumined son-in-law.

By that time, the Midian priest realized he was mistaken in believing that Moses was the son-in-law chosen to free mankind from slavery. But he also now understood that it wasn't slavery to Pharaoh from which man must be delivered—it was slavery to material sense.

During one of their more animated conversations, Jethro began relating ancient legends about a reclusive sect of Jews who lived near the Dead Sea. Supposedly, these mystically inclined Hebrews not only had a profound understanding of spiritual Truth, but also had developed a way to preserve and communicate their knowledge by inscribing their words on a special material they produced from the pith of the papyrus plant. Needless to say, Yaacov was quite impressed and inspired by these stories.

As he continued to spend more time in meditation, additional spiritual principles were clarified for him, and he became even more convinced that he needed to find a way to impart those principles to others. Thus, after four full months of serious contemplation, the enlightened young shepherd decided he had to make the long and arduous journey to visit the unnamed, mysterious sect of Hebrews Jethro had spoken of—the group that was living in the small, isolated village located on a dry plateau about a mile inland from the north-western shore of the Dead Sea.

Reacting much as her sister Zipporah had, Leah also tried to convince *her* husband that he didn't need to take this seemingly unnecessary trip. His place was there at her side; they had a life to build together. And he should not be abandoning her aging father at this critical time when the older man needed Yaacov's help in managing his varied business endeavors.

But Yaacov was not concerned about potential business opportunities. He had a higher purpose in life. He hadn't been sent here just to keep track of a few herds of sheep . . . He hadn't been sent here just to pass the time chatting with local villagers about nothing of any significance . . . *Sent here . . . ?* What did that mean? Were those strange recurring incidents of memory loss trying to tell him something?

Had he come from somewhere else? And if that were the case, where was that "somewhere else?" Eventually, the inquisitive shepherd would learn that he should not have asked the question: *where* was that other place, but, rather *when* was that other place?

Ever since that day when Yaacov had found Moses at the well, he seemed like a different person to Leah. He now had strange thoughts in his head and had been speaking in what sounded like a new language, using many unknown words. So when she finally conceded that he could not be deterred from his contemplated undertaking, she offered to accompany him on his journey. She loved him deeply and didn't want to be separated from him. And what if something unexpected happened and he didn't return? She would never forgive herself for not having gone with him.

But Yaacov would not even consider it. He told Leah he could not do that to her parents. Her beloved family did not deserve to suffer any more pain and sorrow by possibly losing a second daughter. He assured Leah that he would return safely. After all, she was the love of his life, and nothing could take him from her. Yaacov then promised that they would always be together and would live in an eternal bond of Oneness.

"Life is eternal," he said with unimpeachable conviction in his voice. "It is a huge continuous circle that has no beginning or ending. This present life-experience that we are living now can be thought of as merely a set of brackets or barriers placed randomly on that circle—just a small interval in time. So please, Leah, do not be concerned. Together, you and I will partake in a grand adventure in living . . . and we will share it forever, throughout eternity."

And then he realized he had heard similar words before … *but where?*

During his last days in the little village, Yaacov spent a good deal of time with Jethro, discussing his impending trip. He promised his father-in-law that he would return to them.

The shepherd then outlined a few reasons why this was not comparable to Moses' situation. This son-in-law was not going to challenge the greatest power on earth, demanding freedom for an entire nation. He was merely taking a trip across the desert to meet some holy men of God who could help him impart and preserve a very special teaching.

Thus, early one morning in the month of Shevat (February), Yaacov, son of Boaz, embarked upon his long and perilous journey to an unknown land to the north . . . to that mysterious place called *Qumran*.

CHAPTER 12

MORE CONFUSION AND ANOTHER THWARTED ATTACK

Ever since the dirty bomb explosion in Hamburg four months earlier, the *Bundesnachrichtendienst* or BND, Germany's foreign intelligence agency, had been on high alert. With the help of the BfV, the country's domestic secret service organization, every threat was analyzed and every lead was followed to a satisfactory conclusion. And because of that intense level of scrutiny, a second plotted attempt against Germany was prevented.

This time, the plan was to detonate a small nuclear bomb in Berlin. The terrorists had been assembling their weapon in an old warehouse about three miles south of the Tiergarten, Berlin's sprawling urban park near the central part of the city. Among other buildings and institutions, the Tiergarten houses the new German Chancellery, the Bundestag, and the residence of the German President. The notorious Brandenburg Gate, which formerly symbolized the frontier between East and West Berlin, is situated at the eastern rim of the park.

Once the intelligence-gathering services had confirmed their information, the *Militaerischer Abschirmdienst,* or MAD, Germany's military counterintelligence organization, went into action. This agency is the third leg of the country's intelligence community. To complete this delicate and dangerous mission, MAD officials used the full resources of the *Bundeswehr*—the Federal Defense Force.

After just two days of planning, the field operation commenced at 11:40 on Tuesday morning. By twelve minutes after noon, the mission was completed, with six dead jihadists, three live prisoners, and one deactivated and secured nuclear weapon.

N ews of the aborted attack on Berlin spread rapidly throughout the world's intelligence community and newsrooms. This was the third full-scale atomic device confiscated in just three days. So obviously, with that many stymied attempts to nuke major metropolitan areas, people living in those cities were beginning to panic. Some of the principal European capitals were slowly being evacuated. The people who were leaving were primarily those who were willing or able to disrupt their lives, even though there was little specific information available. But in most instances the general populace continued to go about its business just as it had since September 11, 2001. Most people on the planet had become immune to the thought of anything significant happening in their personal lives.

THE PRESENT - ORIGINAL TIMELINE
TUESDAY MORNING - AUGUST 18TH - 8:30 A.M. EDT
CENTRAL INTELLIGENCE AGENCY HEADQUARTERS - LANGLEY, VA

Since the thwarted attempt in Berlin, hundreds of new threats were heard all around the world. On Tuesday morning, CIA Director Scott Cunningham was once again surrounded by his inner circle of intelligence specialists.

"Come on, people, what do we have? Why can't we get something specific? They are making so much noise we should be able to just pick them up on the streets."

Lori Colbert replied, "I know what you mean, Scott. It's really frustrating."

"Good God," Cunningham said angrily. "Israel, and now Germany have found and prevented nuclear attacks in their countries, and we are just sitting around with our fingers up our noses. Why can't we get some dates, times, or loca-tions?"

Dennis Jacoby of NCS then asked, "How are we doing with those prisoners from that nuclear-armed boat, Sean? Have we gotten anything out of them?"

General Larkin answered, "Not too much, Dennis, and we really have worked them over. It appears they are just suicidal low-level operatives doing a dirty job.

"We have also learned that the Europeans are becoming very concerned. They are so much closer to the Muslim world, and any WMDs could be delivered much more easily over there. Now, this interrupted attack in Berlin makes them even more anxious. Hopefully, the Germans may be able to get some information out of the three prisoners they captured.

"Because of all this uncertainty, a few of the major cities in Europe are undergoing a moderate evacuation. Mostly, it's just a voluntary exodus by people who are fearful and may have relatives living somewhere nearby."

Cunningham then said, "As all of you know, the President is in a safe place outside of Washington, D.C., so when I speak to him later today, it will be by teleconference. If any of your departments come up with something more concrete before then, please let me know immediately. I'd like to have some substance for this briefing.

"Think about it, my friends. We've raised the terrorism threat advisory scale to its highest level; the defense readiness condition has been taken up to DEFCON 2; our maritime services have captured a little boat carrying a full-scale nuclear bomb—remember, that was just by accident—and an international airliner exploded while it was about to land in Los Angeles. That is one hell of a lot of terrorist action and reaction, and still no one knows if they are going to try to bring down the whole country."

The Director then concluded the meeting by saying, "I ask all of you to please dig in with your people in the field. We have to come up with something more specific. Thanks for all your efforts . . . I'll talk to you again in a few hours."

CHAPTER 13

JOURNEY TO
THE DEAD SEA

As he had done for Moses on his long expedition to Egypt, Jethro made certain that Yaacov would be well equipped for his trek across the Sinai Desert to the Dead Sea. Though Leah would not be accompanying her husband on his implausible odyssey, Jethro sent two of his best servants along to provide assistance for the young man. The priest didn't want any trouble to come upon his enlightened son-in-law, so he strove to ensure Yaacov's safe return to his deeply distressed daughter. The names of the two servant-helpers were Asher and Nathan.

Riding on camels, while pulling two supply-laden donkeys and driving a few sheep, the three travelers headed out from the little valley early that morning. They also carried some jewelry and other silver trinkets they could barter for supplies. Their initial destination was the ancient village of Taberah, located about 135 kilometers north of the holy mountain.

The first several days of the trip were quite uneventful, as the small entourage made its way northward across the rocky hill country. Temperatures were rather mild and none of them suffered any noticeable fatigue.

Before leaving their village, Yaacov had told the two servants why they were going on this journey to such a faraway place. And once they were underway, the travelers would usually camp near a cave or under a tree after sun-down. But before going to sleep on those evenings, Yaacov also tried to convert the other two men to the mystical life, as he gave them instructions on the spiritual principles that were continuing to unfold in his consciousness. He stressed the infinite and incorporeal nature of God. He explained how wrong the idol worshippers of Moab and Egypt were, and he pointed out that their own people weren't much better, since they thought of their God as some sort of super, man-like being—a potentate who judges and condemns, who rewards and punishes.

"God is an infinite immortal Spirit," he told them—

"But God is also Love. We have heard the legends of Adam and Eve living in a perfect habitat: *The Garden of Eden*. The truth is that we all are still living in that garden; man has never fallen from grace.

"This life that we share is the eternal Life of God being lived in unadulterated harmony and perfection. The outer world of appearances usually contradicts those facts, but that is why we must spend most of our non-working hours in prayer and meditation. It is only in those quiet periods that we can rise above this illusory sense of life and enter the five-dimensional reality of God's Divine Kingdom."

As Yaacov continued to share his insights on a daily basis, his two companions listened intently. Initially, both of them were hearing words they had never heard before. So Yaacov had to explain the strange-sounding phrases. And while Asher was quite receptive to the message, Nathan was a bit reluctant to accept this "radical" teaching, which was contrary to everything he had learned in the past. Yet Yaacov wouldn't let up, because he was on a mission to save the world—or at least, to introduce as many people to Truth as he could.

About four weeks after leaving the Midianite valley near Mount Horeb, the travelers reached the village of Taberah, where they were able to acquire enough food and supplies to last another month. And it was fortunate they did since it took more than three-and-one-half weeks to reach their next stop: the tiny village of Hazeroth.

From there, they headed northeast toward the town of Elath at the northern tip of the Gulf of Aqaba. Once they arrived in that busy city, the three men traded for more supplies and spent four restful days in the area, giving themselves an opportunity to become more refreshed and strengthened for the balance of their trip.

One afternoon in Elath, Yaacov met a traveling silk merchant who told him stories of a strange sect of mystically oriented Jews living near the Dead Sea. This reinforced the information the shepherd had initially received from Jethro. The merchant told Yaacov that the sect didn't go by any name, and the people in the group lived a very austere, reclusive life, spending most of their time discussing spiritual Truth and meditating. The itinerant vendor also said that members of the mysterious sect had developed a way to record their teachings on papyrus and pass the scrolls along to others who were literate enough to read them.

This reinvigorated the fervent shepherd and fortified his resolve even more. He now felt very confident that he definitely was doing the right thing.

As the three adventurers left Elath and continued moving northward, the terrain became flatter and more arid. The daytime temperatures grew increasingly hotter, and the nights seemed shorter. Nevertheless, they plodded on. During some nights, Yaacov slept very little as he spent much of the time in meditation. In his ongoing mystical initiation, he regularly received new insights and inspiration.

Then shortly before dawn one morning while the other two men were still sleeping, Asher let out a loud scream, waking his traveling companions. The young man had just been attacked in his left leg by a horned viper. The leg quickly began to swell, and the frightened servant became very feverish. Yaacov told him just to relax, because the Presence of God was with them. A few moments later, Asher became delirious, and his eyes glazed over. Nathan began to

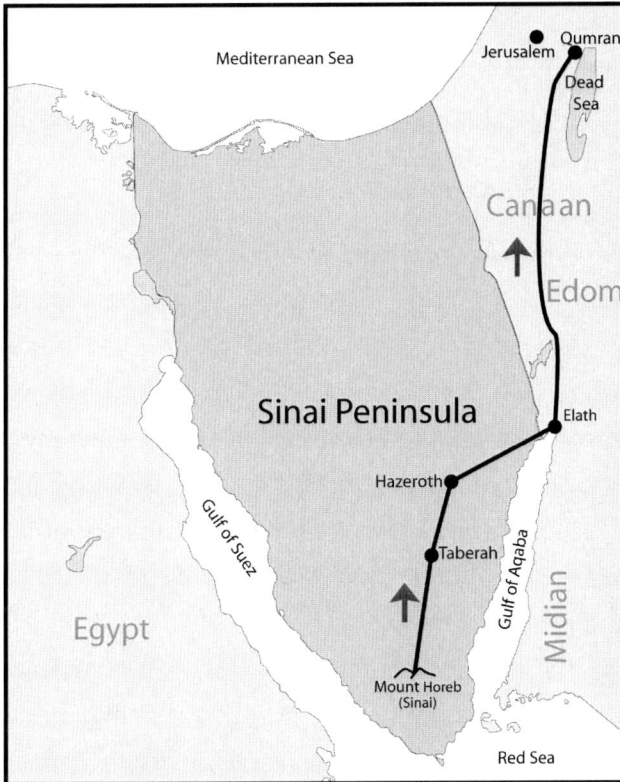

YAACOV'S JOURNEY TO QUMRAN

panic, telling Yaacov of another friend who had been attacked by such a viper and then died within four hours.

The shepherd kept his composure, holding Asher's hand
and speaking to him in a soft, gentle voice, as he told his
friend about the love and protection of God. Yaacov then
closed his eyes and became silent; he tried to feel and experience the divine Presence of God.

From somewhere deep inside his consciousness, a recollection came of an exercise that could lift Asher out of his

physical body. Yaacov realized that the young man's leg was not Asher, himself, but merely belonged to the faithful servant. The real Asher—the essence of his being—was spiritual consciousness and had been created in the image and likeness of God.

Next, Yaacov recalled the words he had heard at the burning bush. The Voice from the fire had told him that he and the Godhead were One, and they shared the name *I*. In other words, God is appearing as Asher. This loyal servant is not a mere physical organism, but really is God incarnate. The Life of God is the Life of Asher . . . The Soul of God is the soul of Asher, and the Consciousness that is God is the consciousness of Asher. God is the substance of this man's being, and they are One.

Soon, the thoughts stopped coming, as Yaacov rested in a deep and glorious silence. After about twenty minutes of basking in that divine *peace which passes all understanding*, the shepherd felt his hand being squeezed. Opening his eyes, he saw Asher sitting up and looking at his two companions with a grateful smile on his face.

Asher's fever was gone, and the swelling in his leg had subsided. Meanwhile, Nathan, who had observed this entire episode, was astounded. He had just witnessed a miracle.

From that point forward, he would become a willing disciple of his enlightened Master. The young servant finally began to comprehend the message Yaacov had been preaching. But he didn't realize that nearly fourteen centuries in the future another illumined Master would present a similar message of Oneness, which would also be very misunderstood. And those misunderstandings would ultimately lead to holy wars that could even end the life of mankind as it exists on this planet.

The three travelers spent the balance of that day resting at their campsite. Because of Asher's seemingly miraculous recovery, they were able to resume their journey early on the following morning.

As they continued traveling northward, the next forty-five days were more routine and not as hectic as the earlier part of their trip had been. Most of their daytime hours were devoted to moving together toward their now unified goal, while the remaining time after dark was spent discussing new spiritual principles that Yaacov was continuing to receive in his meditations.

And finally, after months of grueling travel, the memorable day came when the three trekkers arrived at their destination—a dry and desolate, sparsely populated village northwest of the Dead Sea called *Qumran*.

CHAPTER 14

PLANNING
AND STRATEGY

THE PRESENT - ORIGINAL TIMELINE
TUESDAY MORNING - AUGUST 18TH - 11:30 A.M. MDT
NORAD UNDERGROUND OPERATIONS CENTER
CHEYENNE MOUNTAIN, CO / CIA HEADQUARTERS - LANGLEY, VA

When President Thompson left the White House to fly to the NORAD Underground Operations Center in Colorado he was joined by Joint Chiefs Chairman Daniels, the Director of Homeland Security Domenic Fiorenza, and several high-ranking cabinet members. Other important players were continuing to work in Washington, D.C. with the understanding that they would come to Colorado if and when they were needed. On Tuesday afternoon, the President's group was connected by teleconference with Scott Cunningham, a few people from the intelligence agencies, and the five other members of the Joint Chiefs of Staff.

After Cunningham briefed them on the aborted attack in Berlin and told them he had no further specifics on any potential threats in the United States, President Thompson said, "A key decision we have to make now is whether to start evacuating our major cities. I don't want to cause a panic for all those people who are living in areas that are not in the crosshairs of any probable action. Yet at the same time, I don't want to leave them vulnerable if something does happen."

Speaking from Langley, Lori Colbert said, "As usual, I'm the eternal optimist who doesn't want to overreact. I suggest we wait a few more days before doing anything that drastic. Remember, we already have enough tension in the air with raising the security level to *Imminent,* and with Wall Street being closed. All business financing through the capital markets has been shut down; any IPOs that were planned have been stopped in their tracks; people's IRAs and 401Ks are going to hell, and they don't know if there will be a bottom. And even worse, millions of those same people could die if we don't disrupt every potential attack that's being planned here. Remember, we have to be right every time . . . the bad people with bad intentions only need to be right once or twice. That scares the heck out of me."

Admiral Casey McGraw spoke up next. "As terrifying as all that sounds, Lori, just think of how horrible it could be if worldwide intelligence hadn't done such a good job. We apprehended the three original terrorist groups who were still in the planning stages in the U.S. And then there were the three nuclear attacks that were prevented in Israel, New York and Berlin. If all of those had come to fruition, the world would be quite a different place today, and we would be discussing how to retaliate."

President Thompson then said, "Okay, enough about what might have been. We have to deal with realities. Scott, if you hear of any real threats against a specific city or landmark, let's have everything in place for immediate action."

Turning toward the Director of Homeland Security, the President asked, "Domenic, how quickly can you arrange to get everyone out of our major metropolitan areas?"

"It all depends on how imminent an attack might be," Fiorenza replied. "As you know, we already have an evacuation plan in place, but it will be impossible to vacate most big cities. How do you get all those people out of Manhattan? They have to go over bridges and through tunnels. The same thing is true of San Francisco, with their bridges. Although in that case, people could still drive south toward Silicon Valley. And what if they target Las Vegas? You couldn't get enough airplanes in there to get all those tourists out quickly enough. So what do those people do, rent cars and drive into the desert? There aren't that many rental cars available.

"There is no way that evacuations can work in an orderly fashion. Any such move would generate a huge amount of panic and disorder, and could cause its own repercussions. It would be like the stampede when someone yells 'fire' in a theater."

Scott Cunningham then said, "Domenic is right, Mr. President. As cold and heartless as it sounds, it would be virtually impossible to evacuate all of our highly populated metropolitan areas. Aside from the cities Secretary Fiorenza has already mentioned, where could people go if they live in Chicago, Philadelphia, Los Angeles, Boston, Detroit, Houston, Dallas, Atlanta, Denver, or Phoenix? Heck, we couldn't get all the residents out of Milwaukee, Minneapolis, Pittsburgh, Charlotte, St. Louis, or Washington, D.C."

"Jesus Christ," Marine Commandant Fabretti shouted out. "Whatever happened to fighting real wars, where you know the enemy and can see the whites of his eyes? But I'm telling you, Mr. President, if I were in your shoes, I would push all those red buttons if they really do hit one of our cities."

Thompson replied, "The level of response will be determined at the proper time, Tony. Our job now is still to prevent anything we can, and to keep some semblance of order in the country.

"Having said that, we can't just sit here with our hands in our pockets doing nothing—"

Before the Commander-in-Chief could finish his thought, Director Cunningham's cell phone rang. After getting the message and hanging up, he said, "Mr. President, we just received word that one of the prisoners from that 'pirate ship' is starting to squeal. Apparently he does know something, or else he is just faking it to get us to stop the interrogation. Nonetheless, he claims they are going to hit Washington D.C. by tomorrow or Thursday."

"That's terrible news, Scott," Thompson responded. "Well, if we can't get all the residents out of there, let's at least get most government workers out so we can continue to function afterwards. Scott, I will have Air Force One available for you, the Joint Chiefs members still there, and other key people that will be named. Everyone should be ready to leave by 11:00 tonight.

"And Domenic, we must find a way to start moving the citizens to safety."

CHAPTER 15

QUMRAN

NEAR THE DEAD SEA IN THE LAND OF CANAAN, 1340 BCE

With their long, exhausting journey across the Sinai Peninsula finally completed, Yaacov, Asher and Nathan arrived in the sparsely populated village of Qumran and slept for nearly two days. By the morning of the third day, Yaacov was moving about the area, trying to ascertain where to find the scribes and other members of the reclusive Jewish sect he had heard about. He soon learned that they lived and worked in the limestone cliffs above Qumran where numerous caves were located.

When he asked for directions, most of the villagers couldn't give him much help, other than to point up toward the hills at the end of the valley. So on the morning of his fifth day in Qumran, the enlightened shepherd from Midian took the last steps on his unlikely journey of discovery and sharing.

After ascending the hills, Yaacov found an area where a few pastoral-looking people were standing in a group, chatting quietly. He requested to be introduced to the leader of the sect.

When asked why he wanted to meet the man, Yaacov told them he had an important mystical message that must be preserved and recorded. He said it was a teaching that needed to be transmitted to others.

Among the small group was a rather old, heavily bearded man who was quite stooped over and used a walking stick for support. After listening to this tale for a short while, the old man motioned for Yaacov to follow him, leading the shepherd inside one of the caves. Upon arriving there, Yaacov saw four scribes working on scrolls of papyrus by the dim light of eight torches. Several of them looked up at him curiously as he passed by.

Then, after going through a narrow cave opening to another small cavern, Yaacov saw an even older, frail man wearing just a loin cloth and sitting on a bed of straw in what appeared to be a very Spartan living area. The stooped-over guide introduced the eager visitor to the second man whose name was Eliahu. The guide then exited the room, leaving Yaacov to be thoroughly scrutinized by his host for a few minutes.

While that was happening, the enthusiastic shepherd experienced an eerie sensation of familiarity toward the old man. *Why did it feel as though he had met him before?*

Finally breaking the silence, the group's stoical leader asked, "How can I help you, young man?"

"I have an important message that I must share."

"And what makes your 'message' so important?"

"I just know that it is . . . I was given the *Word of God* while standing before a burning bush on a holy mountain. I was then told that I must share the teaching I had received with all of mankind."

"All right, why don't you tell me a little about your teaching. How is it so special?"

"I have seen the misery of so many people living in this world of material concepts, and I have also learned that the outer world we perceive with our physical senses is an illusion. Yet at the same time, there is a divine, spiritual reality standing right behind it. And that transcendental reality is where God is living. It is the *Kingdom of God.*"

"That is very interesting, young man, please tell me more," Eliahu said with a nod of his head.

"I have learned that God is Life itself. Furthermore, since there is only one infinite Consciousness, I have experienced the Presence of God within me. I discern this universal, infinite Being as the sum and substance of my soul. It is the eternal Life of God living as my individual Life."

"And you heard all of this from a 'burning bush' up on that mountain you told me about earlier?"

"Yes, but I have also heard some of these principles in my daily meditations."

"Oh, you meditate daily?"

"Yes, I do, with my wife."

"I see . . . You have a wife. Then why are you not with her now, instead of coming to a place like this? What is her name?"

For just an instant, Yaacov paused without answering. *What is his wife's name?* From the distant past, he heard the word, "Kathy." He used to meditate with Kathy. *But who is Kathy?*

Regaining his composure, the shepherd replied, "My wife's name is Leah. And she did not come with me, because she needed to stay behind and help her family."

But then Yaacov could not remember ever sitting in meditation with Leah. While she did not discourage him from his new teaching, she also did not fully understand everything he was saying.

While Yaacov was pondering these conflicting thoughts, Eliahu broke the silence again by asking, "And where *did* you come from?"

Yaacov responded enthusiastically, "I have come here after a very long and difficult journey. I came from the Land of Midian, in the valley at the foot of Mount Horeb."

"Ah, yes, I have heard of that place," commented Eliahu. "There are ancient legends which claim the presence of God dwells on that mountain . . . that it is a very sacred site."

"Those are not just old legends," Yaacov interrupted. "I can testify that the Spirit of God does dwell there. And that Spirit spoke to me and my brother-in-law Moses."

"Oh, so now you not only have a wife, but you have a brother-in-law. Do you also have six children who need your support—and maybe ten cousins?

"You see, Yaacov, we are a very pious group here. We all have given up our outer lives in the busy and frivolous world of cause and effect. We have relinquished our earthly goods and our carnal desires. We spend many hours every day in the silence of meditation. I do not see how you could do that. So therefore, I do not believe that we can help you at this time."

"But that is not fair," Yaacov pleaded. "I have already given up everything just to come here. My journey across the desert wilderness was long and dangerous. I may never get back home to see my wife and her family again. But I came here in spite of those obstacles.

"I need to do this. I need to experience the life you all lead. I *need* to share my mystical message of Truth."

"Do you have a place to stay here in Qumran, Yaacov?"

"No, sir, I do not. I wondered if you could—"

After further scrutinizing the eager shepherd, the sect's elderly leader raised his right hand and interrupted. "All right, young man, you may remain here for a few days. We will make a place for you in the living quarters of our scribes. You may also join us for our evening meditations tonight. If you conduct yourself satisfactorily, we will let you participate in our discussion groups and daily class work."

"Thank you, Eliahu," Yaacov responded courteously.

"Oh, don't thank me yet. This is merely a temporary trial period. If you do not fit in here, or cause any disruptions, we will ask you to leave immediately."

"You can trust me, Eliahu, I promise to conform and to obey your rules."

So the old leader of the sect led Yaacov to another cave area where small patches of straw were placed on the floor. Apparently, this was where the scribes lived and slept.

That evening, Yaacov shared a meal with the scribes in a little grove just outside the caves. The men were very quiet as they ate their food. Each of them appeared to be satisfied just to sit in his personal contemplative silence. Then, a short while before sunset, the group gathered together for their meditation. Again, no words were spoken, as each seemed caught up in his own mystical contentment and peace. For Yaacov, that meditation was one of the most enlightening he had ever experienced.

The man named Binyamin, who was in charge of the scribes, took an instant liking to their Midianite guest. After just a few days, he and Yaacov began exchanging their thoughts and ideas. And as the young shepherd continued to attend their meditations and discussion groups, his voice became louder and soon was carrying more influence.

Seeing the response to Yaacov's message, Binyamin and Eliahu started spending a good deal of their time with him discussing mystical Truth. This uninvited stranger had brought a whole new dimension to the group's discussions and communal life. He was presenting ideas and concepts that even they had not heard before. And what strange words he was using.

As the days turned into weeks, Yaacov was readily accepted as a member of the sect. And soon, the leaders agreed that the scribes would begin transcribing and writing the message he was dictating.

But along with all the positive things that were happening in the Midian shepherd's new life, he once again was having those memory lapses during which he felt an attraction to another time and place. *What was that name that came to him when Eliahu asked him about meditating with his wife?*

Then there were the words and phrases he used when he discussed his esoteric spiritual principles. At times, his new friends looked at him as though he were speaking in a foreign tongue. They had never heard terms such as: *transcendental consciousness, the Grand Circle of Eternity,* or *five-dimensional reality.* His references to *the illusory outer world of sense perceptions* also brought questions and a measure of disbelief from his listeners.

So to be certain that the message would be clearly chronicled, Eliahu instructed Binyamin to personally work with one of the other senior scribes in producing Yaacov's manuscript.

When work on the document was finally reaching an end point, the group agreed that the scroll should be entrusted only to those people who would be receptive to such a thought-provoking teaching. For that reason, they decided to place it in a clay jar and store it in an out-of-the-way location in one of the caves. Then, when they wanted to retrieve it later for duplication or distribution, certain members of the sect could readily find it. And if it wasn't needed then, maybe some other explorer might discover the scroll in the far distant future.

Satisfied that his cherished message would now be available to those who would understand and accept it, Yaacov began thinking about going back to Midian to rejoin his beloved Leah and her family. But before he could embark on that journey, his evening meditations took him to even higher levels of mystical awareness. He often reflected upon the exercise he had used when he became an instrument for the healing of his good friend Asher.

In that situation, the enlightened shepherd had seen how Asher's limbs, organs and bodily functions did not constitute the servant's being but, rather, belonged to Asher. Following that line of thinking, Yaacov then realized the same thing must also be true of himself. So he began practicing the exercise almost nightly. While doing that, he received even stronger confirmation that his own true identity was con-sciousness—an individualized manifestation of the One infinite Consciousness. And as he continued to practice the exercise, he regularly began having out-of-body experiences. He also started hearing voices that were giving him instruc-tions. One of those instructions told him that it now was time to go home.

At first, Yaacov assumed that *home* meant back to Midian and Leah. But the Voice said, "No, you belong to another place and time." Then, in a later meditation, he heard the words: "Yaacov, you must go back to Kathy and Shi-mahn—"

"But I don't want to leave Leah," he replied.

The Voice said, "You won't be leaving Leah, because Leah is Kathy."

And while this caused Yaacov a great deal of confusion, the words were stated with such conviction and clarity he didn't know how to refute them.

And then one evening it happened.

The illumined shepherd from Midian found himself outside his Yaacov body, floating high up in space, drifting toward what appeared to be the center of the Universe. He soon was soaring through an ocean of stars and bright lights.

He saw the Grand Circle of Eternity and not only became immersed in it, but actually became an integral part of it. This brought back more memories of that other place. He then started hovering over all those parentheses on the infinite Circle. While many seemed inviting, just one of them had a very special attraction for him.

The attraction to that lifetime was so strong that he commenced drifting down toward it. And as this illumined soul gradually coalesced with that parenthesis, the Yaacov identity began to fade, and Eric once again became the host selfhood.

CHAPTER 16

THE RETURN HOME

MONDAY AFTERNOON, AUGUST 17TH - 2:05 P.M. - TIMELINE NO. 2
SHIMAHN'S ASHRAM - NAKCHU PREFECTURE -
NORTHERN TIBET AUTONOMOUS REGION

After realizing who I was, and where I was, or more importantly, where I belonged, I embarked upon the voyage back to the present in Shimahn's Tibetan ashram. The reverse trip was much like my initial journey in time to the 14th century before Christ. I once again soared through the bright lights and experienced an immersion into the Grand Circle of Eternity. Soon, I was able to see my various parentheses on the infinite Circle. But this time, there was a difference. The parenthesis I originally had left behind in the 21st century was illuminated much more brightly than all the others, so I didn't have to do any searching or make any choices. This time, I was able to just drift down into that very inviting place and, in what seemed like only a brief moment, I was home—

Almost simultaneously, I found myself sitting once again in my chair in Shimahn's library. After opening my eyes and taking a deep breath, I stood up, opened the door, and stepped back into the living area where my wife and my teacher were sitting in meditation.

Kathy was the first to notice my presence, as she said, "Oh, Eric, you're still here . . . Apparently it didn't work."

She looked so innocent and beautiful sitting there that I immediately walked across the room, extended my hands to help her up from the chair, and held her tightly in my arms. She was somewhat bewildered by all my passion since, from her perspective, I had been gone for only about twenty minutes.

While I was still hugging her, Shimahn replied, "No, Kathy. Look at his face. Your husband has been on a historic journey . . . Tell us about your experience, Eric."

Stepping back from my affectionate embrace, she looked at both of us incredulously, and asked, "Are you suggesting that Eric has gone back in time, and now has returned to the present?"

I nodded my head. "Yes, Kathy, I have been gone for almost eight years."

"That's unbelievable," she said with her eyes wide open. "Where were you?"

"This is the part that you really won't believe . . . I was living in the 14th century before Christ . . . I met Moses and was with him at the burning bush on Mt. Horeb."

Shimahn then questioned, "Do you feel this was a significant experience, Eric? Did you do anything that might have altered future events?"

"It's hard to know at this time . . . But—"

Before I could finish my sentence, Kathy interrupted abruptly. "Just hold on here, gentlemen. You're telling us, Eric, that you met Moses . . . *that* Moses? The great patriarch who delivered the Hebrew nation from slavery and gave us the Ten Commandments? The same man who wrote the first five books of the Bible and parted the Red Sea? What are you going to tell us next, that you carved the Ten Commandments in stone for him?"

Even though my wife was a very receptive soul who previously had shared numerous spiritual adventures with me, she still was quite taken aback by my implausible revelation.

I then responded, "No . . . Uh, yes . . . I mean I can't answer all those questions with just a 'yes' or a 'no'. I knew him before he gave us the Ten Commandments. And I cannot be certain that he wrote any books of the Bible . . . You see, he was my brother-in-law."

"Your brother-in-law?" she gasped. "Are you saying that the Biblical Moses was married to your sister? You don't even have a sister."

"No, Kathy, he was married to my wife's sister."

"Your wife's sister? Does that mean you had a wife before me . . . or was it after me?"

"Well, yes and no . . . because actually it was you."

"How could she have been me? I didn't go back there with you?"

"You didn't have to go back, because your soul was already there, but inhabiting a different body. Your name was Leah, and your oldest sister Zipporah was the wife of Moses... And, oh, by the way, your father Jethro was a kind, generous and wise man."

Kathy didn't respond audibly, but just shook her head in disbelief as Shimahn then spoke up. "Eric, you say that you were with Moses at the burning bush?"

"Yes; it was an indescribable experience."

"Was the holy name given to you while you were there?"

"Yes, it was. But I don't think Moses truly understood it this time either. He believed his mission was to go back to Egypt to try to convince Pharaoh to let his people go.

"Honestly, Shimahn, that is not what the Voice told us to do. We were instructed to assimilate the hallowed message and then share it with all of mankind. As I understood the admonition, we are supposed to give the sacred name to all those who will be able to comprehend and accept it."

Shimahn asked, "While you were there, did you do anything about that?"

"Of course," I replied with a smirk on my face. "I wrote a book about it."

"You wrote a book?" Kathy cried out. "How did you do that? Did you have a yellow legal pad and a ballpoint pen with you? Did you invent a word processor while you were there?

"Who needs Bill Gates and Steve Jobs, when you have old Eric here sitting up on a mountaintop writing stories 1,350 years before Jesus was born?"

Hearing her glib remarks, it was obvious that Kathy wasn't yet willing to accept my account of the events. She then asked mischievously, "What was your name when you lived as a Midianite? Were you still Eric, or were you Bill or Steve, oh great inventor of writing instruments?"

Come on, Kathy, don't you think you are being a little facetious? My name was Yaacov, son of Boaz, which in English is translated as Jacob."

"If you did write something down," Shimahn asked, "how were you planning to transmit it to anyone else?"

"I went on a long and arduous journey to Qumran near the Dead Sea. I met some scribes there who belonged to a reclusive sect of Jews. They helped me get the document written on papyrus, and then they stored it in a cave in the area. I have no idea if it has been preserved for all these years."

"Apparently it has not," Shimahn said. "Or if it has, I certainly am not aware of it."

He paused for a moment, and then haltingly pondered aloud, "But if you put it there during your recent trip back in time, it couldn't have appeared before about one half hour ago, because, until you left here, everything followed its original timeline. Now that you have created the document, it could only appear in this new timeline that we are living in after your return from the past."

Just when it seemed that Kathy was beginning to accept what had happened, Shimahn made those last comments, which really confused the two of us.

"Could you please explain that again?" I requested.

"Well, just think about it, young people. All of us have been living in a specific timeline up to about two o'clock this afternoon, when Eric went back to the 14th century BCE. Because he was there in that older parenthesis, he could have created a new timeline from that point forward by changing some important events. But if our young time traveler did not make any dramatic changes back then, everything that followed would have been approximately the same. That timeline would not be any different from the original one that we already have experienced.

"But I do have one question, Eric: Do you know if Moses returned to Egypt to challenge Pharaoh while you were there?"

"Yes, he did. I tried to talk him out of it, but he just wouldn't listen to me."

"Maybe it's just as well that he didn't listen to you. Then everything of significance during that time period was much the same, so there was no major altering of history as we have always known it. But you did produce your papyrus scroll. Yet that could not appear until this new timeline evolved—the timeline that has just been created by your recent return to this present.

"So if your writings are going to have any impact on the future, that won't happen until someone discovers the scroll and then translates and distributes it sometime after today.

"Can you think of anything else of significance that was different, Eric? Were any other important events changed?"

"None that I can remember, sir. But even if nothing much was changed, the whole journey in time was a remarkable experience for me."

"Well then, Eric, it appears that as dramatic as your sojourn to the past has been—getting to meet Moses, hearing the voice of God at the burning bush, along with all the other remarkable experiences you may have had—nothing occurred that will alter the very difficult future we still are facing today."

As we continued to talk, Kathy became even more accepting of what had happened. But that made her want to ask additional questions.

She said, "Shimahn, if Eric has been gone for almost eight years, what happened to you and me in that future period? Or even more importantly, what happened to all the problems in the world during that time?"

He replied, "You and I lived on in the reality that followed the timeline we were living in about one half hour ago—the exact moment when Eric left this parenthesis. And what followed was a very catastrophic series of events. I have some distinct recollections from that period."

"You do?" Kathy asked. "How could you? I don't remember anything."

"I would not expect you to, Kathy; and you can be grateful that you don't remember what happened. It was a horrific experience."

"But how would you remember events from an alternate reality?" I asked Shimahn. "That's the future, not the past. It's a period of time that hasn't even happened yet."

"There is no need to explain all of that now, Eric. Just trust me on this one."

"That's amazing, Shimahn. But as I mentioned earlier, Kathy—or at least her soul appearing as Leah—was there in the Midianite Valley, and we loved each other very much. And her sister Zipporah became Moses' wife. Doesn't that send chills up your spine, Kathy, knowing that your own sister was married to Moses?"

She didn't reply, but just stared at me blankly.

"Oh, and there is one other interesting thing that happened during that time . . . Actually, Moses wanted to marry you instead of Zipporah. You—living as Leah—were his first choice. But instead of marrying Moses, you chose me. What do you think of all that?"

"I don't think I can answer that question at this time, Eric, since I don't recall ever meeting Moses, or having him propose to me."

I then spoke again, even more animatedly than I had been doing. "And Shimahn, you also were there. When I went to Qumran, I believe that you, living in an earlier incarnation, were the leader of the reclusive sect of Hebrews who helped me transcribe my message into a written manuscript. And for what it's worth, you were quite old in that life, too. Maybe not 88, but you certainly lived into your late seventies.

"And here's another intriguing aspect of that episode: I remembered you, but you didn't seem to remember me. Why would that be?"

The Master responded, "When you entered that parenthesis, your soul may have just interacted with the people there for the first time. It is possible that you were recalling me from this present lifetime which you had just left, but I could not remember you because, most likely, you and I had never met previous to that encounter. It is not just a coincidence that we have connected in several lifetimes. You have many soul mates aside from your wife, and you will always be together with those people who are of your own spiritual household.

"It is also possible that you are a much older soul than I am, Eric, which is another reason why I may not have recognized you from any earlier meeting."

Shimahn then leaned back in his chair, took a deep breath, and said, "But now for some more important issues, my young friend. Since you haven't done anything yet that would significantly change the past—thereby leaving us with the same cataclysmic future—you must go back again. And you must do it now, because there is no question about it. We definitely are up against the clock. As I mentioned in my original invitation for you to come here, the future of mankind really does hang in the balance. I now have confirmation that the situation is even more calamitous than I thought it was."

CHAPTER 17

ANOTHER HISTORIC
JOURNEY IN TIME

MONDAY AFTERNOON, AUGUST 17TH - 3:10 P.M. - TIMELINE NO. 2
SHIMAHN'S ASHRAM - NAKCHU PREFECTURE -
NORTHERN TIBET AUTONOMOUS REGION

S ince Shimahn had actually lived through, and remembered, what he described as an extremely cataclysmic future, he stressed the urgency for me to go back in time once more—and to do it as soon as possible. It appeared that he didn't want the two of them, or anyone else, to live through that future again. So I gave Kathy a warm embrace and shook my Master's hand, as I entered the library for the second time that day and seated myself once more in my "launching chair."

By that time, I was getting quite proficient at rising up and out of my body, and making the ascension into the Grand Circle of Eternity. So shortly after closing my eyes, I found myself floating peacefully through the Cosmos and soon entered the Infinite Circle. After gently hovering there for a while, I looked for an inviting parenthesis to which I felt a strong attraction. As in my first experience, there was one that seemed to be beckoning me above all the others. So I just drifted down toward that lifetime and gradually settled in to the silence and darkness below.

As the soul, recently known again as Eric, entered his new host body, he heard the sound of several contentious voices loudly discussing some controversial issues.

JERUSALEM, JUDEA
AUTUMN OF 49 CE

The gathering was referred to as the Council of Jerusalem, or Apostolic Conference, and was held around the time of the Feast of Tabernacles. Paul and Barnabas had just concluded a private meeting with the Apostles Peter, James and John. The followers of Jesus had long been debating the question of whether circumcision was required for Gentiles to be allowed into the church. At that meeting, the group agreed that, going forward, circumcision should not be necessary and, at the same time, they endorsed the ministry of Paul and Barnabas. The Council then suggested that Silas and Judas Barsabas travel with Paul and Barnabas to Antioch to deliver a letter written by James to the Christian brotherhood in that community. The letter summarized the decisions reached at the Jerusalem Conference.

Antioch—also referred to as Syrian Antioch—was an ancient city, founded near the end of the 4th century BCE by

Seleucus, one of Alexander the Great's generals. As a cradle of early Christianity, Antioch was the place where the followers of Jesus were called Christians for the first time.

After the group of missionaries arrived in Antioch, Paul and Barnabas had an excruciating disagreement over whether John Mark should participate in their next journey, because the young man had deserted them on their last trip. The argument became so intense that Paul and Barnabas agreed to separate, with Barnabas taking John Mark to Cyprus, and Paul taking Silas on his heralded second missionary journey.

In his first expedition through the Gentile Greek world, Paul had established churches from Syrian Antioch and Seleucia in the east, to Perga and Pisidian Antioch in the west. On this second journey, he would be starting up several new congregations and giving support to many of the old ones he had founded in his earlier travels.

Leaving Antioch near the end of 49 CE, the first stop for Paul and Silas was Paul's hometown of Tarsus. It was there in that thriving commercial centre that the future apostle— then known as Saul—received his first instructions in Judaism and learned his craft as a tentmaker. Later, Saul would travel to Jerusalem and, in his own words, "be educated at the feet of Gamaliel," a noted Pharisee and a member of the Sanhedrin. The Sanhedrin was a legal tribunal made up of 71 judges or sages and literally functioned as the Supreme Court of ancient Israel. It was the final authority on Jewish law. In further describing himself, Paul claimed that he was "a freeborn Roman citizen; a Pharisee of the Pharisees."

From Tarsus, along the way toward Derbe and Lystra, the two dedicated missionaries did fruitful work to strengthen the churches in Syria and Cilicia. They rode in boats whenever they needed to cross a large body of water, but for most of the land excursions, they walked, because that is what holy men of Asia did: they walked long and far. The first portion of this second missionary journey was primarily over land, so it would require a good deal of tedious walking.

Paul was a balding, short and delicate man who was quite homely and had a few physical handicaps. He walked with an accentuated limp, because his left leg was nearly an inch shorter than his right leg. Yet he was able to handle the long walking trips in spite of that limitation. He also was an epileptic who suffered periodic brain seizures, which often left him totally exhausted and unable to perform his missionary work for days at a time. But his vigorous zeal to share the Christ message lifted him above even that potentially debilitating affliction.

Silas, on the other hand, was quite tall for that era, standing a robust five-feet, ten-inches in height. Outwardly, he was a quiet man who, through the centuries, was treated benevolently by historians. Silas was a Hellenized Jew and, like Paul, also had Roman citizenship. His well-proportioned Greek face was partially covered by a short trimmed beard, and though he was strong enough to be a laborer, blacksmith, or field hand, he was extremely literate and well schooled in classical Greek and Roman literature. So he spent much of his time theorizing and debating with some of his brilliant, erudite friends about abstract metaphysical principles.

However, in the midst of those intellectual discussions, the young scholar often became puzzled by the strange words and thoughts that periodically were coming into his mind from an unexplainable source. Sometimes, the intruding thoughts appeared to be coming from a different time and place. For that reason, he questioned Paul's characterization of the message of Jesus of Nazareth. Even though Silas had never heard the Master speak, he perceived Jesus' teachings from a more esoteric and mystical standpoint.

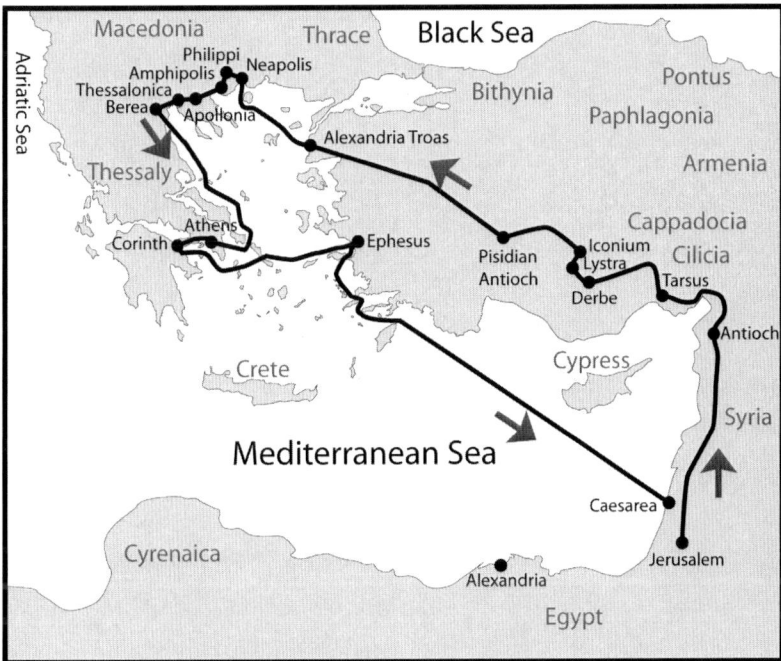

PAUL'S SECOND MISSIONARY JOURNEY
THROUGH THE PAGAN GREEK WORLD

As the two tireless missionaries traveled from city to city, the crowds attending Paul's lectures were growing daily. By that time, this Apostle to the Gentiles had been preaching his interpretation of the Nazarene Prophet's message for more than fifteen years. To Paul, Jesus was the Christ, the only begotten Son of God who had been sent here to redeem the man of earth from his sins and, ultimately, from eternal damnation.

But while Silas listened to Paul's sermonizing and appreciated the size of the crowds the apostle was drawing, the younger evangelist was becoming more disturbed by the words he was hearing. Silas believed that his God was an incorporeal God of Love—an infinite Being who saw everything that He had created, and declared it to be very good. To Silas, the specific event that the world referred to as *Creation* was really *Revelation*—the revealing of the infinite Consciousness manifesting and unfolding Itself as the reality of all existence. In other words, Silas' God appears individually as the true identity of every man, woman and child. Therefore, this God would not punish His children, no matter how bad their transgressions and, hence, there was no need for redemption.

After their long days of work among their followers, the two men spent many evenings discussing their conflicting theories. Paul believed that mankind had been condemned to an eternity of pain and suffering because of the fall of Adam and Eve, and the only source of salvation was to follow, and accept, Jesus Christ as Lord and savior. But Silas' God of Love could never condemn His own children to such a fate.

Silas' God was not a potentate who judges and condemns, who rewards and punishes.

Yet even though Silas carried those deep-seated feelings within himself, he tried not to be too vocal about them and usually offered tacit acceptance of Paul's preaching—at least in public.

After several months of traveling and evangelizing, the two missionaries reached the city of Lystra. During their visit there, they met another young follower named Timothy, who joined their party and accompanied them on the next segments of their trip through Phrygia and Galatia.

Because of his very thin frame and gaunt face, Timothy appeared to be much older than his chronological age. And unlike Silas, who had some strong opinions of his own, Timothy was a true believer of Paul's message. After just a short time together, the celebrated apostle became so impressed with Timothy that he began referring to him as "my own son in the faith." Paul also praised Timothy for his "great knowledge of the Scriptures."

Moving north and west from Lystra, the three evangelists visited Iconium and Pisidian Antioch, establishing more new churches and again reinforcing old ones along the way. The party then planned to travel across the province of Asia to the coastal city of Ephesus, but Paul believed he had received a message from the Holy Spirit, forbidding him to go there. Instead, they turned northward, following the Roman Road for a long journey to the important port city of Alexandria Troas, located about twenty miles from Homer's famous city of Troy.

Troas had a magnificent scenic setting on the northwest coast of Asia Minor. While there, Paul and Silas often marveled at God's glorious creation, as they spent several relaxing evenings watching the breathtaking sunsets over the sparkling cobalt-blue water of the Aegean Sea. Following a few weeks in Troas, they sailed to Neapolis on the north shore of the Aegean via Samothrace, a Greek island located about half way across the sea. From there, they walked along a western route on the *Via Egnatia*, the great military highway that linked Rome to the East. Then, after two more months of walking and proselytizing, they arrived in Philippi, a bustling city in eastern Macedonia in northern Greece.

Originally named Krinides, the town was conquered in 356 BCE by Philip II of Macedon, the father of Alexander the Great. He then renamed it *Philippi* in his own honor. By the year 50 CE, Philippi was the easternmost town of Roman-occupied Europe. So this was the first time Paul had been able to preach the gospel on European soil. But the city also became well known for an important event in the lives of Paul and Silas.

Because Philippi had very few Jews and no synagogue, the three traveling men stayed in the home of Lydia, a devout Jewish woman that Paul had baptized. Lydia was a dealer in dyed cloth, and was also referred to as a purple dye merchant. Furthermore, her household was the first in Europe to be converted to Christianity. But shortly after moving in with Lydia's family, an unpleasant incident put an end to the apostles' brief stay in Philippi. One evening, as Paul and Silas were on their way to Lydia's house, they crossed paths with a young slave girl who was possessed with an evil spirit. Apparently, she was a sooth-sayer who attached herself to the evangelists and began following them around, disrupting their lectures.

Paul became quite frustrated with the situation, so he exorcized the demon from the girl. That upset her employers who had been making a good deal of money from her fortune telling. The girl's employers then caused a great uproar in the city. As a result, Paul and Silas were arrested for causing a disturbance, were publicly beaten, and were incarcerated in prison. Because both men were Roman citizens, this was an illegal act performed by the magistrates. Nevertheless, after receiving custody of the two beaten men, the jailer had their wrists placed in chains and their ankles in leg shackles. Then he had them taken to the deepest reaches of the inner prison and had their feet secured in stocks.

During that experience, Silas tried to convince Paul to accept the Truth of Being as *he* understood it. Paul had been imprisoned before, but this arrest seemed very unjust. In his opinion, he and Silas had done nothing wrong, yet they were beaten, and treated as though they had committed a capital crime.

Speaking softly to his mentor, Silas said, "Please realize that the Presence of God is always with us, Paul. We cannot blame any man or organization for our current plight, or for any other negative situation in which we may find ourselves. Each of us is an individualized expression of God. In other words, we are God incarnate. And yes, this means that, like Jesus, we too have a divine identity."

Paul, meanwhile, wanted to lash out at someone. He couldn't understand why God had forsaken him again. But Silas continued to console him, trying to get the zealous apostle to relax and feel the heavenly presence.

They discussed their conflicting ideas on the subject for several hours until Paul fell asleep. Silas then closed his eyes in meditation and instinctively tried to achieve a level of awareness in which the Spirit of God was flowing *in*, *as*, and *through* him. The young man clearly understood that he was a spiritual being living in the five-dimensional reality of God -consciousness. Without too much effort, he achieved a remarkable level of silence and peace. While resting in that peace, he realized that his true identity was not confined to just his present physical body. As he continued to reason along those lines, the illumined evangelist quickly found himself outside of his body, soaring high into space. Soon, he was surrounded by bright lights and experienced a sensation of supernal joy.

After basking in that mystical ecstasy for a period that he could not measure, Silas gently drifted downward and back into his body. Arriving there, he just continued to rest in the deep, peaceful silence. Suddenly, the ground beneath him started to shake. The vibrations became very intense, waking the other prisoners who began screaming in fear, as some of the walls tumbled down. Most of the inmates expected to be crushed by the falling stones, but then a phenomenal thing happened. Though the walls and ceiling of the prison had collapsed, no one was injured, and the chains and shackles that had been binding the men broke apart and dropped to the ground. Without them knowing what had caused it, they all were set free.

In spite of the sudden release for all the prisoners, none of them tried to escape or leave the facility. Even the jailer was unharmed by the falling debris. Yet, when he saw the remaining doors and walls standing open, he assumed that most of the inmates would just walk out, leaving him to be blamed for the mass exodus. Because of the shame he then would feel, his first reaction was to kill himself. But when he came into contact with Paul and Silas, he sensed the overwhelming power of their souls and realized that, somehow, they must have been the cause of what had just happened. The jailer was very humbled after witnessing how the Presence of God could be brought into an individual's human experience and could then free the person from any form of temporal material power.

Wanting to learn more about their teachings and to spend more time in their presence, he invited the two men to his home for dinner that evening and then became a regular attendee at the Philippian church they had established.

Later that night, Paul and Silas had a long conversation about the apparent miracle that had occurred. Paul believed that his God in heaven was looking down upon them and simply answered his prayers, setting them free as an act of grace. Silas disagreed, since he knew that his mystical experience and ascension into the transcendental five-dimensional consciousness was the catalyst for the event. And though the two friends spoke for hours, it was a disagreement that could not be settled at that time.

Two days later, Timothy joined Paul and Silas, as they left Philippi, continuing their long missionary journey. Their next destination was another Greek city then under Roman rule: Thessalonica.

CHAPTER 18

A MYSTERIOUS
DISCOVERY

The tour group had been in the area since early in the morning, learning the history and significance of the Dead Sea Scrolls' discovery. Led by famed British archaeologist Lindsay Ainsworth-Jones, the group was visiting several of the now legendary caves.

At his level of prominence Ainsworth-Jones seldom spent his time conducting tours of the caves. Usually, he was out at the excavations and digs doing what he did best: finding, analyzing, and translating objects of antiquity from the distant past. Not only was the six-foot, three-inch, sandy-haired explorer a renowned archaeologist, but he was an author of several best-selling books on the subject. In addition, he had been the most interviewed person in his field, often appearing on talk shows such as those hosted by Oprah Winfrey, Larry King and Geraldo Rivera. He also was a regular featured expert on archaeological programs broadcast on the BBC in Europe, as well as the Discovery and History channels in America.

However, on that fateful Tuesday morning in August, something inside Ainsworth-Jones' soul motivated him to participate in the day's tour. And the attraction was so great that the celebrated archaeologist also asked his assistant, Bradley Stratton, to join him.

Since his crew had recently finished excavating their most recent dig, nothing consequential required his attention for now. So Lindsay decided to give a special treat to that day's visitors to Qumran. He would add his insights, knowledge, and reputation to the usual patter provided by the regular tour guides.

At the moment, the group was visiting Cave 3, the hideaway in which the mysterious *Copper Scroll* had been uncovered. After entering the dimly lit cavern with a group of sixteen tourists, the noted archaeologist addressed his audience. "This cave was discovered by local Bedouins in March of 1952," he said. "Some of the most famous manuscripts found here were: *The Copper Scroll, Jubilees*, a portion of *Lamentations*, and *The Hymn of Praise*. *The Copper Scroll* is unique in that it is the only one not written on papyrus or parchment. The scroll lists 67 hiding places throughout the ancient Roman province of Judea. According to the scroll, many of these secret caches were underground and held substantial amounts of gold, silver, copper, aromatics, and some still-undiscovered manuscripts. Unfortunately, no one has yet found any treasures in these mysterious hiding places."

After describing other important characteristics and the historic background of Cave 3, Ainsworth-Jones and Stratton answered a few questions before leading the group to Cave 4. The most famous of the Dead Sea Scroll caves, number 4 is also the most significant in terms of finds. More than 14,000 fragments from about 550 different manuscripts were retrieved there. Cave 4 is made up of one large chamber, which opens into two smaller ones. Discovered by Bedouins while archaeologists were digging at adjacent ruins, most of the manuscripts found there were in tatters, and more than 80 percent of them had been looted and, later, had to be repurchased from Bedouin traders by the government of Jordan.

Ainsworth-Jones, who had participated in numerous tours of the Qumran caves in the past, led this current group to all the regular points of interest. But this time, as he entered Cave 4, something seemed different; something felt out of place. After half-heartedly giving his standard presentation, the acclaimed archeologist asked Bradley Stratton and the two guides to escort the group to their next stop, while he lingered in Cave 4 for a few moments.

Without too much effort, he saw it standing there behind a small ledge. Gleaming like a beacon on a hill, the object called out for his attention. Right before Ainsworth-Jones' eyes was a very old, twenty-two-inch-high clay jar. Bending over to lift the jar, Lindsay saw that it contained what looked like an amazingly well preserved scroll of partially fragmented papyrus.

Good God, what is this? he wondered. *Where did this come from? Thousands of people have visited this cave during the past sixty years, and there has also been a huge amount of looting during that time. How could anything still be here that hadn't been found before?*

Stepping out to the edge of the cave, the stunned archaeologist used his cell phone to call Stratton. "Brad," he shouted excitedly, "I have just found something incredible. Please have the guides reassemble the people on the bus and have the driver take them back to the tour center in Jerusalem. But I need you to stay behind and join me in Cave 4. We have to talk about a remarkable discovery. I promise you won't believe your eyes!"

While Stratton was getting the tourists back on the bus, Lindsay carefully slid the edge of the scroll partially out of the jar, just to see if he could read any of the inscriptions. By the time Stratton reached the cave, his mentor could barely control his enthusiasm. Without being concerned about how this object could have been overlooked in this cave for all those years, Ainsworth-Jones said, "I have only seen a fragment of the edge of the scroll. But if I am not mistaken, my initial assessment indicates that this document is written in a Hebrew dialect that was prevalent in the fourteenth century BCE. In other words, this might be contemporary with the time of Moses."

Stratton's mouth dropped open and his eyes widened, as he then said, "How is that possible, Lindsay? The oldest papyrus or parchment documents found in these caves were created in the first or second centuries BCE. Did the Essene

Jews actually have possession of some writings of Moses? Or even more intriguing, could we possibly trace the Essenes' sect all the way back to Moses' time?"

"I don't have any answers at this moment, Brad, just a ton of questions. And we will need to do all the usual testing for authenticity. But before we tell anyone about this, why don't you call John Farnsworth at the dig and have him drive the mini-van out to pick us up. Oh, and also tell him to bring some heavy moving pads."

CHAPTER 19

PAUL'S SECOND MISSIONARY JOURNEY CONTINUES

MONDAY AFTERNOON, AUGUST 17TH - 2:40 P.M. - TIMELINE NO. 2
SHIMAHN'S ASHRAM - NAKCHU PREFECTURE -
NORTHERN TIBET AUTONOMOUS REGION

After waiting and meditating for about thirty-five minutes, Shimahn and Kathy entered the cool darkness of the library. As was the case during Eric's first attempt at time travel, they found no one in the room. And just as before, Kathy was quite puzzled about what may have happened. But again, Shimahn assured her that her husband was safely on another voyage back in time.

What he didn't tell her, however, was that, unless Eric was successful on this mission, the two of them, along with the rest of mankind, might have to live through another horrendous future, just as they had in the original timeline. Hopefully, this time it wouldn't be for almost eight years, and hopefully, they both would survive that period again. Yet at this moment, all of that was out of their hands.

The best thing they could do now would be to spend a good deal of time in meditation, trying to achieve an awareness of the five-dimensional reality of God-consciousness, thereby living above the conflict. And though they might still be *in* the world, in this new timeline, they would not necessarily have to be *of* the world.

THESSALONICA, MACEDONIA
SUMMER OF 51 CE

After Paul and Silas were set free from the prison in Philippi, Timothy rejoined them and the three devoted missionaries continued their long journey. Along the way, Timothy asked how they were released so quickly. Paul replied, "It was an absolute miracle, Timothy. I had been praying for most of the night. Then shortly after I fell asleep, God answered my prayer by initiating an earthquake that broke the chains and shackles on everyone and set all of us free."

While Timothy was extremely impressed with Paul's account of the event, Silas remained silent. The loyal friend did not want to say anything that might embarrass, or contradict his illustrious companion.

In the next phase of their journey, the three evangelists once more traveled westward via the Egnatian Road, making stops in Amphipolis and Apollonia before arriving in Thessalonica, the historical city and chief port of the Aegean Sea. Paul then spent three weeks preaching in the city's synagogue. He established a Jewish-Gentile church in the area, but it had a strong Gentile majority.

Though Paul continued to give the people his interpretation of the message of Jesus Christ, Silas was becoming more and more troubled with that message. Many evenings after concluding their work among the converts, they again had long discussions on their differing points of view. Late one night in an especially revealing exchange, Silas asked, "Paul, do you believe that God is infinite?"

"Of course I do."

"Well, how can you believe in an infinite God—which means God is all that exists, literally filling all space—and then accept the existence of some other presence or power?"

The apostle was silent for a few seconds as he looked up at the clear, starry sky. He then replied, "I really had not thought about it from an analytical or scientific perspective."

"That perspective is not merely scientific—it is logical," the younger man stated affirmatively. "You cannot have an infinite God, and also have some other powers. All power must flow out from the one infinite Being that we call God. The power of God is in direct proportion to the all-ness of God."

Silas became silent for a moment, as he wondered where he had heard that phrase before. Then he continued. "But remember, Jesus also taught that God is Love. And no one has a better understanding of that than our dear friend John. I'm sure you recall John's words when he was speaking in Jerusalem. He said, *'Let us love one another for love is of God, and every one that loves is born of God and knows*

God. He that does not express love does not know God, because God is Love. There is no fear in Love, but perfect Love will cast out all fear.' Doesn't that capture the essence of what Jesus was teaching?"

"Uh, yes it does, Silas," the apostle responded in a gentle tone. "But Jesus also told us that God is a loving Father."

"That is correct, my friend. However, he then referred to God as *'your Father'* and *'my Father.'* God is the only Being—the only Life, the only Consciousness. And that One Being is appearing as the individual identity of each one of us. We do not exist separate from God but, rather, live in eternal Oneness with God.

"Paul, do you remember the last prayer that Peter and John told us they had heard Jesus pray? The Master said: *'And now, O Father, glorify me with Your own Self, so that we can again share the glory that I had with You before this world was created.*

"*'I have manifested Your name unto the men which You gave me. They were Yours, but now You have given them to me. So they are not of the world, even as I am not of the world. And I do not pray for just these alone, but for all those who will follow and will believe Your message of Truth. I ask that they may be one just as You are in me, and I am in You—that they also may be one in us. And the message that You have given me, I have given them . . . that they may be one, even as we are one . . . I in them, and You in me, that they too may be made perfect in this Oneness.'*

"Don't you agree, Paul, that this is the most important instruction Jesus gave to us? All men are One with God and with each other. The Spirit of God lives *in, as,* and *through* each of us. And that is why the Master also could say, *'I and my Father are One.'*"

"Silas, I bow to your wisdom on this. I will try to bring more of this idea of Oneness into my teaching. Thank you, dear friend."

Despite his disagreements with Silas, Paul was well received by the people to whom he was preaching. But his success with his church in Thessalonica roused the jealousy of the Jews in the area, causing them to protest and agitate at some of his sermons and lectures. The situation became so tense that, one evening, the house in which the evangelists were staying was attacked by some of their adversaries. Fortunately, the three men were able to escape unharmed. Then, to avoid further trouble, the converts helped Paul, Silas and Timothy leave the city by night and head south to the small, ancient town of Berea.

Berea was an out-of-the way village that was less visible and less hostile. As a result, the Berean Jews were much more receptive to the message, as both Silas and Paul preached in the synagogue. But shortly after the missionaries' arrival, a number of Jews from Thessalonica came to Berea to disrupt some of Paul's sermons. When that happened, the apostle was encouraged by his concerned supporters to leave the area. Heeding their advice, he headed to the beautiful and scenic eastern coast of Macedonia, where he was able to get on a ship and set sail for Athens accompanied by a few of the faithful. Meanwhile, Silas and Timothy stayed behind in Berea to continue advocating their respective messages.

Each of the young evangelists appealed to a different type of follower. Timothy attracted those people who liked the message of Paul. Silas, on the other hand, drew a more cerebral group—those Greeks who read and studied the esoteric teachings of Socrates, Plato, Aristotle, and the other great philosophers. Though it had been more than 400 years since the three celebrated Greek intellectuals did their teaching and writing, their words still lived in the hearts and minds of Silas and his free thinking friends. So rather than merely accepting the teachings of Jesus as they were interpreted and handed down by the original disciples, Silas perceived the Galilean Prophet's words through the perspective of the older philosophical giants. As a result, the young scholar did not just preach to the people, but allowed a free and open dialogue in which there was an exchanging of ideas. Speculation and theoretical discussions were rampant at some of those gatherings, yet Silas always brought them back to his basic message of the infinitude and all-ness of God. Starting from that standpoint, everything else that he said flowed quite logically, and his erudite group accepted that interpretation as the *Living Word*.

While the younger men were spreading their respective messages throughout the area around Berea and Thessalonica, Paul had reached Athens and was appalled by what he saw. There were statues and idols, temples and shrines wherever he looked. Among this clutter of deities, he came across one altar dedicated to *"the unknown god."*

As a practicing Jew, Paul had been taught from childhood not to have any other gods before the One God of Israel, and not to make or worship any graven images. So with all this idolatry in Athens as a backdrop, and standing in the shadow of the Acropolis, the noted Apostle to the Gentiles prepared himself to give one of his most memorable and renowned sermons, as he decided to address the Athenians from a highly elevated spot in the middle of the city. It was a place called Mars Hill by the Romans, or The Areopagus by the Greeks. The Areopagus was a rocky marble hill standing about 115 meters high and located a slight distance from the entrance to the Acropolis. As a place where court was held concerning questions of religion and morals, the site has also been referred to as the *Hill of Ares*, because according to legend, Ares, the Greek god of war, was tried there by the Gods for the murder of Poseidon's son.

Though Paul was reacting to all the godlessness he had seen in this idolatrous city, he also was being influenced by his metaphysical discussions with his good friend, Silas. As a result, Paul's sermon on Mars Hill, more than any other he had given, emphasized the omnipotence and omnipresence of God. This speech was his first in which he truly outlined the incorporeal nature of the Godhead. For that reason, he chastised his listeners for their worshipping of any unknown gods.

In stressing the Deity's omnipotence, he said, *"God that made the world and all things in it, seeing that He is the Lord of heaven and earth, dwells not in temples made with hands. Neither is He worshipped with men's hands, as though He needed anything, seeing that He gives to all of us our life, breath, and everything else that we need."*

And to illustrate God's omnipresence and man's Oneness with the Deity, Paul gave his audience one of his most profound teachings. He said, *"For in Him we live, and move, and have our being; as certain of your own poets have said: for we are also His offspring."*

His listeners were awestruck by the words emanating from the apostle's mouth. Some liked this new, highly esoteric teaching, while others did not. But for Paul, this was the beginning of a more mystical message that would flow, at least in part, through some of his later letters to his churches.

After giving that remarkable sermon, the apostle spent a short time in Athens with the followers who had accompanied him. In general, Paul was a free spirit, and even though he hadn't fully accepted the pure mysticism being advocated by his friend Silas, he tried to listen to the Spirit for guidance in his daily life and in his travels. Just as he believed he had been instructed not to go to Ephesus in the previous year, he now sensed that he was being led back to the southwest to rejoin Silas and Timothy. So during the next few days, the apostle finalized his plans to travel toward the Macedonian city of Corinth, the political capital of Achaia or Southern Greece. Corinth was also famous for being the site of two historic pagan temples: one to Apollo—who was the legendary son of Zeus—and the other to Aphrodite, the Greek goddess of love.

CHAPTER 20

TESTING AND TRANSLATING

Beginning their translation efforts at 2:45 Tuesday afternoon, Lindsay Ainsworth-Jones and his staff continued working late into the night. The discovery of the new papyrus scroll he had found in Cave 4 at Qumran created so much excitement that they all wanted to learn more about the document. In order not to damage the scroll by too much handling, they needed to prepare it and make copies from which they could do their translating. Fortunately, the manuscript seemed amazingly well preserved—almost as though it had been written only recently—and was not too fragile.

Shortly before 4:00 p.m., two specialists from the Israel Antiquities Authority in Jerusalem were brought in to help with the verification and authentication of the scroll. At the same time, a few fragments of the papyrus were shipped by overnight express mail to the Laboratory of Archaeometry in Demokritos, Greece for radiocarbon testing.

As the translators continued to work on their copies of the document, they became more and more amazed and totally confused by what they were reading. Everything about this scroll seemed wrong. If it truly was from the 14th century BCE—and the Hebrew dialect implied that it was—the words were completely inconsistent with that time frame.

The manuscript was titled: **The Book of Jacob, Son of Boaz.** The first lines at the beginning of the scroll were: *"I Jacob, son of Boaz. received this message at the burning bush on the holy mountain. I now pass these words on to you and all seekers of Truth."*

After reading those statements, Brian Willoughby, the head translator, pondered out loud. "What the heck is that supposed to mean? Is this guy telling us he was with Moses at the burning bush on Mt. Horeb. Or is he possibly Moses himself?"

His curiosity aroused even more, Ainsworth-Jones eagerly looked over his translator's shoulder so that he, too, could see the words. "Well, if nothing else, Brian, this at least gives corroboration as a second source to the burning bush narrative."

Several hours later, Willoughby remarked, "This is crazy, Lindsay! There are statements here that could not have been a part of the vocabulary of someone who was writing 1,350 years before Jesus was born. Many of these metaphysical words and phrases sound too modernistic for that time period."

After about another hour of translation, Willoughby shouted out again, "This is unbelievable . . . The writer refers to the space-time continuum. How could he use that terminology so many years before Einstein gave us his theories? Who on earth wrote this thing? And when did he write it?"

Ainsworth-Jones asked, "Are you absolutely certain of that, Brian?" as he again perused the translation of the copied document and skimmed through some of the amazing terminology inscribed there. But this time, all he could say was, "Wow!"

Willoughby and his assistant, Cynthia Trowbridge, continued to read aloud some of the phrases they were translating. He said, "This sounds like some present-day, new-age guru is writing these things. Listen to this:

"*'God, as Life, is the Divine First Cause and must be Self-existent. Hence, Life must be eternal. Existence cannot be transformed into nonexistence, Consciousness cannot become unconsciousness, and Life cannot terminate in death.*

"*'There is only one Life, and It is eternal. There is only one Consciousness, and It is infinite. There is only one Ego or Soul, and It is the substance of all form. This Divine Life-force is manifesting Itself in an infinite variety of forms and is unfolding and appearing as the individual Life-Soul-Consciousness that I am and that you are.'*"

Five minutes later, Cynthia Trowbridge followed up. "How about these lines.

"*'God is not just* within *your soul, but actually is the substance* of *your soul. Therefore, your Soul is infinite. God does not just* give *you life, but actually is living* as *your Life, the essence of what you are. Thus, your Life is eternal; it never began and will never end.*

"*'You are not the misidentification known as mortal man or the man of earth but, rather, the form that God assumes in individual expression. Consciousness is the substance, and body is the form as which this Consciousness appears. Consciousness, soul and body are one and indivisible.'*

"Pretty remarkable stuff, isn't it?" Cynthia commented.

The team of translators continued working until Lindsay interrupted them shortly before midnight. "Well, my friends, I know how much each of us wants to keep on digging in to this scroll. But it's really getting late, so why don't you all get some sleep, and come back here around 9:00 tomorrow morning. Thanks for your quick response to all of this and your dedicated work this evening."

"No problem, Lindsay, it's our pleasure." Brian Willoughby said. "Who wouldn't want to find out just what this thing is? This might be one of the greatest discoveries in archaeological history!"

CHAPTER 21

PAUL, SILAS, AND TIMOTHY IN CORINTH, MACEDONIA

EARLY 52 CE

L eaving Athens by the Sacred Way—the road running from Athens to the coastal city of Eleusis—Paul then sailed westward across the Saronic Gulf to Corinth. On the voyage through the Gulf, he passed between the islands of Aegina and Salamis. For ships arriving by that route, a great lighthouse and the Poseidon temple guided the vessels into the Port of Cenchrea.

Once he was comfortably settled in Corinth, Paul sent two of his loyal followers to summon Silas and Timothy to join him. Receiving Paul's message and realizing that their work in Thessalonica and Berea was finished, the two young evangelists readily followed the wishes of their illustrious mentor.

Corinth was an ancient city that dated back to the Neolithic Age of approximately 5000 to 6000 BCE. During the Classical Greek Era, the city rivaled Athens and Thebes in wealth and trade. But Rome had destroyed the old Corinth in 146 BCE. Then in 44 BCE, Julius Caesar re-founded Corinth as a Roman colony. By the time Paul, Silas, and Timothy arrived there in 52 CE, Gallio was proconsul, and the city was again noted for its wealth, as it had become the seat of government for Southern Greece. The first thing the missionaries noticed upon their arrival in Corinth was the reminder of the city's past. There were many rock piles throughout the area, which were ruins of the old city's ancient walls. While Athens was the intellectual center of Greece, Corinth had become the commercial center. The city's prosperity was colorfully described by the historian Strabo who wrote, *"Corinth is called wealthy because of its commerce, since it is situated on the Isthmus and is master of two harbors, one of which leads straight to Asia, and the other to Italy."*

Similar to the responses in other places they had visited, Paul's missionary zeal also attracted good-sized crowds in Corinth. But just as had happened in Thessalonica and Berea, the strong Orthodox Jews rejected the apostle's teaching and often disrupted his meetings and sermons.

During the time that Silas was still preaching in Thessalonica and Berea, he had been spending many of his evenings in meditation and prayer. As he gained a greater realization that his true identity was consciousness, and not a physical body, his meditations occasionally produced out-of-body experiences. But now in Corinth, those experiences were happening with even more frequency. Furthermore, for the past year the young evangelist had been having memory lapses, during which he could not remember much about his human history. Silas often felt he was out of place there—that he belonged somewhere else. So it was no surprise that cool, dry evening in the month of Nissan (March) when the soul of the youngest apostle not only rose up and out of his body again, but also began soaring high into the night sky until he found himself floating amidst a huge display of lights, planets and stars, at what appeared to be the center of the Universe.

The next leg of this cosmic journey had Silas feeling a strong attraction to another time and place, and a lesser affinity to the world he had been living in for the past three years. And then, without any warning, he glimpsed the Grand Circle of Eternity. He didn't know what it was, but soon he was immersed in that Circle and saw the array of intriguing and inviting parentheses below him. He began to feel a strong attraction to one of those sets of brackets and started drifting toward it. But then seemingly out of nowhere, he heard a voice say, "No, Silas! It is too soon. You have not finished your work yet. You must come back to Corinth."

Hearing those words made it seem as though a spell had just been broken. And then, as quickly as the experience had started, there was an even stronger attraction. Something was pulling him back to the world he had known most recently. And because the allure was so intense, he did not fight it, but willingly allowed his soul to drift out of the Cosmos and down into the Grecian sky, as he slowly descended back into the body of Silas—friend and traveling companion of Paul, the Apostle to the Gentiles.

Later that week, Paul introduced Silas and Timothy to his two newest and closest friends, Aquila and his wife Priscilla. The couple had recently come to Corinth from Rome and had two traits in common with Paul. They were Jews who also had Roman citizenship, and they were tentmakers by trade. So to help provide sustenance for himself, the apostle moved into the home of Priscilla and Aquila, joining them in their tent-making projects.

On the following Monday, the three people invited Silas and Timothy to their home to share the evening meal. And it was then that Silas first saw her. Priscilla and Aquila had a nineteen-year-old daughter named Sabina. Instantly mesmerized by her beauty, Silas thought she was the most gorgeous creature he had ever seen. Her long, silky black hair, her large dark eyes, and her flawless skin with its soft golden-olive tone, made her a perfect replica of any Greek or Roman goddess. As soon as their eyes met, Silas knew he had found his soul mate, and her warm infectious smile indicated that she had the same feeling toward him.

Even Sabina's parents immediately recognized the magic between their only daughter and this young missionary who had the complete faith and trust of their dear friend. Soon, the two young people were spending most of their waking hours together, and Silas was quite happy to see that Sabina willingly accepted his unique interpretation of Christian mysticism. So it was just four months later that

Silas—the friend and traveling companion of the Apostle Paul—and Sabina, the beloved daughter of Aquila and Priscilla, were married. The ceremony was performed by none other than everyone's special teacher and confidant, the dedicated apostle from Tarsus.

Paul spent one year and six months in Corinth, because it was the perfect place for him to use as a base while he spread the Gospel throughout western Greece and Macedonia. The city was still young and dynamic, and shared many characteristics with his hometown of Tarsus. In addition to sustaining himself by working with Aquila and Priscilla, Paul had good success in converting the Gentile community to his version of Christianity.

For Silas, it was a period of quietude and introspection, as he settled in to his new life with Sabina. Yet something deep within his soul was telling him to continue spreading the mystical message that was coming through in his meditations. And like his mentor, Silas also was an educated and literate man. He was capable of writing letters, books, and other documents. But the only message he wanted to write about was his unyielding belief in the all-ness of God and man's inherent Oneness with the Deity.

After Paul had fulfilled his ministerial duties in Corinth, he believed he had been directed to leave there and sail to Ephesus, an ancient Greek city on the west coast of Anatolia—modern-day Turkey. When the apostle made his trip there, Ephesus was the second largest city in the Roman Empire and was famous for its Temple of Artemis, a pagan shrine to the goddess Diana and one of the Seven Wonders of the Ancient World. Artemis and Diana are two names for the same goddess, with Artemis being the Greek name, and Diana being the Roman version. The whole temple was constructed of marble, except for the roof, which was made of wood, but covered with tile.

Paul's impending trip to Ephesus created a difficult decision for Silas and his new young wife. Priscilla and Aquila had agreed to join the apostle on his journey. Hence, Silas and Sabina would have to either go along with them, or stay behind in Corinth to begin their own life together, without the support of her parents. The tent-making husband and wife released the young couple from any feelings of guilt by assuring them that it was all right to stay behind. Aquila and Priscilla promised they would return to Corinth after Paul's work in Ephesus was finished.

Comforted by those words, Silas and Sabina decided to build their married life in the city where they had met. But before they came to that decision, the enlightened evangelist had to assure his wife that the two of them could survive without the help of her parents. He told her, "Sabina, please remember how Jesus instructed his disciples to go into the world *'without purse and scrip.'* He showed them how everything they needed would be provided for them as an act of grace. Actually, he taught them how to demonstrate the incorporeal nature of true supply. And the best example he gave of that was when he himself fed the multitudes from what appeared to be only a few loaves and fishes."

Sabina just adored Silas and always loved listening to him, as he offered his spiritual words of wisdom with such fluent conviction. He continued. "True supply is an activity of our consciousness. We have an infinite abundance of supply within our souls. Everything we need will always be provided for us, if we just trust in the omnipotence of God functioning in and as our lives." Silas explained that he could employ his literary talents and evangelistic efforts to support them and, if needed, Sabina could use the tent-making skills she had learned from her parents to supplement their income. But most of all, they had to trust in the power of God that was ever-present within each of them.

Paul, meanwhile, spent only a short amount of time in Ephesus, because he felt compelled to return to Jerusalem for new discussions with the hierarchy of the church there. So after leaving Ephesus by boat, the apostle, along with Timothy and two of their newest converts, sailed over the Great Sea to Caesarea in the land of Judea. Because there were no actual passenger ships in Paul's time, the group had to travel on a cargo ship in the limited space available. That portion of the trip took about seven days. From Caesarea, they made the tedious overland excursion, but this time did not have to walk the entire distance. Paul and his companions were able to ride on donkeys loaned to them by a wealthy member of the coastal Christian community. And though he made numerous stops along the way spreading his Gospel message, this Apostle to the Gentiles would eventually come back to the place where the entire odyssey had begun: the Holy City of Jerusalem. When Paul and his converts arrived there, his long, second missionary journey throughout the Gentile Greek world had been satisfactorily concluded.

CHAPTER 22

TERROR IN THE HOMELAND

THE PRESENT - TIMELINES 1 & 2
TUESDAY, LATE AFTERNOON - AUGUST 18TH
CHICAGO, IL

Rashid Abdul-Nasser was born in Saudi Arabia on May 16, 1967. In the spring of 1980, his parents migrated to the United States and settled in Chicago, Illinois. After graduating from high school, Rashid became a loner who drifted around aimlessly, committing a few petty crimes, but never getting caught. So he had no criminal record. By 1991, he had learned about Osama bin Laden and his radical Islamist movement. Becoming fanatically intrigued with al-Qaeda, the impressionable introvert contacted the Imam of his local mosque on the south side of Chicago to learn more about the group. Fortunately—or unfortunately—for Abdul-Nasser, his Imam was one of the numerous ultra-radical clerics operating in America. Seeing the fire in the young man's eyes, the Islamic recruiter-of-terrorists arranged for Rashid to travel to Afghanistan. And it was there that he had an opportunity to see bin Laden up close and become totally immersed in the notorious militant's operation.

After spending three years in training at the al-Qaeda bases in Afghanistan, the newest American jihadist was sent back to the United States with a long-term, sinister plan and enough funding to support himself and to attend flight-training school.

Within a few years, Abdul-Nasser had achieved a level of proficiency that allowed him to qualify for commercial pilot ground school. Then, after logging his minimum of 250 flight hours, Rashid earned his commercial pilot certificate. Having a singular vision and no social impediments such as a wife or family, the young Muslim soon received an up-to-date medical certificate, his instrument rating, and a multi-engine rating. Rashid Abdul-Nasser was on a mission. He spent whatever amount of time was required and worked as hard as he could to master his chosen profession. And soon he qualified for an airline transport pilot certificate.

During that same period, Abdul-Nasser enrolled in several night courses at a local community college, so he would also have some college credits on his resume.

With all those credentials in hand, the young man took advantage of every opportunity to log flight hours. By late 1996, he had the requisite qualifications to secure a pilot's job on a small regional carrier in the Midwest. It was a time when airlines were relatively unregulated and air travel was still booming. Major carriers were doing mergers and acquisitions. Furthermore, there were no real suspicions about ethnicity, and Abdul-Nasser did everything he could to fit in as a regular American. Being of average height and weight, he was clean-shaven, except for a small mustache. He was well-dressed and well-spoken. Having come to the United States as a young teenager, he spoke English with virtually no accent. He also gave the impression of being a "nice guy," even though he seldom socialized with anyone.

Because of all that determination and planning, as well as his obvious competence, Rashid Abdul-Nasser was hired by United Airlines as a pilot-in-training in March of 2000. After completing many rigorous weeks of that program, the young Muslim passed his line check and then was released to operate scheduled flights for the airline as a crew member.

Rashid had become just one of the group to his co-workers, so even after September 11, 2001, no one looked askance at him. Yet behind the façade, there was a singular militant commitment to the radical jihadist cause promoted by Osama bin Laden. It was amazing how a person could have so much patience and dedication and could keep all that hatred and passion bottled up for a decade and a half. During those years, he accepted any job assigned to him without complaint. He flew the worst routes on the most inconvenient schedules. But it didn't matter, because he had no life outside of this project. Throughout, Abdul-Nasser was quietly establishing his seniority with the airline and slowly moving up the ranks until he had achieved the position of captain.

All of his flights went very smoothly, without any incidents. He never uttered an incendiary word. And that is why no one could have forecast what he had been planning for that very warm Tuesday afternoon in August.

United Airlines Flight 908, an Airbus A320 with 112 people aboard, departed from Denver right on time at 12:42 p.m. and was scheduled to arrive at Chicago's O'Hare International Airport at 4:15. The sky was clear, there was no wind, and all systems were *"go"* as the flight began its initial descent.

What the air traffic controllers and the security people didn't know was that Rashid Abdul-Nasser had a small four-ounce tube of breath spray in his pocket that didn't contain any breath spray. Instead, the container was filled with liquid cyanide. About eight minutes before touchdown, Rashid asked his co-pilot, Jim Bachman, to look at an object he was holding in his hand. As the older man leaned toward him, Abdul-Nasser quickly pointed the tube directly at Bachman's face and pressed the spray valve. Holding his breath to avoid inhaling any of the toxic mist, Rashid turned his head abruptly to his left and put on an oxygen mask. As expected, the cyanide had its desired result as the co-pilot writhed in instantaneous convulsions. Within seconds, he was in a coma and, shortly thereafter, suffered cardiac arrest. Death followed in just a few minutes.

The airliner was in the last stages of its descent when Abdul-Nasser lied to the controllers, telling them his landing gear was locked and wouldn't open. He said he would have to take the plane back up and circle again for another attempt at unlocking the gear. Then before the controllers could respond, he was heading east-southeast. Once they saw that action, an instantaneous sense of panic gripped the workers in the control tower. But there was nothing they could do; everything was moving too fast. As soon as he approached the shore of Lake Michigan, the pilot made an abrupt right turn toward downtown Chicago.

Willis Tower—formerly the Sears Tower—was the tallest building in the Western hemisphere. The skyscraper was one of the most recognizable landmarks in the Chicago skyline and rose to a height of 1,450 feet. Completed in May of 1973, Willis Tower was the world's tallest building for 25 years until the Petronas Towers in Kuala Lampur, Malaysia, were built in 1998.

The tourists visiting the Sky deck that afternoon were the first to see the airliner coming at them from the north. *Surely this can't be what it looks like . . . ? He's getting too close!* A few employees working in the offices and shops that occupied the more than 3.8 million square feet of office and retail space may also have seen it coming. But before anyone could react, the unthinkable happened. Just as had taken place on 9/11 all those years ago, an American commercial airliner flew directly into one of the nation's great landmarks. But this time the plane hadn't been hi-jacked. The pilot had been on a long-term deadly mission of suicidal madness.

The sound of the explosion could be heard for miles. Massive amounts of shattered glass, concrete, and steel flew in all directions. The aircraft impacted the skyscraper at the 79th floor. There was virtually no chance for anyone working in the building above that level to get out. And even people on the lower floors faced the danger of being hit by the smoldering falling debris.

Within minutes, first responders were on the scene. Members of the Chicago Fire Department arrived there just as quickly as their peers in New York had done on that horrible day in September of 2001. And once again, there were remarkable acts of heroism.

As soon as news of the tragic incident reached President Thompson, he was on the phone with CIA Director Cunningham and the Director of Homeland Security.

"How much do we know about this?" the President asked.

"Very little at this time, sir," Domenic Fiorenza answered. "But more information is coming in every second. We have checked the entire passenger manifest and haven't found any suspicious characters. There is not even one Middle-Eastern name on the list. However, there is a somewhat troubling circumstance. The pilot's name was Rashid Abdul-Nasser, and he was born in Saudi Arabia. All that we have on him so far is that he seemed to be a nice quiet man who kept to himself and never caused any problems."

Cunningham then asked, "How could a guy who was born in Saudi Arabia and had a name like that ever become a pilot? Was there a background check?"

Fiorenza answered, "He was hired by United in March of 2000, a year and a half before the attacks on the World Trade Center and the Pentagon. He apparently had done all the right things to qualify for the job and, since then, has never made a radical utterance that would draw any suspicions.

"Still, our people are digging deeper into his background and are checking out his residence as we speak. Maybe we'll find something there and, then again, maybe we won't. But if he isn't the cause of this, we are at a dead end for now."

The President then said, "I will have my press secretary and speech writers get something together as quickly as they can. I need to address the American people to assure them that this was an isolated incident and there is nothing more coming."

Meanwhile, news channels all over the world were broadcasting the story and, most likely, would be for the next several days. Pictures on the TV screens of America had graphic comparisons of the Twin Towers going down in New York on that world-changing day in 2001, and this new attack in Chicago.

After a shaken President Thompson hung up the phone, White House Chief of Staff Donald Bergstrom asked, "Mr. President, what would you think of going to Chicago in a day or two to give some comfort to the victims' families and the people of the area? You remember how George W. Bush stood in front of that pile of rubble in New York and spoke through the bullhorn. That was one of his crowning moments."

"Don, this is no time to play politics or to grandstand. I'm certain the people of Chicago and of America know how I feel at this moment . . . No, I take that back . . . They couldn't possibly know how helpless and impotent I feel.

And I certainly don't want to show any public signs of weakness. So let's give it a few days to see what we can learn about this incident and, more important, to be sure that we stop anything else that may be planned."

At 8:00 p.m. Eastern Daylight Time, the Administration had all news and traditional broadcast networks preempt their regular programming, as President Thompson addressed the nation and the world. Standing at a podium in front of a medium-blue background at the NORAD Command Center, the President looked directly into the camera with a distraught expression on his face, and said:

"Good evening, my fellow Americans . . . I am addressing you tonight with a heavy heart . . . I especially want to extend my deepest sympathy to the courageous people of Chicago and to all of you who had friends and loved ones aboard United Airlines flight 908 that crashed into the Willis tower a few hours ago. Though our country's intelligence agencies and our Department of Homeland Security have done a remarkable job of preventing any similar attacks since September 11th of 2001, this one did get through our defenses. And since we recently raised the Terrorism Advisory System's threat level to *Imminent*, we don't believe this was a breakdown in our procedures. First reports indicate that this was just an isolated act, most likely perpetrated by one deranged individual.

"Since this tragic incident just happened a few hours ago, we don't have a great deal of information yet. But I promise all of you that your government is working diligently on getting some answers. I know that most of you are aware of the nuclear devices that have been intercepted in Israel, Berlin and off the east coast of America.

"Worldwide intelligence organizations believe that with those attempts, and now this attack on another U.S. city, we have seen the last of it. It doesn't seem possible that these radical terrorist groups have the wherewithal or resources to have assembled much more of an arsenal than we have already seen. Nevertheless, agents across the Globe are pulling out all stops on intelligence and counterintelligence. I have been in contact with the heads of state of all of our allies. This is a well-coordinated and concerted effort by all civilized nations in the world today. We will get to the bottom of this and will do everything in our power to prevent any further incidents—"

The President made a few more cursory comments, and then closed his short address with the customary: " . . . And may God bless America."

By that time, the American people *had* been reacting to what had taken place during the previous several days. Wall Street was shut down, and no one could predict when the markets would reopen. And even if they did, huge losses would be showing in everyone's retirement accounts. Banks were closing early, as there were panicky customers standing in line demanding to withdraw their savings, because most ATM machines had been overloaded and now were shut down. The airline traffic system was a complete disaster. Most flights were delayed, and many were cancelled. Baggage was being lost, and some flight attendants were refusing to fly. The dirty bomb attack in Hamburg, the exploded airliner over Los Angeles, along with the nuclear devices seized in the Gaza Strip, Berlin and the Atlantic Ocean had already taken their toll on the psyche of the citizens of the world. But even more disturbing than the economic ramifications, people across the Globe were becoming extremely fearful for their safety. As a result, much of the nation's economy was grinding to a halt—and all of that was occurring before this attack on the Willis Tower.

CHAPTER 23

THE CHURCH IN JERUSALEM

CORINTH AND JERUSALEM
SPRING OF 53 CE

After arriving in Jerusalem, Paul was initially received quite warmly by the church hierarchy there. No longer were the leaders arguing about circumcision, or whether Gentiles should be allowed to join the Christian community. By that time, they had heard of Paul's dedicated missionary work in his first two journeys around the Greek world. They had received reports from followers who had come back from areas he had visited. And though the Church leaders were impressed with the results he had achieved, they also had become aware of the changes taking place in the apostle's teaching, as he was bringing strange and unfamiliar elements into his message. *What was his basis for doing that?* they wondered. *Where was he hearing such things?*

Many members of the group had always resented Paul, because he was not a direct disciple of Jesus and, more importantly, was an early persecutor of Christians. He had not been there when the Master preached his beautiful sermons. He had not heard Jesus present the Beatitudes while standing on that highly elevated hill near Capernaum on the Sea of Galilee. This outsider hadn't heard the Lord's Prayer or the parables when they were spoken. And even though some of the original followers often argued about what each of them thought he had heard Jesus say, it seemed that Paul was taking some extreme new liberties with the message.

After a rather confrontational meeting with Peter, James, John and some of the other church elders, Paul decided to send for Silas, to get some help in reinforcing and justifying his position. Unfortunately, it would take quite a long time to get a message to his friend in Corinth, and then for Silas to make the trip to Jerusalem. So during that period, the contentious evangelist was on his own in debating the church leaders.

Upon receiving Paul's request, Silas discussed the idea with Sabina. She was very understanding of the situation and agreed to accompany him on the journey. By that time, she had become extremely receptive to the mystical message her husband had been advocating and was thrilled with the thought of visiting Jerusalem, the birthplace of the entire Christian movement.

By the end of the month of Tammuz (June), Silas and Sabina arrived in the Holy City, allowing him to participate in the latest rounds of intense conversations with the early leaders of the Christian Church. Similar to Paul's return from his second missionary journey, the young couple also crossed the Mediterranean Sea in the uncomfortable quarters of a cargo ship, and then rode on donkeys for the land portion of their trip from Caesarea to Jerusalem. But while Paul made a few stops along the way to preach his Gospel message, Silas and Sabina headed directly to their destination and made the trip in a little more than half the time it took the proselytizing apostle to get there.

In the first general meeting that Silas attended, Peter opened the discussion by saying, "Jesus told me he was the Christ, the only begotten son of God."

Paul replied, "Did Jesus say that, or did you say that, Peter? I was told that the Master asked the question: 'And who do you say that I am?' and it was you who responded, 'You are the Christ, the son of the living God.' Is that not true?"

"Well, yes," the Big Fisherman answered, "but Jesus did not deny that when I said it."

"And he should not have denied it," Paul replied. "He was the Christ . . . but so are you!" Nodding his head and pointing a finger at each of them, the animated apostle continued, "And you, too, James . . . and you, John . . . and all the rest of you. And believe it or not, so am I. I know that though I am living now, it is not I, but Christ who lives in me and through me. Every one of us has the Christ living within our soul."

Silas was thrilled to hear Paul speaking in such mystical terms, so he then entered the conversation to support his friend. "I was not there, Peter, but I know what I have learned through inner communion with God . . . Remember, 'Christ'—or *Christos* in the Greek—means "the anointed one." Jesus, living as the Christ, had a divine nature. But as Paul just stated, each one of us has that same divine nature, because the Spirit of God lives in each of us. God did not create us separate from Himself. Instead, the infinite Divine Consciousness is manifesting Itself and is appearing individually as your identity and mine. For that reason, we can say with Jesus, *'I and my Father are One.' "*

"That is blasphemy!" shouted one of the older attendees. "You are claiming that you are equal to Jesus Christ . . . Blasphemy, I say!"

"I am sorry, Ehud," Silas replied empathetically, "but I don't agree with you. Every one of us has been created in the image and likeness of God; therefore, we too are divine beings. And when God incarnates Himself and appears in visible manifestation, He is appearing as the Christ *in, as,* and *through* our individual lives."

And though these arguments could never be won, the Council continued to debate for several more months. During that time, Peter began reacting a bit more positively to some of the suggestions being offered by Paul and Silas. As a matter of fact, the old fisherman took a strong liking to Silas, just as Paul had earlier. And Peter even began meeting the young intellectual in the evenings after the group had adjourned for the day. As a sign of his affection, Peter often called Silas by his Romanized name, Silvanus. Soon, they were spending much of their free time together. Eventually, this relationship would grow to a level where the revered apostle requested that Silas help him write his forthcoming epistles.

After just a few more months in Jerusalem, Paul—the itinerant holy man who always moved as he believed the Spirit was leading him—decided to embark on his third missionary journey throughout the now partially Christian Greek world. For the second time in six years, Timothy accompanied him, but Silas stayed behind in Jerusalem with his beloved Sabina. During that interval in the Holy City, Silas continued having discussions with Peter and the other elders of the church, and spent a restful three years in the area. Having that time together in Jerusalem gave Silas and Sabina a wonderful opportunity to see their love for each other grow even more intense. By then, their relationship was no longer just a strong physical attraction. Not only did the places they visited and the stories they heard about Jesus have a profound impact on them, but the mystical experiences they shared in that magical environment created an eternal bond of love and oneness between them. At the end of that period, the young couple went back to Corinth to resume their life together there, and to once again be with Sabina's parents.

About eighteen months later, Paul returned to Jerusalem. After being in the City of David for just a short time, he caused a disturbance at the temple, which led to his arrest. Despite knowing how controversial he was at that time, the apostle openly visited the Temple with four of his followers. When Jews from Asia caught sight of him, they spoke out against the five men and stirred up the whole city. A mob developed, and the people in that assembly seized Paul and dragged him outside the Temple. When word of the disruption reached the colonel of the regiment, he came to the scene with soldiers and centurions to break up the riot. Once Paul announced that he was a protected citizen of Rome, he convinced the Sanhedrin and the High Priest to have him moved to Caesarea, where he was imprisoned for two years, until a new governor reopened his case. When he was accused of treason, Paul appealed to Caesar for a trial in Rome, which was his right as a Roman citizen.

The benefits of Roman citizenship included the right to vote, the right to sue in courts, freedom from unjust arrest or imprisonment, along with several other protections and privileges. A person with this status could not be bound or imprisoned without a trial, could not be tortured or whipped, and could not receive the death penalty unless he was found guilty of treason. Yet Paul and Silas had undergone scourging in Philippi, which the magistrates later realized was against the law. For that reason, they were preparing to release the two men even before the earthquake had destroyed the facility. An additional benefit of citizenship was that a person could appeal to Rome if he felt he was not receiving justice from his local government authorities.

Understanding those facts, Paul, more than anyone, was quite proficient at using the protections of his Roman citizenship whenever it suited his needs. Speaking about the apostle in his anthology of world history, Will Durant, the famed historian, wrote: *"Never before or since has citizen-ship been so jealously guarded or so highly prized."*

While in Caesarea, Paul had an opportunity to plead his case in a final hearing before King Herod Agrippa—who was visiting the city—and Porcius Festus, the procurator of Judea. Because the apostle had already appealed to the Emperor, the two men heard his case and then sent him by boat to Rome where he would spend the last years of his life under house arrest.

Shortly after Paul's incarceration, Peter decided that he also would go to Rome, but he was going voluntarily and willingly, not as a prisoner. Peter believed the Gospel message could be spread there, especially among the sizable Jewish population. On his way to Rome, the apostle visited Silas and Sabina in Corinth. It was there that Silas helped Peter formulate the themes for the epistles he was planning to write. Then, after spending about one week with the young couple, Peter continued his journey.

While Paul's voyage to Rome was quite adventure-some—with him even getting shipwrecked along the way—Peter had a much more leisurely trip there. Nonetheless, in the end, and despite their many previous differences, the two most important figures in early Christianity were unexpect-edly bound together again, as both of them would spend their last years at the very heart and center of the pagan Roman Empire.

CHAPTER 24

THE CHURCH MOVES
TO ROME

THE ANCIENT CITY OF ROME
62 CE

After Peter left Silas and Sabina in Corinth, the happy couple settled in to a quiet life in the wealthy, cosmopolitan city where they had met. Silas regularly preached his mystical message to anyone who would listen, while continuing to receive new spiritual insights in his meditations.

All of this was taking place during the reign of the tyrannical Roman Emperor Nero, who had been hand picked by his great-uncle Claudius to become heir to the throne. Upon Claudius' death in 54 CE, Nero, at the young age of sixteen, became emperor of the greatest nation on earth. His early reign was strongly influenced by his mother Agrippina. Many historians believe Agrippina poisoned Claudius, and some even suspect that her son may have had a role in the atrocity.

About two years after Peter left Corinth, Silas and Sabina heard some extremely distressing news: Peter had also been arrested, so now both he and Paul were incarcerated in Rome. And a few months later, the couple received an impassioned personal letter from Peter asking if Silas would come there to help the old fisherman complete his epistles.

Even though the two young people were quite content with their life together in Corinth, they also felt a strong commitment to helping their good friends who were in need. But since the journey would be long and potentially dangerous, Silas believed he should go to Rome by himself. And the fact that they hadn't had any children yet made the decision for him to go much easier. But Sabina did not want to be separated from him. Speaking softly to her husband, she said, "You are my life, Silas. If something were to happen to you, I would not want to go on living. I want to go with you on this trip."

But Silas realized just how perilous a place Rome had become for practicing Christians, and he did not want to expose his wife to the hazards and vulnerability of being there. He promised that he would be cautious in all of his dealings, and would come back to her. "Sabina, any separation now is just temporary. You and I have a divine destiny to share eternity together. I will never leave you alone . . . I promise to return from this trip, and we will again have a wonderful life, as we then begin building our own family . . . I love you, my darling," he said, as he held her tightly in his muscular arms.

Sabina's parents also pleaded with her to remain with them in Corinth, but it took several days of those discussions before she reluctantly agreed to stay behind. So following a tearful farewell early on a cool, damp morning in the month of Cheshvan (October), the enlightened missionary sadly left his devoted and loving wife, as he embarked upon what was to become his most important journey of that lifetime.

Just as it had been for Peter, Silas had a rather smooth sail to Rome, encountering no physical obstacles or weather problems. Indeed, while he was at sea, the youngest apostle found the gentle roll and sway of the ship so soothing that he had many beautiful meditations. These included several out-of-body experiences in which he felt a compelling attraction to another place and time.

Upon arriving in the Roman capital, he was invited to stay with some good friends he had met during his years in Jerusalem. Many members of the Holy City's Christian congregation had migrated to Rome to be with Peter and Paul while the revered Church leaders were under house arrest.

On his third day in Rome, Silas made arrangements to visit Peter in the living quarters where he was being held. At their first meeting, the intellectual missionary was shocked at how much weight Peter had lost since they had been together in Corinth. Though his quarters were quite pleasant for a confinement facility, something obviously had taken its toll on the aging apostle. His face was gaunt, and he was noticeably weak, as he was walking in a stooped-over fashion, using a heavy wooden cane for support. So Silas tried to give the old fisherman as much help and comfort as he could.

The two men discussed the message Peter wanted to share with the Christian Churches in Asia Minor. Silas was rather surprised that the beloved apostle acted as if he had never heard the younger evangelist's ideas before, even though, while in Corinth, they had discussed including some of them in the upcoming letters. Silas once again tried to convince his old friend to incorporate a more mystical theme. But the resolute Church founder could not be swayed. He had never fully grasped the esoteric Truth in the scholarly man's teachings; he still clung to his belief in the need for salvation from a judging and condemning God. So when the work began, Silas literally became nothing more than a scribe, as he took dictation for Peter's famous First Epistle. However, he was able to enhance the quality of the work.

Being a somewhat uneducated fisherman and laborer, Peter would have been unable to convey any message as fluently as the literate Silas. Therefore after it was circulated, the epistle became noted for the high quality of its Greek language. And even though he had very little influence on the content, the loyal scribe did all he could to provide the first disciple of Jesus with a manuscript of which he could be proud. In addition to the eloquent Greek language, the style was deliberate, and the tone was tranquil and calm. When it became public, the document was well received by all who read it.

Later, a Second Epistle was also attributed to Peter. But Bible scholars do not accept Peter as the author, since research has indicated that the Second Epistle was written long after his death.

During his first weeks in Rome, Silas also found time to visit his dear friend Paul. Surprisingly, the previously zealous, but now rather frail Apostle to the Gentiles displayed a resigned acceptance of his fate. But he, too, still had some letters to send to his friends. Paul's Epistles to Timothy and Titus were written during this period of incarceration.

As he had done with Peter, Silas tried to influence Paul's writings. But again it was all to no avail. Even though Paul had previously shown some interest in Silas' ideas and had included a few of them in his earlier letters and speeches—especially his sermon to the Athenians on Mars Hill—he just could not fully accept the total depth of the mystical message. The concept of a man-like god who rewards and punishes, who judges and condemns, was too ingrained in the two aging apostles.

This really discouraged Silas, because he had heard Paul plead their case in Jerusalem. And in his Epistles to the Ephesians, Corinthians, and Romans, Paul had made some remarkably illumined statements such as:

"There is one body, and one Spirit . . . One God and Father of all, who is above all, and through all, and in you all."

"Do you not know that your body is the temple of the Holy Spirit which is in you? Do you not know that you are the temple of God, and that the Spirit of God dwells in you?"

"The wisdom of this world is foolishness with God. For we look not at the things which are seen, but at the things that are not seen; for the things which are seen are temporal, but the things which are not seen are eternal."

"When I was a child, I spoke as a child, I understood as a child, I thought as a child. But when I became a man, I put away childish things. For now we see through a glass, darkly, but soon face-to-face. Now I know in part, but soon I shall know even as also I am known by God."

"For I am convinced that neither death, nor life, nor angels, nor principalities, nor powers, nor things present, nor things to come, nor height, nor depth, nor any other creature, shall be able to separate us from the love of God."

Silas wondered how Paul's thinking could have changed so much. And although he was frustrated, he gave all the comfort he could to his two good friends; but now, he also decided to take some steps of his own. It was during this very trying period that Silas' evening meditations regularly achieved moments of elevation into the five-dimensional consciousness. As his out-of-body experiences became more frequent, he started having additional memory lapses, during which he had less recollection of his past and often felt out of place in his life in that incarnation. A different far-away life-experience seemed to be beckoning.

At the same time, the young mystic strongly believed that, somehow, he had to get his own message into a more permanent and lasting form—to have it transcribed as a written manuscript. The Truth must be given to mankind. So even though his own consciousness was illumined enough to produce a historical message, he hoped to find someone who could help him in getting the supplies and materials needed to create a lasting document and, ultimately, determine a way to distribute it. To accomplish that task, he spent many of his days searching and inquiring around the ancient city.

In just a short while, the young intellectual became involved with an esoteric discussion group that spent much of its time studying and analyzing the writings of the renowned Greek philosophers. The primary reason they studied the Greeks is because Rome had no original philosophy of its own. Most everything it possessed was taken from Greece, including its art, science and Pantheon of gods. Through his involvement with this learned group, Silas was eventually led to the Roman libraries, where substantial numbers of books—actually scrolls—could be read. And it was at one of the libraries that he met Laurentius Gallus, an exceptionally bright young scholar who had spent most of his early years studying those same world-renowned and erudite philosophers of ancient Greece.

After just a few days together, Silas realized that he had found his perfect disciple, a kindred spirit who immediately understood and accepted his mystical message, and had the same passion for wanting to distribute it to other like-minded souls.

CHAPTER 25

SOME CLARIFICATION AND A PLAN FOR RETALIATION

THE PRESENT – 1930 HOURS MDT, TUESDAY EVENING, AUGUST 18TH -
AFTER THE PRESIDENT'S SPEECH TO THE NATION
NORAD COMMAND CENTER - PETERSON AIR FORCE BASE
CHEYENNE MOUNTAIN IN COLORADO - TIMELINES 1 & 2

The first intelligence reports were just coming in on the United Airlines flight that had crashed into the Willis Tower in downtown Chicago. There was no indication of any hijacking, so it had to have been an act of the pilot, or possibly the pilots working in tandem. Speaking from Langley in a slow serious tone, CIA Director Scott Cunningham opened the meeting by saying, "The co-pilot, Jim Bachman, was a fourteen-year veteran of service with the airline. He was married with two teenage daughters and was a church-going, evangelical Christian. On the other hand, the pilot, Rashid Abdul-Nasser, was born in Saudi Arabia and was a devout Muslim. When the FBI agents went to his house, they found all the signs of a rabidly dedicated jihadist.

The place looked like a shrine to Osama bin Laden and to terrorism. The walls were covered with graphic photographs and newspaper headlines. There were pictures of bin Laden, Ayman al-Zawahiri, and Hasan Mohammed Farouk; there were at least a dozen photos of the World Trade Center towers after the airplanes had hit them. There were several pictures of the Pentagon after the 9/11 attack. And most importantly, there was a suicide note that spelled out the whole plan.

"There is no doubt about it. Rashid Abdul-Nasser is our man. We now know that he had gone to Afghanistan in 1991 to train with al-Qaeda. After three years of preparation and indoctrination there, he was sent back to the United States as a ticking time bomb that would be set off at the proper moment. He was a virtual 21st Century 'Manchurian Candidate.' Because of that, we currently have all the airlines checking their employee rosters to determine if there might be any more like him out there."

President Thompson then asked, "Scott, why would they have waited so long if he has been on the job for all those years?"

"It's crazy, sir, but these people have a lot of patience. They are willing to dedicate many years of their lives to a specific project, especially if it will have a major impact on America. And remember, in the end, the perpetrator is going to die. So by waiting, he just gets to live a little longer."

Cunningham took a deep breath and then, with an even more serious tone in his voice, said, "But here is what may be the most troubling part of the whole episode. The pilot's suicide note also claims this is just the start of what is coming. According to Abdul-Nasser, they are going to bring down many more of our 'pagan monuments' and destroy the heathen world's economies."

"Jesus Christ," General Fabretti shouted out. "Where do you start in retaliation? Do we have to hit the whole damn Muslim world? For what it's worth, you all know that's my first choice."

After looking at the stunned faces in the room, Joint Chiefs Chairman Daniels commented, "Sooner or later we will have to respond. We can't just take this sitting on our hands. And while we don't want to start a nuclear war, if anything of a nuclear or biological nature happens in the U.S., we will retaliate in kind. Initially, we will blast the hell out of the whole mountain range separating Pakistan and Afghanistan. Then if we decide to really make a statement, Tehran will most likely be the first major city we will hit."

"Now you're talkin' my language," Fabretti replied.

President Thompson then said, "Everyone please realize that our first job is still to prevent any other attacks. We have to find a way to stop anything more from happening. And that is why I am once again asking each one of you to pull out all stops on intelligence."

After a brief pause, the President concluded the meeting. "Well, it's getting quite late tonight, so let's adjourn for now and be ready to convene tomorrow morning at 8:00 a.m. Mountain Time. Everyone try to get a good night's rest. I'd like all of you to be refreshed when we get back together."

CHAPTER 26

THE APOSTLES'
FINAL DAYS IN ROME

THE ANCIENT CITY OF ROME
64 CE

By 64 CE, the now-insane Emperor Nero was looking for a scapegoat to take the blame for his many tyrannical actions, especially for the huge fire that had destroyed much of the ancient city. The easiest target for his egregious act was the Christian community.

So by a decree of the Emperor, Christians were rounded up and imprisoned. In some cases, they were even fed to the lions in the Colosseum games. And at that same time, Peter, as a leader of the sect, was charged with treason against Imperial Rome and of preaching about a false god.

Following that pronouncement, it was only a few weeks later that the former Galilean fisherman was taken from his quarters to be crucified. As a final gesture of his loyalty, and as a penance for having denied his Master before *his* crucifixion, the man who was one of the first disciples of Jesus requested to be crucified upside down, with his head facing the ground.

While many of the Christian followers were afraid to be seen in public by that time, Silas could not stay away. He stood openly, right before the inverted cross of his good friend. And then, standing teary-eyed and alone in that very desolate place, the young missionary heard Peter's final words: "Dear God, my heavenly Father, I trust in you. Please take me home now so I may once again sit at the feet of my beloved Lord and Master, Jesus the Christ."

At that poignant moment, the man whom tradition claims was the first bishop of the Roman Catholic Church took his last breath in that lifetime. The next day, Silas, along with some of the other church leaders, buried the body of the most famous disciple in a place that is now the site of St. Peter's Basilica.

With Peter gone, Silas tried to give more attention to his other dear friend, Paul. The young man still hoped to influence his mentor in the writing of his letters to Timothy and Titus. But again, all of those efforts and that beseeching fell on deaf ears. While in the early years of their relation-ship, Paul seemed to be drifting toward Silas' mystical interpretation of Scripture and the nature of God, at that late date in his life, the elderly, but still-dedicated apostle had reverted back to the original message he had preached in his many years of missionary work.

So even though Silas gave Paul some personal assistance at that very trying time, he also began crafting his own document with the aid of Laurentius Gallus, his new, brilliant friend from the Roman library. The young scholar rapidly accepted Silas' mystical teaching as though the words were his own.

Together, the two men spent many hours in meditation, and Silas continued to have remarkable mystical experiences during those sessions. He was able to enter the Grand Circle of Eternity regularly, and to rest in the bliss he would experience there. And while he was in that supernal state of being, the lure and attraction to another place continued to grow. Yet he knew something was wrong . . . it still was too early to leave . . . his work here was not finished.

And then there was the deteriorating situation with his friend Paul. By 66 CE, Nero had increased his persecution of the Christians living in Rome. So it was an easy option for the crazed Emperor to make another powerful statement by executing their last major leader. A few days after Nero's decision, the most traveled Christian of all, the revered Apostle to the Gentiles, was taken to a place in Rome called Tre Fontane and was beheaded.

Because of the tight security, Silas was unable to be with Paul at the end. But he did join a few other followers as they removed the apostle's body from that spot and buried it at a location outside the walls of Rome where the Basilica of St. Paul now stands above his grave.

After Paul's execution, Silas continued to work on his own writings. The manuscript, which he and Laurentius Gallus were inscribing on a parchment scroll, was nearing completion. Although it is hardly possible to turn off the infinite flow of the Spirit of God, at some point, the project would have to be ended so the young man could return to his wife Sabina and her family in Corinth.

But similar to what had happened in another incarnation of this illumined soul 1,400 years earlier, the attraction to a future time and place was so strong, that the intended trip to Corinth would never take place.

Knowing that wherever he was going he would be leaving Rome, Silas entrusted his manuscript to his devoted friend and disciple, Laurentius Gallus. The young Roman scholar promised to preserve the scroll and ensure that it would be stored in a safe place where it could be made available to other receptive souls then and in the future.

So that evening, when his meditation once again took him up and out of his Silas body and into the Grand Circle of Eternity, the most enlightened apostle of the early Christian era finally allowed his soul to give in to the strong pull it was feeling to another place and time—a very brightly lit parenthesis near the far side of the infinite Circle.

CHAPTER 27

BACK TO THE FUTURE
ONCE MORE

THE PRESENT - MONDAY AFTERNOON, AUGUST 17TH - 3:30 P.M.
SHIMAHN'S ASHRAM - NAKCHU PREFECTURE -
NORTHERN TIBET AUTONOMOUS REGION
TIMELINE NO. 3

On my second journey home from the past, I again soared through the Grand Circle of Eternity, the Silas body dropped away, and I became a free soul floating in the infinite Circle. I saw the beckoning parenthesis in the distance and, soon, it became very clear that this was the place where I belonged. So I allowed myself to drift down toward that inviting location and to coalesce with that life-stream. In what seemed like just an instant, I was back there, sitting in my chair in Shimahn's library.

This time, I stayed in that spot for a while to get my bearings. After a few minutes of resting there, I rose from the chair, opened the door, and saw the warm, smiling face of my lovely wife, Kathy. My heart soared with love for her.

Shimahn was sitting across the room and he, too, seemed pleased to see me.

"Was this journey fruitful, Eric?" he asked.

"I certainly hope so, Shimahn." I responded, as I once again walked up to Kathy and held her in a warm embrace. "But I really can't be certain at this time."

Stepping back from my unexpected bear hug, my wife looked at me strangely and said, "I assume the two of you are telling me that Eric has been on another trip back in time?"

"Yes, Kathy," I replied.

"Where were you this time, with George Washington?"

"No, Kathy, this time I went back to a period much earlier than that. I was with the first Christian brotherhood in Jerusalem, fifteen years after Jesus was crucified. I then accompanied the Apostle Paul on his second missionary journey, and I was with Peter and Paul when they were executed in Rome."

"And I'm Mrs. Santa Claus," she said, with sarcasm in her voice. "Don't you think these wild stories are beginning to sound a little unbelievable?"

"You know, Kathy, sometimes I think I liked you a lot better in your earlier incarnations. You didn't give me any trouble in those, but you certainly have an abrasive edge in this lifetime."

"Young people," Shimahn interrupted, "this is no time to get argumentative. I am certain Eric has much to tell us about this historic journey."

"You can say that again, Shimahn. But as with the last trip, I don't know if I accomplished your goals. I'm not sure that I altered anything meaningful enough to affect the future."

The Master then asked, "Based upon what you know of those circumstances from a historical perspective, do you feel anything changed significantly . . . did something happen at a different time, or with a different outcome?"

"Not really," I replied. "Everything seemed the same as I have always understood it to be. Honestly, Shimahn, I did as much as I could to get Peter and Paul to accept our mystical approach to life, but they just wouldn't change their limited thinking.

"They both showed some degree of receptivity for a while, but then in the end, they reverted back to their funda-mentalist approach. They just couldn't grasp the infinite, incorporeal nature of God. Nonetheless, this trip in time was an amazing adventure."

Shimahn then asked, "Were the discussions between Paul and the church elders as contentious as tradition tells us they were?"

"Absolutely," I replied, "but they grew even more contentious when I became involved in the conversations."

"What was your role?" the Master asked. "Who were you?"

"Believe it or not, I was Silas, Paul's traveling compan-ion on his second missionary journey. Peter called me Silvanus, which I believe is a more Romanized version of the name."

Kathy began exhibiting less sarcasm and greater curios-ity as she heard more of my story. She then said, "Eric, if you were Silas, doesn't that mean you were beaten and imprisoned in Philippi?"

"Yes, it does. That was one of my worst experiences in
that lifetime. But the most abominable experience of all was
standing next to Peter as he was hanging upside down on that
cross in Rome. I was the only member of the group who was
there to hear his last words and see him take his last breath.
Crucifixion is a horrible way to die."

"It certainly must be," Kathy replied. "But wasn't Paul
beheaded? Isn't that just as bad, or even worse?"

"It really is a gruesome procedure, but I wasn't there to
witness that act. Paul's beheading was done in a closed-off
area. And as terrible as that method of execution might be, at
least it is quick, and doesn't drag on the way a crucifixion
does."

Shimahn then offered me a cool glass of lemonade—
which I accepted—as he asked, "Eric, if you were in prison
with Paul, how did the two of you get free?"

Sipping from my glass, I said, "It was very much the
way the Bible explains it. We were in shackles and stocks in
the inner chamber of the prison. Paul was extremely upset
about being arrested, because we hadn't committed a crime.
As a matter of fact, he was so irate, I had to speak to him for
quite a while to get him to settle down and feel the presence
of God. After we had been discussing the principles for about
a half hour, he fell asleep. So I just closed my eyes and tried
to achieve the five-dimensional consciousness. For what it's
worth, that was one of the deepest and most powerful
meditations I had experienced during that entire journey back

in time. Then, after resting for a while in the contentment of that supernal peace, I opened my eyes, as the ground began to shake all around us.

"Just as the episode is described in the Book of Acts, there was an earthquake, the prison's walls and ceiling came crashing down, and everyone's chains were broken. Despite all the noise and pandemonium, no one was injured, and no one tried to escape from the facility. Eventually, the jailer realized that something supernatural had happened and he allowed all of us to go free. He even invited Paul and me to dinner at his home that night."

After hearing my discourse, Shimahn said, "So it was you—or rather, you living as Silas—who was the instrument through which the power of God was realized in that situation. How did Paul react to that? Wasn't that enough proof for him?"

"Well, we discussed it for a while, but Paul just believed that his anthropomorphic God was looking down at us from heaven and, for whatever reason, decided to set us free. But there was no chanting or singing by all the prisoners as suggested in the Bible. Most of them were sound asleep."

"Were there any other significant events that happened on the journey?" my teacher asked.

"Nothing that would have changed the future as we have always known it. Timothy and I rejoined Paul in Corinth, and it was there that I met Sabina."

"Sabina?" Kathy shouted out. "Who the heck is Sabina?"

In spite of her remarkable spirituality, I quickly realized that Kathy would not take my next statement very well. "She was my wife," I answered softly.

"You had another wife . . . ? This is the third one, at least that I know about. How is it that it's so easy for you to pick up all these women? Are you on the prowl every time you're away from me for a few weeks?"

"A few weeks?" I responded. "I was gone for almost seventeen years."

"How is that possible?" she asked with astonishment in her voice. "Shimahn, what happened to you and me during all that time?"

"Once again, you don't want to hear the details, Kathy. The world as we have always known it virtually ended. All international commerce had ceased, and most people ended up living in poverty, or in a very limited state of existence. Many worldwide treaties and alliances came to an end, and no nation trusted any other nation again. All financial systems were in shambles and many people reverted back to the barter system."

Bowing his head, the Master took a long, deep breath and said, "You stayed here for about three months, Kathy. But as the world started coming apart, you decided to go home to be with your parents in Ohio."

His voice began to trail off as he continued. "I have no idea of what may have happened to you and your family during that terrible period . . . I don't even know if you lived or died, because I never heard from you again—

"But enough of that!" he said in a louder, more positive tone. "We have to decide if Eric's last journey in time has helped us prevent all of that from happening in our new future.

"What else can you tell us, Eric . . . or should I say, Silas?"

"Yes, Eric, why don't you tell us more about Sabina," Kathy said somewhat derisively. "What did she look like? How did you meet her?"

"All right, Kathy, but before I say anything, please remember that Sabina was you . . . that is, the *you* who is my soul mate, but appearing in an earlier life-experience. I know this must be very difficult for you to accept, but in both of my voyages back in time, I didn't recall anything from this present lifetime. I didn't remember you, Shimahn, our parents, President Thompson, or anyone else. I didn't even remember George Washington or Abraham Lincoln. But even more important, I left the wives I had there to return to this version of you—the one whom I love more than life itself. I will never be going back to see them again, but I will always be here with you."

Initially, Kathy had a rather downhearted expression on her face, but after giving this whole situation more thought, she seemed to become more understanding of what my entire ordeal must have been like. And after she had heard my last statement of how deep my love for her was, she finally lightened up. Yet she still would need time to become accustomed to the fact that I had had two other wives, even though I assured her that, in each case, her soul appearing in another incarnation was the person that I married.

Before we could say any more on that subject, Shimahn cut us off by commenting, "Young people, please let us move on . . . We are in a race against time to prevent some very bad things from happening and only you, Eric, can do anything about it.

"Now once again, my young friend, what else happened that might change the future?"

"Well, I did write another book that presents our mystical principles in a very clear and concise manner. If that has been discovered by now, maybe it has influenced people to live a more spiritual life with less violence."

"I am sorry, Eric, but I don't think that will help us. You see, this new, third timeline has just been created by your latest return here, so no one will have found the Silas manuscript before this afternoon. As I explained in our conversation after your first journey in time, unless you changed something of significance while you were there, we all are living under the same history and timeline as we would have been before you went back. But when you returned here that first time from your Yaacov body—actually, just about thirty-five minutes ago in this present parenthesis—you created an alternate reality and second timeline. It was a life stream with you in it—at least for a short time—as opposed to the other one without you. But then, because you went back to be with the early Christians, the first two timelines continued, but you were not a part of them. However, Kathy and I lived on in both of those parentheses and, as I mentioned previously, they were very disastrous experiences for everyone living on Planet Earth. Now that you have returned from your Silas body, you have created a third timeline. But if you did not do anything in that lifetime with Paul that was important enough to change the previous two outcomes, this new timeline will unfold in a similar fashion and be just as calamitous as the first two.

"Does that make sense to you?" he asked pensively.

My wife and I both nodded our heads as he said, "So we need an event much more significant than just a book you have written that hasn't been found yet."

"I suppose you are right, Shimahn," I replied. "In order to accomplish our goal, we need to affect something even more important from the past. That is why I have also given this a good deal of thought, and have concluded that there are very few previous events we could change that would fundamentally impact this present moment, or the new future."

"For example, if someone went back in time and killed Adolf Hitler, that would not affect this current situation. It possibly could have helped avoid World War II in Europe and the Holocaust, but it would not prevent what is happening now, or what may occur in the near future."

Shimahn quickly scolded me, "Eric, we do not want you going back to perform such violent acts. You cannot murder someone!"

Kathy simply stared at me with her hand covering her mouth, as she had become speechless over all that she was hearing.

I continued. "I understand that, Shimahn. And I wouldn't be capable of doing such a thing. I was just making the point that very few past events are earth-shaking enough to really impact the future. However, I do have an idea that I may want to pursue, but I would like to take a while to think about it. How much time do you feel we have before I need to leave on my next voyage back in time?"

"It would be best for you to begin your next trip no later than seven or eight o'clock tonight. We don't want the good people of the world to have to experience even another few months of such violent conflict—much less several decades—as they did in the first two timelines.

"Will that work for you?"

"Yes, I believe it will. But before going back again, I want to spend some quality time with Kathy. I would like her to join me now for a relaxing stroll on the ashram grounds. We will return here at 6:30 this evening after a nice dinner together. Personally, I have a strong urge to sample some of Mingma's nutritional and tasty cooking. I haven't had a really good meal in years," I finished with a chuckle in my voice and reached out a hand to my lovely wife.

CHAPTER 28

ANOTHER
UNEXPECTED FIND

The small group of visitors had just completed their tour of the ancient Christian catacombs located under the eternal city of Rome. The catacombs are underground burial places for Christians, Jews, and pagans. They are made up of a series of tunnels laid out in the form of a labyrinth. Located under or near the city, they are important, among other things, for the art history of the two great religions. There are forty known subterranean burial chambers in and around Rome.

The Christian catacombs were founded in the second century CE, and excavating of them continued until the first half of the fifth century. Early on, the catacombs were only burial places, where Christians gathered to celebrate their funeral rites. Then later, during the persecutions, the under-ground passages were used as places of momentary refuge for celebration of the Eucharist. But contrary to public belief, the catacombs were not used as hiding places as suggested in some books and motion pictures.

Also, the early Christians did not use the term "catacombs" in referring to these burial sites. Rather, the phrase was later taken from *catacomba*, an old Italian word which meant "a subterranean receptacle of the dead."

On that particular Tuesday afternoon, the gathering of ten or so people had just finished touring the catacombs of St. Sebastian under Via Appia Antica. As they were about to ascend the long staircase, tour guide Mariabella Rosatti saw the object standing deep in a corner, somewhat hidden from view. She had been through these passageways many times before, so at first she was quite puzzled about what it could be; she needed more time to study it. Mariabella asked her assistants to lead the group up the stairs and out of the area, while she stayed behind to further scrutinize what she thought she had seen. She fabricated an excuse that wouldn't generate any questions or concerns from her co-workers. Then, upon closer inspection, Mariabella realized that the object was a very old, earth-colored clay pot, standing about two-and-a-half feet high and containing a tightly wound scroll of well-preserved parchment.

Dear God, what is this? she wondered, *and where did it come from?*

Using her walkie-talkie to reach her assistants, Mariabella heard the voice of Rosalia Fortunato. "Is anything wrong, Mariabella? Why didn't you come up with us?"

"Nothing for you to be concerned about, Rosalia, I'm fine. Uh, could you please call Enrico Sabatini at the Institute of Antiquities and see if he or one of his associates could come here immediately? Tell him it's quite important that I speak to him."

"Why, Mariabella, what's wrong?"

"Nothing is wrong, I just need some answers to a few questions."

"The questions couldn't wait till we get back to the office?"

"No, Rosalia, they involve the catacombs, and he has to be here to see what I am talking about . . . Please call him now, and then take the group back to the tour center."

Afraid to unroll or even touch the parchment, Mariabella just sat quietly on the bottom step, staring at her discovery. She waited not-too-patiently for exactly forty-eight minutes that seemed more like forty-eight hours.

Upon arriving in the underground chamber, the first words out of Enrico Sabatini's mouth were, "What's so important that it couldn't wait until tomorrow morning? It's almost 4:00 on a beautiful Tuesday afternoon. I was planning to go home early today, and you should be out strolling in the piazza with your boyfriend."

Without saying a word, she just pointed toward the object standing in the dark corner.

"What's that?" Sabatini cried out.

"You tell me. You're the expert."

Together, they carried the clay pot out to a more brightly lit area.

"Holy Mother of God!" he said. "Where did this come from? How did it get here?"

"Enrico, if I knew that, I wouldn't have called you. What do you think it is?"

He replied, "Obviously, it's an ancient scroll of parchment sitting in an old clay pot . . . At first glance, I don't know if it's 500 years old, or 5,000 years old. But whatever its age, it does seem to be extremely well-preserved.

"Do you think you can help me carry it up the stairs?"

"I'm going to have to," the attractive tour guide responded sternly, "unless you can conjure up St. Peter's ghost and get him to help us. What are you going to do with it? Where are you going to take it?"

"I believe we need to get it to the Antiquities Analysis Center in Florence. They can give us more answers. And of course, you know the country's rules on ancient objects and other old finds. There are substantial penalties for not handling these types of things in the proper way. Furthermore, this could generate a huge controversy between the Vatican and the government as to who has ownership."

Enrico glanced around the dimly lit chamber, and said, "I will personally drive it up to Florence tomorrow morning and let the proper authorities determine the next steps.

"Thank you for calling me, Mariabella."

CHAPTER 29

THE FIRST BLOWS
ARE STRUCK

It was a beautiful sunny morning in Rome, one of history's greatest cities, which has been nicknamed *Caput Mundi* (Capital of the World) and *The Eternal City*. The summer tourist season was in full bloom; the fountains glistened splendidly under the rays of a blazing sun, and the Holy See went quietly about its business in Vatican City.

The Italian Renaissance of the 15th and 16th centuries CE gave us the remarkable works of art from Michelangelo, Raphael, Botticelli, da Vinci, and other masters; and the Colosseum, one of the world's most popular tourist attractions, still stood as a monument to the glory that was Rome during its greatest days as an empire. So nothing about this day could foretell the horror that awaited the former home of the Caesars.

Fortunately, Enrico Sabatini left early that morning on his drive to Florence. He was extremely anxious to have the scroll analyzed. If there were a large reward for such a remarkable find, he would certainly share it with Mariabella, since she is the one who found it, and had the courtesy to call him.

Meanwhile, another vehicle was going in the opposite direction. After its tedious six-hour trip, the old truck had just entered Rome a short while ago and was moving slowly eastward along Via Gregorio VII. It had just passed Via Leone XIII and was approaching Via Anastasio II. Then without any warning, at exactly 11:46 that morning the blast occurred, and the Rome that the world has known and loved for all these centuries was no more.

At 5:50 a.m. Eastern Daylight Time in New York, reporter Jackson Williams interrupted his network's regular programming with these words: "CNN sadly reports that an apparent nuclear explosion has just occurred in the heart of Rome, very close to Vatican City. While we have confirmed the blast, we have no knowledge as to the strength or power of the weapon, and there has not yet been enough time to assess the damage. First reports indicate that the devastation is horrendous. CNN will keep you updated as we get more information."

At 3:57 a.m. Mountain Daylight Time, President Thompson was awakened by the ringing of his bedside telephone in his new temporary "home" in the Cheyenne Mountain NORAD control center.

"My God!" was his first response. "How bad is it?"

"Sorry, sir, but we don't have any information yet. As you might expect, it is very difficult to get any news out from up close."

"Under the circumstances, I don't imagine we can reach Prime Minister Giordano, but please try . . . See if you can patch me through, Don."

While the President of the United States is often regarded as the most powerful person on the planet, at that world-changing moment, President Thompson sat on the edge of his bed with his face in his hands, feeling completely powerless. Maybe life as the Governor of Florida wasn't all that bad. Yet he had resigned that office before the end of his second term to seek the presidency. It had been a difficult decision, but the elder statesmen of his party felt Thompson was the best candidate for the job. So after long discussions with his wife and daughter, he agreed to run.

He had been swept into office on a wave of negative reactions against the previous administration. In fact, by the first Tuesday of November that election year, it was almost an open rebellion. The bad economy, combined with the previous president's sharp move toward socialism, his perceived weakness on illegal immigration, and his refusal to call Islamic extremists "terrorists," were overwhelmingly rejected by his country's voters.

So at this perilous moment, having been elected as the man the people wanted in charge in a national emergency, Darwin Thompson's first urge was to respond everywhere in the Islamic world. Yet how could he do that without creating an even worse crisis? Within ten minutes, he received a telephone call from British Prime Minister Cedric Knightly.

The President's good friend in London was very somber as he asked, "Do you believe we can retaliate anywhere at this time?"

"Not without some serious repercussions, Cedric. Have you heard any damage assessments yet?"

"Only a small amount. Because of the proximity of the detonation, it appears that Vatican City is gone; and the Pope was in residence. But that also means St. Peter's Basilica, the Sistine Chapel, the Apostolic Palace . . . all the museums, the statues, the fountains, the works of art . . . all of them are gone."

"That is unbelievable. Even the Nazis' plundering of the historic art works during World War II doesn't compare to this."

President Thompson then asked, "Uh, Cedric, have you made any plans to leave London at this time?"

"Well, my security people have suggested it, but I think it would look bad. The Queen and her family have left Buckingham Palace, but I feel that I should stay here. You know, old chap, put up a jolly good front, just as Winston did in World War II. The people need that in times like these, don't you think?"

"All right, Cedric, thank you for calling. Good luck to you, and let's stay in touch over the next day or two. We need our intelligence departments to continue sharing everything at this critical time. Please keep all the lines of communication open."

By 7:00 a.m. on the East Coast, more information about the Rome attack was available, but most of it was coming from the news networks.

Fox News Anchor Jerry Buckner, speaking in a very solemn tone, opened his broadcast with these words: "Early this morning, a fifteen-kiloton nuclear device exploded in Rome, Italy. This was not just a dirty bomb, but a full-fledged nuclear weapon. The epicenter of the blast was less than one mile from Vatican City. As a result, the Holy See and the Roman Curia no longer exist. The Pope, the Cardinal Secretary of State, the visiting cardinals, and all members of the Papal Household, are presumed to have been killed. And of course, the magnificent buildings and monuments of the Vatican are now just a huge mound of rubble."

His voice trembling with emotion, the newsman continued. "On your TV screen are two telescopic aerial photos from about twenty miles away from ground zero. These clearly illustrate the magnitude of the devastation. The picture on the left shows how the area has looked for most of our lifetimes . . . The one on the right gives an idea of how it looks now.

"This is the first full-scale nuclear attack on any nation or populated city since the American bombings of Hiroshima and Nagasaki, Japan at the end of World War II. Metropolitan Rome has a population—I believe I should have said *had* a population—of more than three-and-a-half million people—

"My next guest is noted physicist Dr. Gunther Werner, Professor Emeritus of the Massachusetts Institute of Technology. Dr. Werner was an early opponent of nuclear weaponry and is considered an expert on the potential damage that can be caused by an atomic bomb—"

Then the scientist gave his estimates of the current death toll, how long the radiation would last, and how many people would die in the next several months.

While that was happening, the Dow Jones Industrial futures were showing a potential loss of more than 4,200 points at the opening, with the Standard and Poor's 500 futures being down 312 points. Both of those numbers would represent by far the greatest opening losses in the history of the stock market.

Almost simultaneously, S.E.C. Chairman Bronstein contacted Treasury Secretary Gordon Breckenridge to discuss the situation, and they were able to arrange an immediate conference call with President Thompson.

Because of the downing of the Singapore Airlines flight to Los Angeles, the securities markets were kept closed on Tuesday. However, after that day of rest, the decision makers had planned to reopen the markets on Wednesday morning. But that was before the destruction of the Willis Tower in Chicago. Now, with the nuclear attack on Rome, the three men agreed they should not allow the securities markets to open. Based upon the projected futures numbers, nearly 46 percent of the nation's wealth had evaporated since Friday's close. Furthermore, in Europe the FTSE 100 Index, or "Footsie"—the roster of the 100 most highly capitalized UK companies listed on the London Stock Exchange—had lost 52 percent of its value in just the last two hours before the

British Financial Services Authority could shut down its markets.

In America, the three-man financial brain trust believed it was better to just freeze everything in place with the markets closed indefinitely, than to allow such a visible economic meltdown.

Then, at 9:48 a.m. EDT, all the major news networks began broadcasting a feed from Al Jazeera, the Middle Eastern news network headquartered in Doha, Qatar. Al Jazeera had been quite controversial in the West ever since its inception, and especially in the weeks following the attacks of September 11, 2001, when the channel broadcast video statements by Osama bin Laden and other al-Qaeda spokesmen.

On that Wednesday morning in August, the unidentified announcer said, "Al Jazeera has just received a short video of Hasan Mohammed Farouk, the second-highest ranking operative in al Qaeda. Our sources tell us this tape was recorded less than three hours ago."

The video began with a moment of silence and then a turbaned, heavily bearded man with a cynical, sly smile on his face began to speak in Classic Arabic, with English translations following. He said:

"The long-awaited Jihad has begun! The imperialist infidels are now beginning to suffer the same level of pain the children of Islam have endured for all these years. Rome was chosen first because it was the heart of the heathen religious structure. This is a small return payment for the humiliation and suffering the Crusades brought upon our people.

"The Roman Catholic Church has always wanted a holy war against Islam . . . well, now it has one. And Italy is also paying the price for aligning itself with the *Great Satan* in its illegal invasions of Iraq and Afghanistan. But this is just the beginning.

"The exploded Singapore Airliner and the destruction of the skyscraper in Chicago are merely a foretaste of what is coming. Nations of the world . . . I warn you not to fly your aircraft to America. If you do, they will be destroyed in the air. And to you self-righteous people in the United States who were so proud of yourselves, and were dancing in the streets the night you killed our great leader Osama bin Laden, I ask how many of you will be dancing tonight?"

The speaker again looked directly into the camera with a mean, contemptuous smile, raised his right fist in the air, and shouted, "*Alahu Akbar* . . . Death to the infidels!"

7:48 A.M. WEDNESDAY MORNING - AUGUST 19TH
SAN FRANCISCO, CA

The 1997 Dodge Caravan left its garage in Sausalito at 7:24 a.m. Pacific Daylight Time and headed south on Highway 101. At precisely 7:48, the vehicle had reached its targeted destination at 300 meters south of the north tower of the Golden Gate Bridge.

At 7:32 a.m., the old Ford panel truck exited Golden Gate Park and began its Highway 1 northbound approach to the famous American landmark. By 7:48, it also had reached its destination, 300 meters north of the south tower.

The Dodge Caravan exploded first, creating a gaping hole in the north portion of the main span. The second blast from the Ford truck came just twelve seconds later. Combined, the two bridge detonations carried about two-thirds the power of the explosives that were used to bring down the Alfred P. Murrah Federal Building in Oklahoma City on April 19, 1995.

Twisted masses of steel and concrete were hanging by a thread at each of the points of attack, and a huge portion of the main span plunged into the Bay below, along with dozens of vehicles.

As soon as the alarm came in, most of the resources of the San Francisco Fire Department were deployed to the south explosion site. Meanwhile, the north side of the bridge had to be serviced by the various volunteer fire departments located in Sausalito, Marin City, and other communities to the north. Also quickly arriving on the scene were most of the search and rescue aircraft of the California Air National Guard. Though rescue efforts began early in the morning, they would continue throughout the day and around the clock until all missing people had been accounted for.

As a result of this horrific attack, San Francisco literally ground to a halt. All northbound traffic flowing out of the city was paralyzed.

That Wednesday in August had now become one of the most cataclysmic days in the history of the world.

CHAPTER 30

TRANSLATING AND DECODING
A MYSTICAL MESSAGE

THE PRESENT – WEDNESDAY MORNING, AUGUST 19TH
TIMELINES 2 AND 3
THE ISRAELI ARCHAEOLOGICAL INSTITUTE, TEL AVIV, ISRAEL

There was no reason for Lindsay Ainsworth-Jones to have sent his translators home on Tuesday night, because none of them slept a wink. The mysterious nature of the scroll their boss had found in Cave 4 at Qumran had them completely baffled. For that reason, all three of them were at the Institute twenty minutes early on Wednesday morning.

As soon as they started their work, they were again seeing profound mystical phrases. Among those were statements such as:

"Life is spiritual. It is synonymous with Consciousness. There never has been a physical life . . . There never has

been a physical consciousness. Physicality and mortality are illusions of sense. The Divine I within you is Life Itself. There is no reality in any form of physicality . . . There is no mortality in reality . . . There is only Life living forever as conscious perfection embodied."

Another wisdom said, "The I AM which is God is the I of your being—the essence and nucleus of what you are. It is the Divine Consciousness manifesting Itself at every conceivable level of your individual life-experience."

By 10:30 that morning, the group had a preliminary answer back from the Laboratory of Archaeometry in Greece. First reports from the radiocarbon testing indicated that the papyrus and the ink were from the fourteenth century before Christ.

The document was authentic.

After getting that news, Brian Willoughby commented, "I'm very glad to know this thing is real . . . but that still doesn't make it any less confusing. Have any of you ever seen these kinds of mystical words and phrases in any other contemporary document from that period? Everything about this language seems too current, as though someone from the present is saying these things."

About twenty minutes later, Willoughby let out a shout, "You've got to be kidding me! There's a line here that says, 'Let the Force be with you.' Is that somebody's idea of a joke? Did George Lucas go back in time and write this thing?"

Cynthia Trowbridge then spoke up. "Listen to this section. 'I am not a prisoner of my mind . . . I am not a victim *of the mind's false perceptions. All human beliefs are illusions. They are subjective, erroneous suggestions, which cannot be externalized or manifested in objective form. Therefore, no disease, pain or illness can appear in my body. No lack, limitation or loss can appear in my life-experience. Nothing of an evil nature can occur in this harmonious unfoldment of the Consciousness that I am.'*

"Wow!" Cynthia declared. "I would be happy to sit at the feet of this illumined Master."

Then Laura Markham, the third translator, spoke up. "I agree with you, Cindy. This guy is something else. Listen to this: *'The place whereon I stand is holy ground. It is* My Kingdom, *the spiritual realm of peace, joy and eternal harmony. Then what is there to fear?*

No weapon that is formed against me shall prosper. I will not fear man whose breath is in his nostrils—his erroneous creation theories, his false beliefs about life, his fear of death, nor his seeming descent into the hell of humanhood.

I am a pure, perfect, individual Consciousness, the eternal spiritual Consciousness that is only aware of spiritual reality. Nothing of an evil or diseased nature can enter into, nor defile, this pristine unblemished Consciousness.'

"Gosh, this is some powerful stuff," she declared.

The translators continued working feverishly for the next few hours, unceasingly marveling at what they were reading. But then, at 1:15 p.m., a deep cloud of melancholy and horror fell over the group, as they heard the news from Rome for the first time. The magnificent ancient city had just been destroyed by a nuclear blast.

Suddenly, the new find from Qumran carried far less significance and just didn't seem that important anymore. In the last hour, the world had changed dramatically, so the previously enthusiastic workers decided to break for the rest of that day.

CHAPTER 31

ARMAGEDDON — DAY ONE

News of the nuclear attack against Rome had been circulating for nearly 24 hours. If it could happen there, it could happen here. So both the General Directorate for External Security (DGSE) and the Central Directorate of Interior Intelligence (DCRI) were on high alert.

Though they had worked feverishly through the night for the past several days, the two French espionage and counter-terrorism agencies had drawn nothing but blanks. As a result, when the device was fully assembled in the old warehouse building, there was little that could be done to prevent detonation.

Paris had a large Muslim population, so the jihadists questioned whether they should attack the city. Yet the symbolism of seeing the Eiffel Tower, the Louvre Museum, and the other landmarks coming down was so great, they felt the human sacrifice was worth it. After all, weren't they also dying for the cause?

So at 9:40 that Thursday morning, the device exploded with staggering impact. It was a twenty-kiloton nuclear bomb containing a large amount of fissionable materials. The results were as devastating as the perpetrators hoped they would be.

Before the explosion, the city of Paris had a population of approximately 2.2 million people; the greater metropolitan area totaled more than 11 million. The death toll was expected to far exceed the number of casualties that resulted from either the dirty bomb in Hamburg, Germany, or the more powerful weapon in Rome.

While many of the western governments were still reeling from the nuclear explosion in the Italian capital on the previous day, this attack in Paris was a further blow to the stability of those governments and their respective economies. Most of the world's airlines had stopped flying, and Europe's banks and securities markets were closed. Yet this was not the end of the carnage.

THE PRESENT - THURSDAY MORNING, AUGUST 20TH
LONDON, ENGLAND - TIMELINES 1, 2 AND 3

A little more than an hour later a similar blast occurred in London, England. This one took out Parliament, the Tower of London, 10 Downing Street, and Buckingham Palace. By mid-afternoon, the hearts and souls of both cities had been reduced to huge mounds of wreckage. Nearly three million people had been killed, and the radioactivity reached levels that were dangerous even to those citizens who were farther away from the epicenters of the blasts. In addition, the two cities' world-famous rivers—the Thames and the River Seine—were polluted to unrecoverable levels. The situation had become so grim that the national and international news networks couldn't keep up with all the chaos and pandemonium. Not the BBC, France 24, nor the World News Network's outlets in those countries were able to transmit broadcasts. Only the American networks could get sketchy reports out, and those were being done from a distance.

Meanwhile, President Darwin Thompson heard the dreaded early-morning ringing of his bedside telephone for the second time in two days. He immediately knew that no one calls with good news at that time of the morning. First, he heard the horrific report from Paris. Then, just an hour later, and before he could even get his Cabinet and war council fully assembled, the gut-wrenching call came in, chronicling the nuclear attack in London.

The President's first reaction was sadness for the probable loss of his good friend at 10 Downing Street.

Cedric, he thought, *why didn't you get out of there? I only wish we could have done more to help you.*

But then he had to attend to his own nation's business. *Were these attacks going to continue moving west across the time zones? Was America next?*

Those were questions that only time could answer.

While President Thompson was weighing his options, Joint Chiefs Chairman Daniels was already in the Colorado bunker, as were the secretaries of State and Defense, the Director of Homeland Security, plus a few other cabinet officials. At the same moment, Scott Cunningham and several key people of his intelligence team were aboard Air Force One, heading toward Peterson Air Force Base. Cunningham's flight also carried the U.S. Attorney General, the other members of the Joint Chiefs, and some of the families of those government workers who were either at, or coming to, the NORAD facility.

Soon the full military brain trust of the United States would be reassembled and the nation would virtually have a government in exile, stationed in Colorado. And many of the unwitting citizens of the country didn't even know it was happening. But then the people's leaders had to decide on two different courses of action: one if the U.S. was attacked with a nuclear or biological weapon, and one if it was not. Should the American government hit back for what had happened to its good friends in Europe? Would that really accomplish anything, or just make a few people feel good for a short while? And yet, didn't they owe that to their dearest allies? If a nuclear bomb from Iran had hit Israel, President

Thompson would have kept his promise to that nation, and the United States would have retaliated. So why not strike back now when even greater atrocities had been perpetrated across the world?

By 4:00 on Thursday morning, Scott Cunningham's flight had landed in Colorado. As soon as the complete entourage of military and intelligence people were situated in their lodgings, the full body came together for a meeting at 5:00 a.m.

This was by far the gloomiest of all the gatherings the group had held in the past several days. No one had any absolute answers on the best course of action.

No one, that is, except for Marine Commandant Fabretti. In his mind, he knew exactly what steps should be taken next.

"We owe it the Brits and the Italians—my people—to give them some payback," Fabretti said. "Maybe the French haven't been supporting us so much in recent years, but they did help us win the Revolutionary War.

"We can't just let this stand without a response."

DNI Director Larkin then said, "I agree with General Fabretti. We cannot just sit idly by, taking all of this without hitting back somewhere."

President Thompson replied, "Don't think I am not on your side, gentlemen. I am seething with rage at this moment. I promise you we will retaliate. I just want all of you to know that if we do that, it could be the start of World War III, along with all the potential repercussions such an event will produce. But that is a chance we will have to take.

"Do any of you have additional comments?"

When no one responded, the Commander-in-Chief said, "Okay, I will be speaking with the Russian and Chinese leaders—not to get their permission, but to let them know what we believe must be done. And then General Daniels and I will share our plan for retaliation with all of you.

"Let's meet back here again in two hours."

CHAPTER 32

ANOTHER DOCUMENT TO TRANSLATE

On Wednesday morning, Enrico Sabatini delivered the mysterious scroll from the catacombs to the Antiquities Analysis Center in Florence. Shortly after arriving there, he heard the tragic news about the nuclear explosion in Rome. He was devastated. His wife and four children lived with him in their home located very close to Vatican City. Every attempt he made to contact his family failed. A short while later, the Analysis Center office closed so the workers could go to their homes to follow the story on television, and since he couldn't go back to Rome, Enrico went to the home of Agnese Gambrotti, one of the translators. Because Sabatini was virtually in a state of hysteria, Agnese hoped that she and her husband, along with her sister who lived with them, could give him some comfort and consolation.

But even though the workers in the Center were deeply concerned about what had happened in their nation's Capital, they had two choices. They all could stay home and watch the news reports for several days, or they could come back to their office and hope their work might provide a distraction.

Since none of them had relatives living in Rome, and there was no threat to Florence at that time, most of them chose to return to their desks at 8:00 Thursday morning. Enrico Sabatini had just delivered a remarkable document to their facility, and they were anxious to learn more about it, despite being quite weepy-eyed and sleep deprived.

The title of the scroll was **The Gospel According to Silas,** *Traveling Companion of Paul the Apostle.*

The language was Greek, with a few Hebrew and Latin phrases mixed in. Based upon the dialect used, the scroll appeared to have been produced in the first century CE.

A separate small page of parchment was included inside the wrapped scroll. On that document, were the words:

"Following the instructions of my father, Laurentius Gallus, I, Marcus Gallus, have placed this scroll here in the catacombs of Rome. My father told me that the message in this manuscript was given to us by Silas, the friend and traveling companion of Paul of Tarsus, the Apostle to the Gentiles."

The first lines of the scroll read: *"These are my words, the words of Silas of Corinth, as they have been revealed to me through several lifetimes of meditation and prayer.*

God is infinite . . . there is only one Life, one Soul, one Spirit—one all-inclusive Universal Consciousness. This immortal Being is the sum and substance of all existence and of all reality.

This Universal Consciousness is appearing as the individual spiritual Consciousness that I am and that you are. It is the substance of my being and yours."

After reading those lines, Mario Andolini, the head translator at the Analysis Center, said, "The author of this scroll claims to be Silas, the traveling companion of Paul. If it really is that Silas, the one whom Peter referred to as Sylvanus, this could be an incredible document. It possibly might have been written earlier than the three synoptic Gospels, or at the least, it could be contemporaneous with the Gospel of Mark, if not even earlier than that one.

"But what kind of words are these? Who used all these metaphysical and new-age phrases at the time of Peter and Paul?"

His assistant, Agnese Gambrotti, replied, "And what does he mean by *'several lifetimes of meditation and prayer?'* Does he believe in reincarnation?"

She then said, "This is amazing! Listen to these lines: *'I do not live in the* Kingdom of God . . . The Kingdom of God (My Kingdom) *exists within me, within this infinite, individual Consciousness that I am. And I have dominion over everything that appears in this Kingdom.*

In My Kingdom, *there is only spiritual perfection. Nothing of a limited or imperfect nature exists here. The seeming limitations of physical sense are nothing more than illusions. And because illusions can never be objectified, they cannot even appear in the five-dimensional level of reality where I live, and move, and have my being.'*

"Incredible, isn't it?" she said. "This sounds like some kind of crossover between Christianity and Buddhism. Where did this writer come from? How did he learn all these ideas so long ago?"

Andolini answered, "I don't even want to speculate, I just want to relish what I am seeing here. With all the bad news in the world today, there hasn't been much to enjoy lately."

As they continued to translate more of the scroll, the workers couldn't believe their eyes. Never before had they seen such words and phrases come out of that time period.

Many of them seemed too modern—even metaphysical in nature.

A short time later, Agnese Gambrotti wondered aloud, "Just who is this Laurentius Gallus? Obviously he is Roman. And if Silas was his friend, then this guy must also have known Peter and Paul. Yet I have never heard of him before. Do any of you know who he might be?"

The other workers just shrugged their shoulders. Then, before they could really make a serious dent in the manu-script from the catacombs, the bad news from Paris came in.

The world-famous City of Lights had just gone dark—and this time, maybe forever.

"What is going on?" Agnese asked. "Has the world gone mad? Yesterday it was Rome; today it is Paris. What's next?"

She didn't have to wait long to get the answer to her question. About the same time the translators agreed they were not in the mood to continue working, they heard about the bombing of London. And that was enough for them to decide to close the Analysis Center until the following Monday, provided the world was still rotating on its axis at that time.

CHAPTER 33

MAKING PLANS FOR THE FINAL JOURNEY

*MONDAY EVENING, AUGUST 17TH - 6:30 P.M. - TIMELINE NO. 3
SHIMAHN'S ASHRAM - NAKCHU PREFECTURE -
NORTHERN TIBET AUTONOMOUS REGION*

A fter Kathy and I had strolled around the ashram grounds and then enjoyed what to me was a most delicious dinner, we returned to Shimahn's living room at 6:30 on Monday evening. During our time together, I had an opportunity to settle Kathy down about my other marriages in past incarnations. I once again pointed out that, when I returned to those old parentheses, I had virtually no recollection of this life in the 21st century. I was not being unfaithful to her, because I didn't remember her. But even more important, she—her soul living in another body—was the woman I had married. "And furthermore," I said pleadingly, "you should be happy that we now have absolute confirmation that you and I truly are soul mates, and *will* be together throughout eternity."

Kathy seemed to accept my explanations and was more positive about everything in our final discussions that evening.

Shimahn began our conversation. "Eric, I hope I haven't been wrong about all of this. But reflecting upon what you said this afternoon, I am not certain there is any event you could change that would be significant enough to alter the terrible future we are facing. We don't want you going back to assassinate people such as Muhammad or Osama bin Laden and, other than an act of that magnitude, I don't know what else would be effective.

"And equally important, there is very little chance you would have lived in close enough proximity to anyone who was that important to this situation. Also, based upon my understanding, I don't believe you can choose a specific lifetime in advance, if you would even know when or where it was."

Kathy then commented, "You know, Eric, Shimahn might be right. Maybe there is nothing you can do to alter the future. And it scares me to death to think of you out there in some vast timeless wilderness, trying to get back to us here in twenty-first-century Tibet.

"This may sound selfish, but the three of us have enough knowledge and mystical awareness to rise above so many of the problems we face in life. Might it not be wiser for us just to drop this idea and spend as much time as we can living above the fray, in the five-dimensional consciousness?"

"In general, I agree with both of you," I replied. "But since I did go back to those other parentheses, I now have a better perspective of the evil that abounds in this world of cause and effect. I have witnessed up close the greatness of the Roman Empire. But I also have seen what happens when there is an abuse of that power, as in the case of the tyrannical rule by a deranged person like Nero.

"Because they called themselves Christians, people were being slaughtered—fed to the lions just for sport. And for those who were crucified, it also was a horrible death.

"This world as we know it today has no chance for survival. And it all has come about so quickly. Just think of the world in which our parents were raised. It was a beautiful, peaceful place relative to what is going on now. Even the psychopathy of Hitler and the excessive cruelty of Stalin were beaten back. But as you mentioned in our first meeting, Shimahn, we now are confronted with a new level of unmitigated evil. And to make matters worse, these people have possession of weapons of mass destruction that are many times more powerful than any armaments those other tyrants had in the past.

"So for those reasons, I feel I must go back one last time. And to set your minds at ease, I truly believe I know what I must do now, and where I must do it."

"What is it?" my wife asked enthusiastically.

"Sorry, Kathy, I don't want to speak about this unless I really can accomplish it. So just as Shimahn replied to us when we wondered how he could recall events from some future alternate reality, I say to both of you: just trust me on this. I am certain of what must be done.

"And by the way, if I am right about what I am planning, it won't take years to accomplish my task. I expect to be gone for just a week or two."

And with that, I again gave each of them a hug and walked through the library doorway, as I winked and said, "See you soon in the next timeline."

CHAPTER 34

ARMAGEDDON—
DAY ONE, CONTINUED

The military brain trust of the United States had gathered once more in its "government-in-exile" location inside Cheyenne Mountain. President Thompson was outlining what he called a "limited, but firm, nuclear response" to all the attacks and attempted attacks of the past forty-eight hours. But before the group could hear the entire plan, the telephone on the big table began to ring. Because of all the tension in the air, the ringing seemed louder and more alarming than normal.

Then the caller gave the dreaded, but not totally unexpected news . . . The unthinkable had just happened.

There had been a nuclear explosion in Washington, D.C.

Instantaneously, most of the women in the room began weeping uncontrollably . . . and it was only a matter of seconds before many of the men joined them in their sorrow.

CIA's Scott Cunningham seemed to take it the hardest. It was his responsibility to prevent something like this from happening. Yet it had happened—and on his watch. The national hero couldn't express strongly enough how much shame and sense of failure he was feeling at that moment, as he bowed his head in silence.

After about three minutes without a word being spoken, the President said furiously, "All right, let's scrap the plan. This is beyond the pale. General Daniels, if you and the Joint Chiefs agree, let's step it up to plan B.

"We will throw so much radiation at those goddamned mountains between Afghanistan and Pakistan that no form of organism will be able to live there again for decades. Then, yes, we'll do just what General Fabretti suggested a few days ago. We're taking out Tehran, Damascus, and Riyadh . . . Does anyone object to that?"

No one said a word, but all the military men made strong, affirmative gestures.

"Just so all of you realize how serious we are," Thompson continued, "the bomb that we confiscated from the pirate ship, and the explosions in Rome, Paris, and London were of the 15- to 20-kiloton variety. We are hitting back with weapons yielding 400 to 500 kilotons.

"Let's see how many of those Islamic bastards are still breathing after we start doing that. As we have stated many times during the past several days, America has been trying to avoid initiating World War III. But now, these lunatics have done it, and we are merely responding and defending our homeland."

None of the people in the room had ever seen the President lose his cool to that degree. But Generals Fabretti and Larkin couldn't have been more pleased. In fact, they would have been in an uproar if the President had not responded in this manner.

The next issue was to assess the damage in the nation's Capital. Again, the news networks were the best source for up-to-date information.

According to the announcers, there now was some slightly better news in the midst of all the horror going on in the world. Contrary to first reports, it had been determined that the device detonated in Washington, D.C. was in fact a dirty bomb, and not a full-scale nuclear weapon. Other than getting that small dose of semi-good news, it would be days before any real assessments could be made. However, unlike the weapons exploded in Rome, Paris, and London, the bomb in Washington would not create anything close to the same level of devastation and radiation.

But that did not make a difference in America's response to another jihadist attack on the homeland. The level of retaliation outlined by President Thompson was going to be carried out. The bombs would begin raining down on the Afghan-Pakistani border by 9:00 that evening. The three major Islamic capitals would be destroyed a short while later.

And for some inexplicable reason, there would be a certain group of people in this world who now would feel a lot better than they had earlier that morning.

As a very wise oracle once said, *"Madness begets madness."*

CHAPTER 35

THE FINAL JOURNEY
IN TIME

For several days, Shimahn had been telling us of the calamitous future the world was facing unless I could change some significant event that would in some way alter that future.

I already knew that if we can lift ourselves into the five-dimensional consciousness, we also can rise above the inherent evils of this world of sense perceptions. In *My Kingdom*, there are no evil circumstances. In the divine reality of God-consciousness, there are no wars or rumors of war. There is only the all-harmonious unfoldment of the one infinite Being that we call God. So taking physical footsteps to try to prevent any problems seemed a bit contradictory.

I also knew that Kathy and I, along with Shimahn, could be safe in our little cocoon of mystical consciousness way up there in the Himalayas. Yet, together, we had embarked upon this journey into the unknown, and I already had made two trips back in time.

Therefore, I did not want to give up now, especially because I believed I knew exactly what had to be done to solve the problems the world was facing.

So for the third time on that very same Monday afternoon, I entered Shimahn's library to attempt what, hopefully, would be my last journey to the distant past. But this time, instead of making a quick exit out of my body and soaring easily into the Grand Circle of Eternity, I spent more time in the chair, trying to visualize the spiritual nature of all existence and to feel a divine Oneness with God. I wanted to take this next trip enveloped by a full realization of peace and contentment, knowing that the work had already been done.

After resting in that state of celestial bliss for at least twenty minutes, I finally allowed myself to exit this body once more and to rise into the infinite Circle. From there, I hovered over my various parentheses for a longer time than usual.

I knew what my objective had to be, but I also wanted to be certain there was a place for me in the destination I had in mind. So I continued to drift in that supernal state of harmony, waiting to find the parenthesis I was seeking. And then I saw it, beckoning me from a distance. Suddenly it was illuminated more brightly than all the others.

This enlightened soul drifted down to that inviting place and allowed itself to slowly coalesce with that other life-stream until there was no more Eric, and only a new, very old identity. Arriving in that chosen destination, he then opened his eyes to the most lush, serene and beautiful habitat that God had ever created.

CHAPTER 36

ARMAGEDDON—
DAY TWO

THE PRESENT - 8:00 A.M. FRIDAY MORNING, AUGUST 21ST
NORAD COMMAND CENTER - PETERSON AIR FORCE BASE
CHEYENNE MOUNTAIN IN COLORADO - TIMELINES 1, 2 AND 3

After the bombs had been dropped in the Middle East, there was the expected malevolent reaction among all Muslims across the world. They had always believed that America was the *Great Satan*, and now they knew with certainty. Only the Americans could be evil enough to have perpetrated such acts of irrational violence against innocent citizens of sovereign states.

Meanwhile, back in the United States, most of the nation's commerce had come to a complete, grinding halt after the dirty bomb attack on Washington, D.C. The airlines had stopped flying, truckers had stopped driving, most retail stores were closed, and factories were barely operating. All banks were closed, along with the securities markets, which had never reopened since they were shut down on the previous Monday. Ninety percent of the nation's labor force was staying home to watch the unfolding events on television. Even the public schools were closed. It seemed that the only people still working were healthcare providers, police and fire department employees, along with television news announcers.

President Thompson made two more brief statements after his address following the Willis Tower attack. In one, he authorized a National Day of Mourning for the following Monday. Mostly, the President was trying to assuage the fears of the nation's citizens. Initially, the U.S. government released limited information on the retaliatory bombings in the Middle East. The leaders wanted to assure the American people that they were responding, without giving too much information to the enemy. But they also felt compelled to make a strong statement to both the Islamic world and to anyone else who intended to attack the homeland or the country's interests around the globe. *This will never happen again!*

After the European attacks, Rome, Paris, and London had become uninhabitable places. The devastation from the explosions was hideous, and the radiation fallout had created serious contamination of the water supplies and the animal food chain.

Since all three nuclear blasts were detonated on the ground, the air bursts produced more radiation fallout than would have been created from an explosion high in the air. But because this type of radiation decays relatively quickly, it was expected to be about five or six weeks before it would be safe for rescue teams and construction workers to reenter the cities. Even under those difficult conditions, temporary hospitals were set up as close to the cities as possible. In practically no time, they were filled beyond capacity, literally bursting at the seams. The Red Cross and other charitable organizations were also doing all they could but, because of the radiation, no one could get close enough to make any significant difference.

On the other hand, the effects of the United States' bombing of Tehran, Damascus and Riyadh, with weapons that were twenty times more powerful, would be immeasurable. The scope of the blasts of the 400- and 500-kiloton bombs would destroy everything in those cities and a good portion of any adjacent areas.

By 8:00 on Friday morning, the U.S. military command had regrouped in its Cheyenne Mountain bunker. Joint Chiefs Chairman Daniels opened the discussion.

"We have definitive evidence that the three Islamic capitals we hit last night are now gone. Furthermore, no Taliban or al-Qaeda member will be able to use those mountains between Pakistan and Afghanistan as a sanctuary for a very long time. We have pummeled those hills and caves with a huge amount of explosive radiation. As a result, we have basically destroyed those terrorist groups' ability to function again in that area. However, there still are many cells operating around the world in other countries. We are hoping this action will put an end to this insanity. But only time will tell."

It didn't take long to get an answer to that statement. By 9:30 that morning, the entire cabinet had joined the military leaders at their meeting site. As they were discussing how to restore some semblance of normalcy to the country and its economy, the telephone on the conference table rang again.

Another heart-stopping moment of sadness and anger gripped the group when they heard the news. There had just been a second nuclear-type explosion in America. This time it was Las Vegas, Nevada, that had been hit. The detonation took place right in the heart of the Strip, just north of Flamingo Avenue. But this time the initial report got it right. It was another dirty bomb.

So while the long-term radiation effects should be less than would occur with a more powerful nuclear weapon, the immediate damage from the explosion would still be many billions of dollars. At least twenty-two of the world's finest hotels and casinos were brought to the ground, and tens of thousands of people had been killed or wounded, or would suffer from radiation effects.

"Those bastards!" shouted General Sean Larkin. "Mr. President, I believe we have to hit them back at a ratio of five or ten to one. For every one of our cities they hit, we take out ten of theirs."

"I'm with you, Sean," said General Fabretti. "Does anybody disagree with that?"

Most of the attendees shook their heads, which meant they agreed. President Thompson was about to outline Plan C—the next higher level of retaliation—when the table phone rang again.

Everyone in the room froze in stone-cold silence. After four agonizing rings, the President pushed the speaker button.

The caller told them there had just been a powerful nuclear explosion in the Port of Los Angeles. This one was a real atomic bomb. A huge mushroom cloud was hanging over the city, as the weapon had been detonated from a boat in the harbor.

"Son-of-a-bitch!" Thompson shouted out. "All bets are off now." Looking at the Joint Chiefs Chairman, the President said, "Show us the plan D list, Jack."

General Daniels clicked the mouse on his computer, and everyone looked up at the big screen. He said, "We are targeting the largest cities in these countries, as well as any important infrastructure locations or nearby terrorist training sites."

The screen listed the following names: Pakistan, Yemen, Libya, Afghanistan, Nigeria, Bangladesh, North Korea, Ethiopia, Sudan, Somalia, and Algeria.

President Thompson then said, "In addition to last night's attacks, we are going to hit other cities in Iran, Syria, and Saudi Arabia, plus anyplace where Al Jazeera broadcasts originate. And, General Fabretti, as you suggested, we are also taking out Mecca and Medina. For now, we are holding back on Egypt, Jordan and Indonesia until we see how things play out after this round."

Looking around the room, he asked, "Any comments or questions?"

Once again, everyone was in total agreement with the plan.

So the process of retaliatory mass destruction was implemented as ordered. And thus began the beginning of the end of the quality of life the Western world had known for the last 100 years in timelines 1, 2 and 3.

In that violent future, these terrible actions and reactions continued to rage, as they escalated into enormously savage and bloody holy wars.

Any Christians or Jews found in the now-devastated Islamic countries were arrested and executed. Any Muslims living in western, Judeo-Christian societies were incarcerated for life in austere concentration camps.

And the argument over who should control Jerusalem raged on for decades. Soon it was realized that this round of the *Battle of Armageddon* did not produce a winner . . . There were only losers.

These are the generations of mankind—the original descendants of Adam and Eve. This is the result of a life lived amidst the pairs of opposites—that false concept of life that is the battleground for good and evil. This is the life that was lived in timelines 1, 2 and 3.

Mankind lost its way in this world of material sense and was unable to recover, because it continued to deal with every problem at the level of the problem—an eye for an eye, and a tooth for a tooth . . . that is, until two ancient scrolls were eventually translated, and the mystical message contained within them began to be distributed. At first, the distribution was a slow process going from one awakened soul to another. Over time, those awakened beings discerned the Truth enumerated in the scrolls. Soon they began to practice that Truth and, then, would gradually discover a way out of the black hole of spiritual darkness. These newly enlightened beings would then become *Children of the Light* and, ultimately, would find their way back to the five-dimensional consciousness and the Grand Circle of Eternity.

Yet, there was one more opportunity to avoid all of this carnage. There still was one important journey that was being traveled. It was a journey that, if successful, could produce the 4th timeline.

CHAPTER 37

IN THE BEGINNING

THE GARDEN OF EDEN
SOMETIME BETWEEN 10000 AND 15000 BCE
LOCATED NEAR THE FERTILE CRESCENT - ANCIENT MESOPOTAMIA

These are the words from the Great Revelator, disclosing the true account of creation. It is the divine revelation of Infinite Consciousness unfolding and manifesting Itself as the substance and reality of all that exists.

"In the beginning was the Word, and the Word was with God, and the Word was God. The same was in the beginning with God.

All things were made by Him, and without Him was not any thing made that was made.

In the beginning God created the heaven and the earth.

And the earth was without form, and void; and darkness was upon the face of the deep. And the Spirit of God moved upon the face of the waters.

And God said, 'Let there be light,' and there was light.

And God said, 'Let Us make man and woman in Our image, after Our likeness: and let them have dominion over the fish of the sea, and over the fowl of the air, and over the cattle, and over every creeping thing that creeps upon the earth.'

So God created them in His own image, in the image of God He created male and female—the two aspects of His Divine Self.

And God blessed them, and God said unto them, 'Be fruitful, and multiply, and replenish the earth and subdue it.'

And God saw everything that He had made and, behold, it was very good.

In Him was life, and the life was the light of men.

And God saw the light, that it was good.

'I am Alpha and Omega, the beginning and the ending,' said the Lord.

'They must know from the rising of the sun, and from the west, that there is none beside Me. I am the Lord, and there is none else.

'I have provided the earth for them as a five-dimensional spiritual creation and have placed my sons and daughters upon it.

'I am their Life. I am their Soul. Through them, I express the infinite glory and majesty of My Being, for we are One.

'All of this is the divine unfoldment of My immaculate, infinite Consciousness. I AM that I AM.'

This is the absolute Truth of Being as given by the Great Revelator. But a false concept of this reality has been lying dormant in the universal mind of man. When it was awakened in that mind, this fallacious ideology claimed that God is not an all-powerful creative Consciousness—that God is not the sum and substance of all existence.

Instead, this second account of creation asserts that God is not infinite, and that mankind must live amidst the conflicting dualisms created by the pairs of opposites—that both good and evil are real.

Following are the words of the False Prophet. These teachings and events provided the foundation for man's subjection to material sense—the erroneous concept of life as it was lived in the 1st, 2nd and 3rd timelines.

"And the Lord God formed man of the dust of the ground, and breathed into his nostrils the breath of life; and man became a living soul.

And the Lord God said, 'It is not good that the man should be alone; I will make a helper for him.'

And the Lord God caused a deep sleep to fall upon Adam, and he slept . . . And out of the rib of Adam, God created a woman to live with him and be his equal. Together, they should procreate and bring forth sons and daughters.

And the Lord God planted a garden eastward in Eden; and there He put the man and woman whom He had formed.

And out of the ground made the Lord God to grow every tree that is pleasant to the sight, and good for food: the Tree of Life also in the midst of the garden, and the Tree of the Knowledge of Good and Evil.

And the Lord God took the man and woman and put them into the Garden of Eden to dress it and to keep it.

And the Lord God commanded them saying, 'Of every tree of the garden you may freely eat:

'But of the Tree of the Knowledge of Good and Evil, you shall not eat of it: for in the day that you eat thereof you will surely die.'

Now the serpent was more sinister than any beast that the Lord God had made. And the serpent said unto the woman, 'Has God told you that you may not eat of every tree of the garden?'

And the woman said unto the serpent, 'We may eat of the fruit of the trees of the garden except for two: the Tree of Life, and the Tree of the Knowledge of Good and Evil.

'And of the fruit of the Tree of the Knowledge of Good and Evil—the tree which is in the midst of the garden—God has said, "You shall not eat of it, neither shall you touch it, lest you die."'

And the serpent said unto the woman, 'You shall not surely die:

'For God knows that in the day you eat thereof, then your eyes shall be opened, and you will be as gods, knowing good and evil.'

And when the woman saw that the tree was good for food, and that it was pleasant to the eyes, and a tree to be desired to make one wise, she took of the fruit thereof, and so did eat it. As a result, her descendents would be destined to live forever under a false concept of life in an illusory world of material sense. They would henceforth be governed by the pairs of opposites."

And thus ended the sayings of the False Prophet.

Following is the history of the new heaven and new earth, as revealed by the Father of Mankind in the 4th timeline.

"The woman was about to eat the fruit when she heard the haunting voice:

'Please don't do it, Mother! Do not eat the forbidden fruit!'

Dropping the fruit to the ground she asked, 'Who is speaking? Where are you?'

'Please don't eat of the fruit, Mother. I am your son, Abel. I beg you, Mother, please do not eat the fruit of that tree!'

'How can this be . . . ? My son Abel is dead. He was murdered by his brother who has now been banished from us.'

'But we can still change all of that, Mother. We do not have to go through that again.

'Cain killed his brother in another lifetime . . . a different timeline.

'I have come back here to meet you before you make that dreaded mistake. Now we are here together again at the base of the tree. You can still make the choice not to eat the forbidden fruit.'

'Why should I not eat it, my son? The serpent told me that it would make us like gods, who would know good and evil.'

'The serpent is a liar. If you eat that fruit, all of your children will be born in sin, and you will be condemning them and the children of all mankind to lifetimes of pain, misery and sorrow.

'God created us perfect, in His own image and likeness. God is our Life. God is Love. This Life and Love of God flow through every fiber of our being. We live in a perfect habitat: The Garden of Eden.

'But all of that will be taken away from us if you eat of that fruit. The serpent has lied. You will not be like the true God who knows only good. Instead, you will become en-chanted with the pairs of opposites; you will always believe in good and evil. And that will have you worshipping false gods.

'As a result, my brothers, sisters and I, along with all the rest of your descendants, will forever be banned from the garden. We will live our lives in fear and suffering. Brother will rise up against brother. Nation will rise up against nation, and the world will destroy itself with wars of unimag-inable bloodshed and horror.

'If you eat the fruit of the forbidden tree, even I will not live to fulfill my true destiny. Your family will be divided, and one of your other sons will forever be banished from you.

'Mother, you can save us from all of that by not eating the fruit from the Tree of the Knowledge of Good and Evil.'

'But my son, even if I do not eat the fruit, someone else may do it sometime in the future. What can we do to prevent that from happening?'

'We must destroy the tree, Mother. I will go to get my father and my brothers. We will find a way to destroy the tree. Please do not eat the fruit while I am away.'

So Adam and his three sons came to the place where Eve was resting next to the tree in the midst of the garden.

Seeing her there, Adam said, 'What is this that you have done, woman? Have you eaten the fruit of the forbidden tree?'

'No, my husband, I have not yet eaten it. Our beloved dead son has been restored to us. He is very wise and has told me not to eat the fruit.

'But now we must find a way to destroy the tree forever.'

'We do not have any tools with which to do that,' he replied. 'I will not be able to cut down the tree. We will have to build a wall around it and bury the tree in such a manner that no one will ever find it and be tempted by it again.'

And so they did. Using sticks, rocks, and their bare fingers, the couple and their three sons feverishly dug up the fertile ground all around them, working on the project for several weeks. Ultimately, they were successful in burying the forbidden tree under a huge mound of earth. As a result, the Tree of the Knowledge of Good and Evil was removed from the universal consciousness of mankind.

Because of this diligent family effort, a new timeline was created in which man—the generic term for all of God's children—became free. No longer would he believe in good

] 303 [

and evil. No longer would he be a prisoner of the pairs of opposites. Instead, man would come to realize that he had been created in the image and likeness of God.

And since God is Spirit, man is a spiritual being. Since God is Life, that Life appears as the Life of man. There is only one infinite Consciousness. Therefore, man is an individualized expression of that Universal Consciousness."

These are the words of Abel, the enlightened son of Adam and Eve—the Father of all men and women who are living in the 4th timeline. That timeline represents the true spiritual unfoldment of the One infinite Consciousness appearing in all of its splendor and glory throughout Time and Eternity.

And thus, the beloved son of Adam and Eve was now free to reenter the Grand Circle of Eternity. From there, he would return to his rightful place in the new millennium of the 21st Century . . . the place where his historic journeys in time had begun.

EPILOGUE

TIMELINE NO. 4

The land east of The Garden of Eden, sometime Between 10,000 and 15,000 BCE: Brothers Cain and Abel divide the land given to them by their parents, Adam and Eve. Together, they work to harvest it and to keep it. One year later, they further subdivide the land and grant one third of the area to their brother Seth.

Mt. Horeb in the Sinai Peninsula, 1342 BCE: Moses ascends the holy mountain and meets God face to face. He learns the sacred meaning of the holy name: *I AM*. He accepts this important Truth and shares it with all mankind.

The Arabian city of Mecca, August 20, 570 CE: Muhammad ibn 'Abdullah, later know as Mohammed, is born.

Mecca, Saudi Arabia, 610 CE in the month of Ramadan: Muhammad receives his first revelation of the one God and founds the religion of Islam. It is a religion based upon peace and love to all mankind.

Nicaea, Bithynia, 767 CE: At the Second Council of Nicaea, Pope Adrian I brings the leaders of Islam, the Eastern Orthodox Church, and the Roman Catholic Church together to establish a working relationship in which they will honor each other's beliefs and customs. They agree to work toward creating a universal church that will accept the one God of the Universe.

The Middle East, 1102 CE: The leaders of Islam and the Eastern and Western Catholic churches continue their dialogue, agreeing to share the city of Jerusalem as a holy place for each of their respective religions.

Ajaccio, Corsica, August 15, 1769: Letizia Bonaparte, wife of Carlo Bonaparte gives birth to a son, Napoleon.

Paris, France, 1804: Napoleon Bonaparte is elected as President of France. He has a long, peaceful and prosperous reign as he establishes his country as one of the leading nations of the world.

Trier, Prussia, Germany, May 5, 1818: Karl Heinrich Marx is born to middle-class parents. He comes from a long line of rabbis on both sides of his family.

Brussels, Belgium, April, 1843: Following his family tradition, Karl Marx is ordained a Rabbi. Ten years later, he publishes a world-renowned book on Jewish mysticism.

Gori, Georgia, December 21, 1878: Joseph Stalin is born to peasant parents. Because of the poor and unsanitary living conditions, the child dies at the age of seven years.

Braunau, Austria, April 20, 1889: Frau Klara Hitler, wife of Alois Hitler, gives birth to a stillborn son. The boy was to have been named Adolf.

Moscow, Russia, 1922: After a peaceful transition from rule by the Czars to a government of the people, the Republic of Russia becomes a welcome member of the League of Nations and the world community.

Berlin, Germany, January 30, 1933: The Republic of Germany achieves a new level of peace and understanding among its citizens, and continues to be a leading force for cooperation in Europe. Helmut Kleinschmidt is sworn in as Chancellor.

Pearl Harbor, Hawaii Territory, United States, December 8, 1941: It is a typical warm, sunny, day in paradise. The United States naval base at Pearl Harbor is abuzz with excitement. President Roosevelt is stopping there on his way to Japan, where he will be meeting Emperor Hirohito to discuss the two allies' commitment to peace in the world. He will be bringing a special gift to the emperor, as the two leaders are opening a new dialog on how they can trade more effectively with each other.

Warsaw, Poland, November 11, 1943: The Republic of Poland celebrates the 25th anniversary of the establishment of the 2nd Polish Republic. An especially joyous celebration is held in the beautiful resort city of Auschwitz.

Hiroshima and Nagasaki, Japan, August 12, 1945: Sports fans in Hiroshima and Nagasaki are quite excited as the annual intra-Japan soccer tournament is underway. Four teams from each of the rival cities are in the competition.

Washington D.C. and Moscow, Russia, August, 1949: The two great allies begin the process of working together on the use of nuclear power as the cleanest form of energy. They willingly share their technology with the rest of the world, as the air pollution that had begun a decade earlier is halted in it tracks.

Riyadh, Saudi Arabia, March 10, 1957: Osama bin Laden is born as the son of Mohammed bin Laden.

Afghanistan, April 16, 1989: Osama bin Laden is found dead in his home from unexplained causes.

New York, NY, September 12, 2001: It is a beautiful, sunny day in New York City. With the recent rise in stock market values, Wall Street is humming. The magnificent Twin Towers of the World Trade Center are alive with commerce.

Central Intelligence Agency, Langley, VA, The Present: The high-tech global research agency is awarded a medal for meritorious service in its open cooperation with the nations of the world. All of civilization is benefitting from the unselfish work being done by the scientists and engineers on the CIA staff.

Tel Aviv, Israel and Florence, Italy, The Present: Two mysterious scrolls that had recently been discovered are finally translated. The manuscripts redefine the spiritual nature of life, as most enlightened mystics already understand it. But eventually, those words will be shared across the planet. This, in turn, will lead receptive men and women into the light of Truth, and to the life to which they were always destined—a life lived in the spiritual reality of *My Kingdom*.

POSTLUDE

TIMELINE NO. 4

THE PRESENT - MONDAY EVENING, AUGUST 17TH - 7:30 P.M. -
TIMELINE NO. 4
SHIMAHN'S ASHRAM - NAKCHU PREFECTURE -
NORTHERN TIBET AUTONOMOUS REGION

When Eve followed her son's admonition and did not eat the forbidden fruit from the Tree of the Knowledge of Good and Evil, she enabled him to establish a new timeline that was not governed by the pairs of opposites or by any conflicting dualisms. It became a timeline of Oneness. In this new transcendental level of awareness, many illumined souls achieved the realization that God and man are One—that the infinite, Universal Consciousness is expressing and revealing Itself as the reality of all existence and as the individual identity of each one of us. Instead of a life lived under the law, as it had been in the first three timelines, life is now lived under grace.

This is a transitional step toward the ultimate experience of the life Christ Jesus promised we could live. This is a higher revelation of the Son of God; it is the new world order, as it is unfolding in the new heaven and new earth foreseen by the Apostle John in his Apocalypse.

With his mission accomplished, the illumined soul named Abel, Yaacov, Silas, and Eric, made his final journey in time, back to that very serene, inviting place where his odysseys in time had been conceived . . . in the beautiful ashram in Tibet.

When I arrived back in my chair in Shimahn's library, I knew something felt different. The air seemed lighter and, outside, the sky appeared to be brighter. The deep sense of peace that was always in the atmosphere was still there, but now it was all-encompassing.

I opened the library door and stepped back into the Master's living room. Once again, he and Kathy were waiting there for me, as though I had been gone for only a few minutes.

"Welcome back," Shimahn said, "and congratulations."

"Thank you," I replied proudly.

"Where did you go?" Kathy asked. "What did you do?"

With a smile on my face, I lightheartedly said, "I went to visit my mother and had her change her diet."

"What?" Kathy shouted out. "How could that do anything for the future?"

"It all depends on who your mother is," I chuckled.

"Come on, Eric, be serious," she said.

Then Shimahn asked, "Was your mother who I think she was, Eric?"

"Yes."

"Okay, gentlemen, you've had your fun," Kathy scolded. "Now why don't you let me in on your little secret."

Shimahn answered, "Kathy, his mother was Eve."

"Eve?" she asked incredulously. "Do you mean Eve, the first woman—the one who was the wife of Adam?"

"Yes," I replied. "The last time I came back here, I realized that no other event was significant enough to make the kind of impact that was needed.

"I had to prevent Eve from eating the forbidden fruit. She and her husband had been placed in a perfect, immaculate habitat, *The Garden of Eden*. They knew only peace, joy, and harmony. So the symbolic act of her breaking the law of God and then learning that there could be both good and evil is what caused mankind's fall from grace and all of the world's accompanying problems. That is why anything I might have done later to alter some future event would have been irrelevant. We had to purge mankind of its belief in duality.

"The knowledge of good and evil was the root cause of all the problems in the three previous timelines. But the divine unfoldment of God-consciousness is only good. There is no evil in God. The belief in good and evil is a human concept.

"Yet, there still is a chance for the man of earth to go astray because, even though we buried the Tree of the

Knowledge of Good and Evil, it could be uncovered again by someone else. The latent possibility to believe in good and evil will always exist in this world of material sense. And that is why everything in this world has an opposite, or a potential opposite. There is old and there is young; there is white and there is black. Other opposites are healthy and sick, rich and poor, joy and sadness, pleasure and pain, and yes, even living and dead.

"But all of those are man-made concepts; they are part and parcel of the four-dimensional universe of space-time. Therefore, our next mission must be to educate mankind out of its limited sense of existence. My voyage to the Garden of Eden still left us with a physical world of cause and effect, of action and reaction. And even though it is a healthier place with less violence and terror, it still is a limited, illusory sense of life. So evil could still rear its ugly head in the future.

"Our job now is to find other illumined souls who will join us in this quest to achieve the five-dimensional con-sciousness—to help others ascend into the spiritual reality of a life truly lived under Divine Grace. And I believe the three of us should begin that work tomorrow morning."

Shimahn replied, "Eric, you are correct in your descrip-tion of what must be done. But it cannot be done here in Tibet. You have many more journeys to travel. You have many more adventures ahead of you. And those cannot be consummated here in this ashram.

"Now that we have completed this project, you need to go back into the world where the future battles have to be won. There is still so much education needed to bring more receptive souls into the light of Truth. You must continue sharing this message."

Kathy then said, "But Shimahn, Eric has accomplished so much already. And he did it all from right here. Why can't we stay a while longer and continue working together?"

"That would be a bit selfish, Kathy," he replied graciously. "I understand your desire to stay in this serene atmosphere, but your future work needs to be done in the outside world."

"Shimahn is right, Kathy," I suggested. "Even with my remarkable journey to the Garden of Eden, I have merely patched up *this world*—the physical realm of sense perceptions. As a result, we have given mankind a second chance to get it right. But that still leaves most people living a life in spiritual darkness, relative to the infinite potential they all have within their souls. The only thing I have accomplished thus far is to temporarily improve the pictures of the outer world of cause and effect. We now have a more peaceful planet and have avoided some of the calamitous events we were facing. But the man of earth is still living outside the *Kingdom of God*. So now, if we can just convince a few receptive souls to join us on this fantastic journey, we could begin uplifting the collective consciousness of all mankind."

"All right, Eric," my wife said passively. "I suppose you are right. But it seems like we just arrived here."

"It may seem that way to you, Kathy, but I feel as though I have been traveling for about twenty-five years.

"What would you suggest we do next, Shimahn? Where should we begin?"

"I believe you should try to track down those two scrolls you created when you went back in time. I assume that someone will find them in the next few days, and will soon begin translating them. That message must be given to all mankind. And because most people will be enchanted with the words in those documents, they will also want to share them with others.

"And best of all, much credibility will be attributed to those scrolls, because they were written so long ago. They will have an intriguing and mysterious quality to them. Many people will read them or will hear about their content from others. If you or I published a book today with identical words in it, our message would not get the same receptivity and acceptance. So that is the job before you."

Following those final comments, Kathy and I stepped over to our beloved Master as he reached out to us for one final embrace. It was an extremely poignant moment for both of us. The feeling was similar to what I had experienced the last time I saw Nehemiah in Old Jerusalem when I was twelve years old. After I had waved goodbye to the old Hebrew in the Holy City, I felt there soon was going to be a great void in my life—that I would never see him again. And I was right. Nehemiah would pass away some years later, before I had an opportunity to be in his presence once more. Now, leaving Shimahn like this gave me that same empty feeling. Yet this time, the emptiness was also filled with so much love and gratitude for all the joy and wonder my precious Master had given me through the years. Because of him, I have been provided with this fantastic mystical teaching that has truly made my life an adventure in living. And though my original encounter with these illumined beings had always seemed so long ago, now it felt like just yesterday. It appears that Mr. Einstein was right . . . *time really is relative.*

Kathy and I spent most of Tuesday relaxing in the peace and serenity of the ashram grounds. Then early Wednesday afternoon, Tenzing and Mingma escorted us out to the old car-truck. They drove us back to the train station in Nakchu, and waited there until we boarded our train back to Lhasa.

The train ride south was quite relaxing. We once again passed through that part of the country in which the majestic Himalayan Mountains created a magnificent backdrop. Beholding the majesty of those mountain ranges, we could only fantasize about what else might lie within them. Somewhere out there in those snow-capped peaks there may have been a real Shangri-la, similar to the one that was so eloquently described in the story of the Lost Horizon. But for Kathy and me, it seemed as though we had already spent a major portion of our lives in our own special Shangri-la.

And so, as the train rolled on, both of us closed our eyes in meditation and tried to experience the five-dimensional reality of life that exists deep within our souls. This would be the first step on our continuing journey of spiritual discovery—our own personal adventure in mysticism.

ABOUT THE AUTHOR

Don Mardak has been a student of Christian mysticism for more than four decades and has conducted classes on *Living the Mystical Life*. He also has been a successful entrepreneur for most of his working years. As the President, CEO and Chairman of a small public company, Mr. Mardak always tried to apply the mystical principles outlined in this book in his business dealings and relationships. The results have been quite astonishing as, very often, without taking thought or striving for a specific result, the proper person appeared or a meaningful event occurred, which made each day a spiritual unfoldment. His greatest desire is that those of you who truly are receptive to this message will open yourselves up to the inflow of the Spirit. In that process, you will find answers to your deepest questions which, then, will lead you to your own search for Truth and, ultimately, your personal spiritual destiny.

Mr. Mardak lives with his wife Judy in Wisconsin and Florida. They have two grown children and four grandchildren.